Edward W. Gilliam

Thomas Ruffin

A novel

Edward W. Gilliam

Thomas Ruffin
A novel

ISBN/EAN: 9783337000424

Printed in Europe, USA, Canada, Australia, Japan

Cover: Foto ©Andreas Hilbeck / pixelio.de

More available books at **www.hansebooks.com**

Thomas Ruffin.

BY

E. W. GILLIAM, M. D.

Author of "1791: A Tale of San Domingo."

———

BALTIMORE:

NICHOLS, KILLAM & MAFFITT,

1896.

Thomas Ruffin.

CHAPTER I.

CLOUD CAP.

"From our New Orleans commission merchant," said the manager of Cloud Cap, as he stood on his piazza a fine summer morning and opened a letter Lucinda, the maid, had just brought over from the mansion.

Cloud Cap was one of the loveliest, most fertile, best conducted, and most prosperous estates in the far South sixty odd years ago. John Ruffin was its owner. It had long been the seat of a splendid hospitality. The recent death of Mrs. Ruffin had put an end to this, and, with advancing age, John Ruffin's care was now all centred on his son Thomas.

Cloud Cap lay upon a goodly river, three miles above the fine, old-fashioned, hospitable, thriving town of L——, the latter at the head of steamboat navigation, and controlling an extensive back-country trade. Those would have thought the appellation strange, who were unfamiliar with the local traditions. Cloud Cap, indeed, was somewhat of an eminence, yet by no means so commanding as to justify such a title. In fact, the name was not derived from the locality at all, but from a gigantic Indian Chief (Cloud Cap being the English synonym for his Indian name), whose wigwam, in days far away back, stood on this site—the village of his people occupying the river plain below.

The mansion—so roomy and so comfortable, with great airy passages, and broad piazzas, a typical Southern gentleman's home—stood high upon the river's hill, among lordly ash and oak.

Southward half a mile ran the main road, whence a broad avenue—skirted on either side by tidy, white-washed negro cabins—led up to Cloud Cap. Towards the North the hill-side was finely wooded and carefully kept down to the lowest point of the declivity, where it terminated in a magnificent plantation of river low ground.

Mr. Ruffin was a man of affluence and owned a number of plantations; but this, known as the "Indian Field," was the pride of them all. Two crescent curves, formed on one side by the foot line of the hill and on the opposite side by the bend of the river, inclosed an oval area of some 400 acres. It was perfectly level, so that a dog at one extremity could be seen at the other, and famed for fertility. In a former age it had been the site of an Indian village, and Mr. Ruffin would point out to his friends the positions of wigwams here and there, from the superior fertility marking certain distinctly circumscribed spots—due, in his view, to the ashes and bones thrown out by the squaws.

"From our New Orleans commission house," said the manager opening the letter. Evidently it was an interesting and agreeable communication; for his countenance took on a most pleased expression, as he read.

"A sales ticket! Well done, Cloud Cap!" he exclaimed exultingly, as he completed the perusal.

"*John Ruffin, Esq.*" (re-reading the letter and aloud) :

DEAR SIR :—Please find below statement of sales :

400 Bales Cotton at 10c.	$20,000
330 Bar'l Rice at 6c.	5,400
100 Hhd's Sugar at 5c.	10,000
	35,400
Commission at 5 per cent.	628
Net amount,	34,772

This sum, at your request, has been placed in bank to your credit. Please find herewith certificate of bank deposit.

Hope sales are satisfactory. With many thanks and soliciting further consignments, we remain respectfully,

NOTT & Co., *Cotton Factors.*"

"35,000 net! Well done, I say, old Cloud Cap! Where has Cloud Cap her equal? Cloud Cap caps climax! C. C. C. C.! Four C's. What does that mean? Why, that Cloud Cap's the finest estate within the four seas—that is, in all America. Ha! ha! ha!"

The reappearance of Lucinda cut short the thread of the manager's exultations.

"Please, Sir," she said with a curtsey, "Cupid wants to know what time it is."

"Yes, Sir," curtseying.

"Send Cupid to me at once."

"Yes, Sir," responded Lucinda with a low curtsey, as she retired.

"Our carriage driver has been strangely remiss," soliloquized the manager. "His orders were express to have the buggy at the village for Thomas Ruffin an hour ago—8 o'clock. The stage that brings Thomas is due at the village at half-past 8."

As reflections of this character were passing through his mind, from the rear Cupid was approaching—a big, black, bald, ungainly negro, no darling doubtless among dusky damsels, but a true prince among whips. His array was strictly in coachman style, a foil to his ungainliness, and he bore the air of importance usually attaching to a wealthy gentleman's carriage driver.

"How is it you are here, Sir?" cried the manager harshly, as he turned at the sound of Cupid's step. "You had explicit orders to have the buggy at the village at 8."

"I knowed, Sah," replied Cupid, with a profound bow, "de orders wus exquisite."

"Why, then, did you neglect such orders?" asked the manager, sharply interrupting.

"Very sorry," (bowing); "but the carriage-house clock shet down at 7, an' I's jes dis minit found it out."

"Hurry off! hurry off! and don't let Mr. Ruffin see you. Thomas is waiting at the village, if not now on the way in a hired vehicle."

"Yes, Sah! yes, Sah!" responded Cupid, hastily bowing himself out of the manager's presence, as the latter opened a letter from the table, whereon lay the morning mail, and glanced at it.

"More Cloud Cap peals, perhaps—from Thomas Sanford & Co.—the New Orleans house that's coining money so. Ah! there's a rhyme."

"*To John Ruffin,*" (reading aloud):

"DEAR SIR:—Check received. Your funds in bank have been transferred to this house, and placed to your credit. Please find enclosed receipt.

Mr. Sanford, senior member, will personally write you and transmit papers.

Yours truly,
THOMAS SANFORD & CO."

"This is personal, and should have been so marked. Yes, papers came yesterday, as Mr. Ruffin informed me. Nott & Co. had written sale proceeds, and the Boss checked out all his cash to this new hustling house. Hope it's a safe venture. They promise big money."

The manager at once stepped over to the mansion, to hand Mr. Ruffin the Sanford letter. He found him giving directions to the servants, touching arrangements for an expected visit from old friends of his, Adam Peale, and his wife, Martha.

Adam Peale was a Quaker by religion, a merchant by calling, a round-faced, dumpy, kind-hearted, jolly old gentleman. He resided in one of the great

Northern cities—had long had business relations with Mr. Ruffin—and out of these had grown a close friendship, to be emphasized by this anticipated visit to Cloud Cap.

The spouse, Martha, was as true-hearted and good-hearted as her lord, but showed the sharp outlines of form and feature, that usually, for some cause or other, characterize the Quakers—or Friends, if that be better. Not a shadow of disrespect is meant, good reader, in using the former designation.

John Ruffin was a typical Southern gentleman, under the old regime, high-toned, generous, cultivated, and courteous. Physically, of spare habit—angular frame—muscles thin—and skin of a dark or earthy hue. The face gave indications of energy, and movements were hasty and abrupt. He was turned of fifty, but looked older—the general expression, one of subdued sadness. His eldest son had shown a wild, roving disposition, and, some years before the beginning of this narrative, had gone West in search of fortune. Then his letters· began to drop off. Then they ceased. Strenuous, unwearied quest proved fruitless. It was many a day since any tidings had been received, and he was given up for dead. Recently, Mr. Ruffin had lost his wife, a loving and lovable woman, and he was tenderly attached to her—not, however, in that essential and peculiar way he was to Thomas, who now alone remained to him. Naturally, one cannot love his wife as he loves his child. Beyond the qualities that command friendship, the normal relation of husband and wife is sexual only. Between parent and child there is blood tie, and the parent, withal, marks his own self, reappearing in the features and characteristics of his offspring.

The Manager had scarcely left, when the bell rang, the door opened, and Lucinda ushered in the Peales, in full Quaker style and travelling garb.

"Bless me! My city friends!" exclaimed John Ruffin, amidst great hand-shaking. "Why, I expected you by the next boat.'"

"Doth it disturb thee, John," quoth Friend Peale, rallying his host, "that we have anticipated the visit's beginning?"

"No! No! not unless you make it ground for shortening the visit's end."

A hearty ha! ha! ha! greeted the sally.

"Delighted to see you," exclaimed John Ruffin. "A thousand welcomes to Cloud Cap. Here, Mrs. Peale, take the chair of honor," drawing forward, as he spoke, an ancient looking chair—"a family relic of most venerable ancestry, and with a seat wrought by my own hands."

"By thy own hands?" she queried, with a mingled expression of curiosity and astonishment.

"Yes."

"Well! I declare! who'd have thought it!" she exclaimed, as she examined the chair's bottom.

"It's the soft inside shuck, Madam, split, dampened, and twisted."

"We never see the like with us."

"Your North lands can't grow our Southern shucks."

"Where did thee pick it up?"

"In the cabins, when a boy. Shucking chairs is a negro's common source of pocket change."

"Thee has a trade, John," quoth the good woman laughing.

"Something, Mrs. Peale, to fall back on, should fortune fail."

"To have been Cloud Cap's owner," interjected Friend Peale, "and a chair-mender—"

"You consider two states wide apart, perhaps," interrupted Mr. Ruffin, smiling and anticipating the sentiment.

"Yea! ha! ha! ha!" Friend Peale heartily responded.

"Stranger things have happened, Friend Peale. I may yet twist shucks for a living," said the host with assumed gravity. Whereat the jolly Quaker discharged another volley: "Ha! ha! ha! Get out, John, get out!"

"I'm glad the carriage happened to be at the landing," said Mr. Ruffin.

"And the driver, at my request," remarked his guest, "drove hither in a circuit, to show the estate to best advantage."

"Well, Friend Peale, you've often heard, I'm sure, of Cloud Cap."

"Yea, John—when have I sold thee a bill of goods that I haven't heard of it?"

"Ha! ha! ha! Well, now that you have *seen* it, what have you to say?" interrogated the host.

"What the Queen of Sheba said to Solomon."— He paused an instant as if in the effort to recall the exact quotation, and before he could say what the Queen of Sheba said, his ready little wife came to his rescue and broke in, taking her good man's words:

"Behold! the half was not told me."

She immediately saw the discourtesy in Friend Peale's look of surprise, but sought to put a good face on the incident, and replied in smiles:

"Please, Adam, let a *she* say what a *she* said;" and a ringing laugh saluted the bit of pleasantry.

It had scarcely subsided, when Mrs. Peale observed, with the splendid plantation scenes she had just witnessed, vividly before her:

"And *I* thought upon the Royal Prophet's words, as his eye caught the rich harvests of Judea."—

But she was not allowed to finish. Friend Peale was now ahead of time, and taking, in his turn, his wife's words, solemnly but quickly interjected:

"The valleys stand so thick with corn, they laugh and sing."

And to her surprised look and shade of annoyance at the implied rebuke, he still solemnly answered:

"Please, Martha, let a *he* say what a *he* said."

Another ringing laugh from all greeted the hit and smoothed out the little wrinkle, and honors were considered easy between good man and spouse.

"The negro quarters make a village, John," re-marked Friend Peale, still ringing the changes on Cloud Cap.

"And look so clean and nice in white-wash," Mrs. Peale added.

"And the Blacks are so polite," said he.

"And seem contented and happy," said she.

"And the grounds, John, are lovely," Friend Peale continued, multiplying the merited encomiums.

"Well! well! Cloud Cap praises are pleasing," replied Mr. Ruffin to all this; "but you're dusty and tired, and must not be kept from your rooms" (ringing up servant as he speaks). "After rest and refreshment I'll show you round myself, and then I think you'll say with all who have been here, *there is but one Cloud Cap.*"

At this point Lucinda entered with a curtesy.

"Here, Lucinda," said the host, "show our guests to their rooms, and see that the luggage is all right."

In those days the tongues of maid servants were often in their knees, and Lucinda silently responded in a curtsey.

With renewed and mutual expressions of pleasure at the meeting, the Peales retire, and the door which opens for their exit, admits another visitor, who had been in waiting, Mr. Le Wray.

The latter was leading lawyer resident at L——, whom Mr. Ruffin generally consulted. He had been sent for on this occasion touching a matter of special importance.

"Come in, Mr. Le Wray," said Mr. Ruffin, according to a mode of speech not unfrequently addressed to one already wholly "in," as in the present instance; for the attorney was advancing towards the speaker. "I've sent for you," he continued, after exchange of salutations, "to submit certain papers bearing on the provision I wish to make for Thomas."

"Very well, Sir."

"You know I'm an anxious Father."

"Yes, Sir."

"But *how* anxious—*how* peculiar—*how* silly, it may be—you *don't* know."

"No—I don't know that yet, Mr. Ruffin."

"There has never lived a Father, I believe, with a heart so tender, so framed to be anxious—and never a son, I believe, who, while so amiable, is so formed to rouse anxiety."

"Come! Mr. Ruffin, 'twon't do to nurse extremes, Sir."

"I'm peculiar, I tell you—the most peculiar Father on earth, perhaps. It's my *nature*."

"But reason should moderate natural tendencies."

"Can't help it, Le Wray. I'm a fool, perhaps, about Thomas. Would you believe, that, when I think of him in certain relations, I'm filled with inexpressible sadness?"

"You astonish me, Sir!"

"I suffer a kind of agony."

"Mr. Ruffin! What on earth can you mean?"

"Thomas is so unfitted for the world, Le Wray."

"Ha! ha! ha! Such a disparity, Mr. Ruffin, between the manifesto and the conduct of the war. I thought you were about to charge against the lad some heinous offense, or fatal infirmity. Ha! ha! ha!"

"I fear it *is* a fatal infirmity."

Pray, Sir, how is he unfitted for the world?"

"In many ways, Le Wray."

"Will you please specify them?"

"He seems so feeble."

"Let him then nurse his muscularity, Mr. Ruffin. The remedy lies there."

"I don't mean physical feebleness, though his body is not the strongest. I mean a feeble nature, poor child. As lovable and intelligent as he is, I fear in him—and God only knows how it weighs upon me—a softness, a weakness of character, that disqualifies for the world."

"What evidence do you offer?"

"He's so impulsive, so wanting in judgment, Le Wray."

"He's but a youth, yet."

"A whim takes him. Immediately he gratifies it—the thing's bought or exchanged, the bargain made—and immediately he's dissatisfied and unhappy. No stability, no firm opinions, no strength of character."

"Many a fine and successful man, Sir, has shown such whims in youth."

"But Thomas' seem so excessive."

"Educate, educate, Mr. Ruffin. Time and care will wear down and round off the eccentricities—which, indeed, your excessive solicitude must greatly exaggerate."

"Ah! Le Wray, you don't see him as I do, the most diffident and most sensitive of mortals."

"Because I don't see him through a lense of distortion."

"He's full of affection—ready to lean—sighs for companionship—yet all in vain. Excessive diffidence discourages advances. Venturing among companions, excessive sensitiveness makes him a target. He's self-driven from them, and, poor child, ever doomed to isolation."

"You are conjuring up a Thomas, that, in my humble opinion, has no existence, Mr. Ruffin."

"Better, perhaps, had he never existed."

"Mr. Ruffin!"

"Since preordained to special suffering."

"Are you crazy, Sir?"

"Afflicted in his parents, Le Wray."

"On my soul you *must* be crazy, Sir."

"His mother—"

"Mr. Ruffin! Mr. Ruffin!" interrupted the lawyer, "this will never do. Arraign your saintly wife, and the sod scarce rooted over her grave!"

"No! Le Wray—no, Sir!—no! no!"

I've never known one to approach your late wife, Mr. Ruffin."

"Nor I, Le Wray."

"Her self-abnegation, purity, and sweetness—"

"Had no equal," broke in Mr. Ruffin, resolved no one should be before him in his wife's praises.

"She was the charm of her circle."

"Most truly spoken, Le Wray."

"And made religion amiable in the eyes of all who knew her."

"Yes, yes. One so nearly perfect I shall never see again."

"How, then, an afflicting Mother, Mr. Ruffin?"

"She was neurotic and supersensitive, and should never have wed a supersensitive neurotic like me."

"Ha! ha! ha!" responded the lawyer.

"Merriment is out of place, Mr. Le Wray."

"Pardon me, Mr. Ruffin."

"I'm disturbed in mind, even distressed, Sir. The acute cause you'll know later on."

"I pray, Sir, pardon the laugh, provoked by a contrast. You were pressing a *similarity* in respect to your wife's temperament, while I have ever recognized a clear *opposition*."

"A clear opposition!"

"Yes, Sir. You a distinct brunette—she a distinct blonde; and I may add; the fruit of such a union by natural law should be harmonious."

"*Should be!* But is it? Fact outweighs theory, Le Wray—as no one ought to know so well as a lawyer.—Thomas' nature harmonious! How can it be, combining the nervous idiosyncracies of his parents? This very day he returns from school, because life there is a torment. Try as he may, the poor, sensitive, diffident fellow cannot get on with the boys, and is so completely isolated and unhappy, that, should he remain, I would fear for his mind."

"I've seen timid youths make manly men, I could tell you, Mr. Ruffin; but you set your face against counsel and comfort."

"What a mercy! could I think so about Thomas; for I *suffer* because of him."

"When, for the life of me, I can see no adequate cause."

"I bear the child, now alone left to me, an affection so singular that the thought of his helplessness—"

"His helplessness!" interrupted the lawyer. "Sir, you will work yourself into a deranged state. Why such anticipations? The man's hand, I repeat, is not yet all revealed in the lad. Exaggeration and imagination are running away with you, Sir."

"Call me a fool, if you will, but—"

"This Thomas, Sir—so helpless, so feeble in character—may yet take care of *you*, Mr. Ruffin," again interrupted the lawyer, unable to restrain himself at fancies he considered so unreasonable.

"Yes, call me a fool—but the thought of his helplessness, in the possible struggles of life, makes my heart sink from excess of tendernesss."

"But *why*, why worry yourself with any thought of life-struggles—you so amply rich?"

"True. I can provide for him. Thank God! for that resource. Should aught happen, Le Wray, to take it from me *I believe I'd go mad.*"

"Why allude, at all, to such a contingency, Mr. Ruffin? You can't have apprehensions in that direction?" asked the lawyer, with a manner indicating awakened interest.

"No-o," was the reply, in a tone of reservation. "But there are matters to be spoken of presently.— Now, as to the provision for Thomas—"

The sentence was cut off by the entrance of Lucinda.

"Please, Sir," she said with a curtsey, "the overseers is a waitin'."

"Tell them to come in."

"Yes, Sir," she replied curtseying, and retired, to give the message.

These field-overseers were elderly, experienced negroes, known for integrity and farming skill. Each had charge of a gang of laborers. All were under the Manager, and at the head was Mr. Ruffin himself. A thorough master of plantation work in all its details, he took an active part in inspecting and directing, as his time allowed. He had been over the fields the day before, and had instructed the Manager to send up the overseers for special orders.

A moment later they enter, with profound bows and a sense of importance awkwardly exhibited—a half dozen, Amos, Solomon and others—and line themselves against the wall opposite the seats occupied by the Master and his visitor.

"Well, Boys," spoke Mr. Ruffin, "Cloud Cap must do its level best this season."

"Yes, Sah!" they all answer in unison, with the bow that waited on every address to the Master.

"I want it to make me all the cash it can."

"Yes, Sah!"

"See that your gangs do their duty."

"Yes, Sah!"

"Amos!"

"Yes, Sah!" Amos responded with a low bow, as he stepped forward.

"Run thirty plows in the Indian Field."

"Yes, Sah!"

"I want that corn finished up, while the ground's damp and in condition."

"Yes, Sah! De ground's in fine perdition, Sah," Amos replied with a broad grin and bow of unusual strength, elated at his display of speech, and withal visibly stimulating the lawyer's risibles.

"Well, Solomon!" said the Master, addressing the second overseer.

"Yes, Sah!" spoke up Solomon with the bow, stepping forward briskly, as Amos retired to the line.

"Put sixty hoes in the cotton."

"Yes, Sah!"

"Fine day for exterminating grass, Solomon."

"Yes, Sah! Splendid day, Sah, for germinatin'

de grass, Sah!" rejoined Solomon, and with a chuckle of exultation, that, if he had not surpassed Amos, he was up to him at least in the gift of tongues.

"You other Boys!" said the Master, calling up the rest.

"Yes, Sah!" they answer stepping forward, as Solomon now retires to line.

"Go on with the work you were doing yesterday."

"Yes, Sah!"

"That's all."

"Yes, Sah!" answer the "other Boys" as they turn to resume their places.

Mr. Ruffin pauses a moment in reflection, and then remarks:

"You can retire now."

The overseers, not comprehending *retire* remain standing and in a species of bewilderment. To cover their ignorance in a stranger's presence, the Master endeavors by look and gesture to have them leave, while they, not knowing what to do and grinning stupidly, exchange glances with him and with each other.

"Can't you understand!" exclaimed Mr. Ruffin, ending the scene with a tone of irritation. "You can leave now, I say."

"Yes, Sah! yes, Sah!" the overseers make answer, bowing and retiring briskly.

"Fine looking darkies," observed the lawyer, as the door closed behind them.

"With a fine knowledge of farming, too, I can tell you, Le Wray."

"And I can add, Mr. Ruffin, a fine discrimination in respect to language."

A smile from John Ruffin greeted the banter, as he took up the broken thread of conversation.—

"Now, as to the provision for Thomas: He has no aptitude nor fancy, I think, for plantation management. But he has mind, is well educated and fond of books, and altogether, I judge, literature will be his field. I purpose, therefore, to accumulate cash up to $100,000—invest this for him in a life annuity—and leave Cloud Cap in a trust, for his benefit. He can, then, when I am gone, choose a residence in some favorable city, where his literary tastes may be pursued to best advantage, with a fortune needing a minimum of care."

"Well!" threw in the lawyer in a lawyerlike way, tapping the table with his finger and settling down to business, as Mr. Ruffin made a momentary pause.

"To get the $100,000 in the quickest way possible," continued Mr. Ruffin, "I've become a limited copartner in the New Orleans Cotton House of Thomas Sanford & Co."

"How much have you invested, Mr. Ruffin?"

"$50,000—all my cash."

"How much do the Sanfords offer, Sir?"

"30 per cent."

"Did you examine into the Firm's condition?"

"No. Mr. Sanford is a very near and a very dear

cousin, as you're aware, and I accepted his statements."

"In affairs of this sort, it's advisable to watch
even near and dear cousins, Mr. Ruffin. Cousins
have proven cozening, where personal interests are
involved."

"Do you reflect upon my kinsman, Sir ?"

"Not at all, Mr. Ruffin. I'm simply giving my
experience as a lawyer, and in the light of that experience advise you to be on guard. Mr. Sanford is
one of our first citizens, I know, and entirely trust-
worthy."

"Why the caution, then, against accepting his
statements ?"

"He may be deceived."

"He ! the head of the House !"

"The nominal head, but not the active Manager,
Mr. Ruffin. Mr. Sanford is a resident of our town
and often absent from New Orleans, and the state
of affairs there cannot always be known to him."

Mr. Ruffin reflected a moment in a worried way,
and then remarked:

"But, Le Wray, the House, though a new one,
has had remarkable success. Surely, there can be
no danger."

"Yes—and success due to remarkably *bold* speculation, as I hear."

"Why that emphasis on "bold" ? Do you
suppose Mr. Sanford would countenance illegitimate business ?"

"Not illegitimate in the sense of being *per se* dis-
honest."

"In what sense then?"

"That of undue hazard."

"Why suppose undue hazard *here?*"

"A promise of 30 per cent. in cotton means rash
speculation, if it means anything, Mr. Ruffin. The
House has leaped into wealth by taking heavy risks
and making hits. But tides ebb, as well as flow."

"I wish I had consulted you before investigating,"
said Mr. Ruffin, with an expression of alarm mani-
festly gathering on his countenance.

"Have you heard any rumors, Sir?"

"Why?—Have you, Le Wray?"

"Have *you?*"

"Yes, to speak the honest truth; and I'm really
alarmed. Some days ago I received outside advices
reflecting on the House, and at once wrote Mr. Sanford, now in New Orleans. I'm looking any moment for an answer. And yesterday's mail brought
another letter repeating these adverse reports."

"I'm glad your Copartnership is limited, and
affecting but a fraction of your means."

"And this brings up the very matter for consul-
tation. Please see if this copartnership instrument
is correct. Mr. Sanford had it drawn. These rumors have disturbed me, *and I must be reassured
I'm not involved beyond the sum invested.*"

Mr. Le Wray carefully examines the paper, and
returns it with the remark:

"It's all right, Sir."

"Well! I'm relieved!" exclaimed John Ruffin, stretching himself back in his seat with an air of the greatest satisfaction.

"But, Mr. Ruffin, the validity of the limitation clause rests on two conditions."

"Ah! What are they?" eagerly asks the client.

"First: You are to take no active part in the management."

"I've taken none."

"Second: Publication must be made."

"Publication!" cried out Mr. Ruffin bending forward, as alarm again loured over his features.

"Yes. Has this been omitted?"

"Mr. Sanford said nothing about publication," the client evasively answered, postponing the negative, to take in the turn matters had assumed, and the signs of alarm visibly increasing.

"Have you made then, or caused to be made, no publication of the transaction?" pointedly asked the lawyer.

"None, Sir," was the faltering reply.

"Then, Mr. Ruffin, this paper is absolutely nil as far as a limited copartnership is concerned, and your entire means are involved in the fortunes of the Sanford House."

"My God!" broke forth John Ruffin, rising from his seat with a blanched countenance.

"Be calm, Mr. Ruffin. Don't lose your head. Matters may not be bad after all."

"What d'you advise?"

"To leave at once for New Orleans, or rather write there, and have publication made."

"But suppose something has happened, Le Wray?"

"We'll not *suppose* something, till we *know* something," the lawyer rejoined.

He had scarcely ended the sentence, when the door opened and friend Peale and his wife in high feather came bustling into the room with Thomas.

"Here he is! here he is! John Ruffin," exclaimed Mrs. Peale.

"And a happy lad he seems," added her good man.

"O dear Father!" Thomas cried out, "I'm *so*, so glad to see you and be home again."

"My child!" the Father exclaimed, embracing his son.

"Here's a letter, Father, I brought from the village."

John Ruffin seizes the letter, tears it open, and with an awful light in his eyes reads aloud :

"Thomas Sanford & Co. fail for over half million!"

"My son! my son! We've lost all and are beggars!"

"What!" Thomas blurted out, unable to take in the situation, yet profoundly agitated by a sense of something dreadful.

"We've lost Cloud Cap and all our fortune, my child, and are beggars," faltered the Father.

"O Father!" cried Thomas, bursting into tears

and seizing his Father's hand, ''never mind ! never mind ! I can help you.''

But the words are unheeded ; for John Ruffin faints and falls into his son's supporting arms.

CHAPTER II.

My earliest recollections are those of a beautiful and happy Southern home. I mean particularly our country home at Cloud Cap. I remember my Mother's often telling me, when a child, I had soft, wavy brown hair, and large, dark, tender eyes. From the first my education received very careful attention. My father superintended my Latin, himself a classical scholar, and I had besides the best tutors both in town and country. But in the late Spring and early Autumn and all the Summer through, I was free, I may say. I had a frail appearance, and my Father encouraged in every way the development of my physique. I had a fancy for "chopping," and became an expert woodman. My Father provided me with axe, maul, wedges, and gluts, specially my own, and many a goodly tree did I fell and cut and split and cord for Winter fuel.

The foundation so laid for firm muscles and compact bones (though really I never *looked* strong) proved of signal advantage in after years, when unusual demands were made on endurance. What I

have since seen in books, I experienced in my own
person, that one of the two cardinal helps (the
other, a cheerful spirit) towards successful passage
through the world, is a sturdy frame, a body strong
to bear.

At seventeen I was tall and well taught, yet singularly shy and reticent in the presence of strangers. The face of my fellow man, though in stormy
mood, I can now confront, I hope, with commendable firmness. But at that time I was timid and
shrinking to a most painful degree—due, as my
Father said, to having lived so entirely at home,
under tutors and with those always considerate and
tender; and for rubbing out these wrinkles the experience of a Boarding School he considered advisable. That it was for the best so I thought, too, to
whom he fully explained his reasons. Alas! it
proved the beginning of sorrows.

Those there are, doubtless, for whom a Boarding
School process *is* desirable—who come out smooth
and shiny. But others are rubbed raw, harmed
irrevocably. I warn the parents of oversensitive
children. Don't attempt rubbing out the wrinkles
through an average Boarding School without having
gauged the child accurately. My Father had not
sounded my depths, or he would have been the last
on earth to send me among a lot of rough, vulgar,
unfeeling boys, to have my supersensitiveness
played upon and deeped into melancholia, which
would have become insanity, I veribly believe, had
not my stay at school been cut short suddenly.

But the dark side of Boarding School life was now hidden. I saw only the other. All that my Father said as to the advantages, I believed. I became interested in the preparations for departure. As dearly as I loved my home, I took positive pleasure in seeing my abundant outfit packed away in a stout leathern trunk. If a misgiving was expressed now and then, they would reassure me, saying "Selrachts" was not so far off, and should anything happen they could at once reach me.

The last visit to L—— was to see the Sanfords. Thomas Sanford was a man of character and of fortune. As stated in the preceding chapter, he was senior member of the New Orleans Cotton House of Sanford & Co. He was my Mother's first cousin, their mothers being sisters, and the closest intimacy existed between the families. Cousin Thomas was my god-father. I was his namesake, and a special favorite. My reception on this particular occasion was of the warmest kind. Good wishes were showered upon me. Cousin Thomas predicted scholarly successes. Aunt Sanford—a well-preserved matron of the olden school, with an air of distinction, and gracious winning manners—gave appropriate counsels. From each I received a memento. But what I valued most was a little token from my Cousin Amy.

Amy Sanford was just one year my junior. We had been play-mates from infancy, I may say, and were great friends; yet till this hour I had not known the strength of the bond. We made frequent and extended visits to each other, and in the summertide especially Amy would often be at Cloud Cap for days together. There was no daughter in our family, nor son in the Sanford's, and we, in a sense, respectively supplied the want. Amy had full, bright-brown eyes, and a wealth of chestnut hair, and had she been far less winsome, she would have held still the key to popularity in the interest uniformly manifested in the affairs of others. Into all the amusements of my boyhood she entered with zeal—with far more than I did into her's; and among the first things she did on each successive visit, was to go the rounds with me to my partridge-traps and hare-snares, and to see my dam and corn-stalk flutter-wheels down at the branch.

I speak of Amy, as she was in earlier days. With increasing years the perfect freedom of childhood had declined—not from any untoward or hardening influences, like those batterings and deceivings of the world that transform ingenuous youth into spirits of suspicion and ill-will, withdrawing into themselves, and coiled up serpent-like, to strike aggressors. No, no. The process was altogether natural. Amy was now in her 16th year, rapidly expanding into rounded lines of even greater beauty. She had passed into that period of life, when the consciousness of sex, dawning on the pure in heart, raises its barriers, and the merry-hearted, demonstrative girl of yore is inclined instinctively towards shyness and reticence. Besides, habits of intimacy had been affected necessarily by absence at a Northern School (a celebrated Quaker institution), where, it can be added, her studies had been pursued with *eclat*. My Father had recommended the school to Cousin Thomas; and he himself knew it through his Quaker friend, Mr. Peale, a prominent member of the board of trustees.

Whatever the cause. the change was external and no more. Our sentiments towards each other—or rather, *my* sentiments towards Amy, since I could speak for myself alone—had not altered, only deepened, and begun to assume a form, the true character of which I did not then altogether understand. About one thing, however, there was no misapprehension. My parting with Amy had more of pang than with any of the others. On this occasion she stood apart, the least demonstrative person in the company. Yet her fine eyes shone with an expression I often dwelt on afterwards; and as I kissed her warm lips she placed in my hand a locket holding a pressed Moss rosebud—her favorite flower, and from "our bush," she said—the bush we had planted away back and had long cultivated together.

Next day I was to leave, at 4 P. M. "Selrachts" was not so far off. Yet I was not to go in our own carriage, but in the public stage, and alone, thrown at once on my own responsibilities.

That morning my Father took occasion to repeat the counsels he had impressed upon me. On one point he put special emphasis, as the first lesson every boy should learn : The importance of moral courage to bear ridicule. He pointed to examples

in his own school and college careers, where upright
youths had been self-ensnared from inability to face
a laugh. He knew, he said, for the first week or
two I would be dismally homesick, but that I must
bear up like a man—that a happy faculty of adaptation had been given us—that he felt sure my conduct
would win the esteem of my teachers and make
friends among the boys. He was sure, too, from the
training I had received and amount of ground gone
over, that I would make a commendable record in
my studies—that the ambitions and rivalries and
triumphs of the class-room would rouse and interest
me—that I would become engrossed in a new order
of ideas, and be soon, he doubted not, contentedly
fitted in to my surroundings. He would lay stress
on it, that, in sending me to this school, the purpose was to make me self-reliant, to give me tough-
ness for brushing and pushing and rubbing through
the world—in short, to make a man of me ; and
while, he knew, there would be hardnesses, to en-
dure these hardnesses was the very end sought.

The parting hour was at hand. Preparations to
the last detail had been completed. The thought
of change, with hopeful possibilities, is exhilarating, and in a state of happy excitement I took leave
of every body and every thing, animate and inani-
mate, at and about Cloud Cap—met the coach on
time—and at 4 rumbled out of L.—

Thoughts come and go, a thousand thoughts. I was
not unhappy. Rather otherwise. I soon found
myself watching the clouds. From the earliest re-

collections this have I done with singular interest.
Probably, because my mother was wont to tell me,
that, in the divine economy, the angels have charge
of the winds and the clouds. I would watch and
watch them, and imagine personal form and movement. It was in the thirties, the 27th of September, but a fine summer-like afternoon. A lively
breeze tempered the blazing sun. Bodies of cumu-
lus summer-cloud floated lazily here and there, with
lower strata of smooth leaden hue, supporting massy
sunlit coils of dazzling whiteness, like radiant banks
of snow. I watched the clouds and fell into rev-
eries. Time sped. It grew dark, and out of the
giant depths of the clear Heavens the stars shone
forth with unusual splendor. Still I was watching
the heavens and dreaming. At length drowsiness
drew on—recoil from excitement. The coach's gentle jog over sandy roads aided the tendency. Presently I slept, and soundly.

At 6 next morning we had breakfast at a famous
way-side inn, kept by one Mrs. Barclay. Here à
change of whip was made, and sixth change of
teams, and soon we were bowling along again. I
felt mannish and splendid. Noon dinner was taken
at another country inn, with another change of
teams. Two hours later, from a hill-crest, the spires
of Selrachts College were seen to the right above the
top of an intervening wood. Three-fourths of a
mile further on the stately façade came full into view.

The edifice, fronting southward, occupied a slightly elevated site, two hundred yards from the road—

the intervening area being set in grass, and adorned with lawn trees and shrubbery and flowering plants of various description. This area a winding carriage way cut in twain. On either side of this way ran the graveled walks. A space, northwest, level and bare, made an ample play-ground. East of the grounds, up to the main road, were the kitchen gardens. Southward, beyond the road, lay broad, well cultivated fields. Westward stood a body of dark forest.

The college was of stone, four stories high. A main centre portion—of sixty feet front, and standing out from the long wings in massive piazzas upheld by a succession of arches—terminated laterally in two short towers, surmounted by dumpy, quadrilateral spires.

An imposing pile. Its genius was an accomplished German, Wilhelm Von Selrachts. As Lamertine has observed in his life of Fenelon, there are two qualities in rare combination, but which must coexist, to make a really great teacher, *the power to command, and the gift of pleasing.* These in eminent degree Von Selrachts possessed, and had not death cut short his career, his fame would have been as broad as the country.

He received me with a winning air of benevolent authority, adding certain pertinent observations, suggested by what my Father had written him, I am sure—observations upon the peculiar trials before me. Presently I was introduced to the Dominie having immediate supervision of the boys with

whom I was to be classed. His name was Du Big-
lau—verily, a *low*, lean, little Frenchman, yet truly
big in amiable directions, the most sympathetic and
kindliest of men.

First impressions were not unfavorable, even good.
I ate supper in the spacious refectory and went to
bed with far less of homesickness than I had anticipated. It was long before I could close my eyes.
For hours I lay wide awake in the great attic dormitory, with scores of sleeping boys about me.
There were throngs and throngs of thought. They
gathered mainly about the next Xtmastide. With
us and in our circle it had ever been a season of the
greatest gaiety. How bright would be the next! I
would be at home! And how improved! How joyfully would my dear Father and all greet me!—
Finally sleep came, and with it behold! a dream:
It was the Xtmastide at home, and I stood by Amy's
side, cutting, as of your, cedar and holly twigs for
her nimble fingers to bind into wreaths for the
Xtmas altar. I awoke. Again I slept. Again I
dreamed—yet less and less distinctly. Towards
morning I had passed into sound slumber, broken
by the early college bell.

I rose unrefreshed. Excitements had passed away.
A lonely, helpless, despairing sort of feeling came
creeping over me ; nor did the incidents of the day
tend to dispel it. Unfortunately, at this juncture
the reputation of the college for discipline had
drawn thither an unusually large percentage of
rough, rude material. My experiences now began.

It was a few moments past breakfast, in the recreation room, when my teacher, calling me up, introduced me to a lot of these fellows. Whereat I blushed like a girl, averted my head, cast my eyes down, and looked askance at the boys, in a timid sort of way—an old trick of mine with strangers. To behaviour so unexpected and silly the natural response was a burst of laughter. I drew back dreadfully confused and mortified. The Dominie spoke up kindly, accompanying me, as I retired, completely downhearted, to the solitude of the study-hall. He remained with me the rest of the hour, never alluding to the blunder, but seeking to divert my mind by explaining, with an interplay of wit and anecdote, the mode of teaching at the college, &c., &c.

The bell rang for recitation, and presently in the class room I gave another "exhibition." It was the weekly review in mental arithmetic. The questions had been going round, simple questions, thought I to myself, and getting many more misses than I would have supposed—when all at once the Dominie, looking at me kindly, called my name and asked *me* a question. I had not dreamed of such a thing. I had been told it was not usual to be called up on one's first appearance in class, and the peculiar circumstances of my case made the call the more unexpected. In this departure the Dominie was moved by the best motive, as he afterwards explained to me. At the matriculating examination the evening before, he had asked, if not this identical question, yet questions of precisely similar character, and I had given such ready answers, he felt sure I would answer this, and acquit myself so creditably, as to offset the impression make by the *faux pas* at the introduction.

The question struck me like a thunderbolt. I rose mechanically, my whole body visibly agitated, my face pale as a ghost's, and, in tremulous voice, asked a restatement of the question— partly, to gain time for reflection—partly, because, in the confusion overwhelming me, I had not in truth clearly apprehended the Dominie's words. The latter realized my predicament and put the question again, very slowly, very clearly, very distinctly, giving at the same time a smile of encouragement. All for naught. I had enough intelligence left to see the Dominie's friendly animus, and my inability to meet expectation augmented the confusion. I stood regarding him with a stupid stare. I tried to think, but was totally unable. I had not the least control over resources. A sweat oozed from every pore. My agitation was visibly increasing, when the Dominie, with expression of distress at having unwittingly set a trap, relieved the situation by answering the question for me—whereupon I shot back into my seat in a gush of passionate tears. The boys responded with a ripple of derisive laughter. This the Dominie instantly checked, and, saying I was not well, bade me seek relief in the open air.

I went out, and beneath some dense, low-branched cedars, which grew on the slope near the play-ground of the smaller boys, threw myself down in agony of

spirit, supersensitive creature that I was. Vexed
with myself, mortified to the last degree, I made a
great vow.

By the noon recreation hour I was composed.
Immediately I sought the Dominie—insisted upon
his plying me with questions at once—told him I
had vowed to overcome this foolishness—and that
such a discipline before the class would be a means.

He commended the resolution—warned me with a
twinkle to be ready—felt sure I would do well,
&c., &c.

The Dominie promptly redeemed the promise.
The questions began coming that very afternoon. I
had a mastery of the subjects, seeing the ground
had been covered under tutors. Answers were cor-
rectly given, if timidly. With every recitation I
gathered confidence; and soon it became apparent
to the class I was the first scholar among them.

My proficiency delighted the Dominie, of course;
but won the pointed ill-will of three or four boys
whom I had thus turned down. They had been
standing abreast at head, and struggling against
each other for the medal. Ambitions now merged
into a common hostility towards me; and the Dominie
himself unwittingly supplied an engine of persecution. The circumstances were these:

Within the week of my matriculation our class
received an addition in a tall, awkward, country
lad. The first day of his appearance at recitation
the usual question was put by the Dominie:

"What is your full name, Master Berryson?" he

asked, as, pencil and class-book in hand, he made ready for an entry.

"Benjamin Opedyke Berryson," replied the lad.

"Is Berryson spelled with a 'y' or an 'i' ?"

"*We* spell with a 'y,' " said the lad.

"Some spell it with an 'i,' then?" remarked the Dominie, noticing the emphasis.

"Yes, Sir."

The Dominie wrote down the name, and, as he completed it, spoke it to himself, slowly, disjunctively, and in a musing way (B.—O.—Ber.-ry.-son), scrutinizing the entry. Then suddenly looking up, with humor dancing in his eye, remarked:

" 'I' and 'y' often replace each other, Master Berryson."

"Yes, Sir," the lad responded.

"And with this exchange did you ever reflect how your name reads backwards?"

"No, Sir."

"In 'No, Sir,' you make a beginning," said the Dominie with a broad smile, "since the back reading is *No-Sir-re-bob.*"

A roar of laughter followed.

"It's a habit of mine to read names backwards," continued the Dominie, "and I make some funny finds. A few sessions ago we had in the class Edward C. Ivon—E. C. Ivon—a sharp, wide awake, city chap, who knew a thing or two. *Novice* is the name backwards."

Another roar greeted this.

"And then we had Eldridge L. Peets—E. L.

Peets—a dumpy, squat little fellow. The back reading is *steeple.*"

Another roar from the benches.

The incident at once aroused interest in reverse renderings. Every name was turned about for a find. To get a fling, those boys tried my own, who thought they had a grudge against me. Without avail, however, till the next day, when a remark let fall by the Dominie came to their aid. He was explaining the Greek alphabet. Speaking of *gamma*, the letter answering to our "g," he remarked casually, that its form (γ) resembled somewhat the lower half of the English "*ƒ.*" Forthwith these boys tried my name with "g" replacing "*ƒ*," and got a skit on me in "niggur"—pronounced by them "neegur!"

As distinguished from epithets purposely insulting, mere nick-names originate in a certain degree of congruity—at least without it are scarcely maintained. The ideas investing my own personel and "niggur" were absolutely opposed; for I was rather frail-looking—unusually clean and neat—and at a glance distinguished by a peculiar air of sensitiveness and delicacy. The term was so utterly incongruous it had no proper breath of life—a nothing—a reed shaken by the wind—a nine day's college fad; and I should have extinguished its furtive indirect utterance by indifference.

The fates willed otherwise. I was so excessively sensitive—born without a skin, as Hume said of Rousseau. I felt the fling profoundly, and winced under it in such a way as to egg on the set of boys I have spoken of. Scarcely, too, had they begun using "niggur," when an incident gave the term currency. That is, the Prefect came to my aid—over the left. Having sharply threatened the flout, he was prompt to punish the first man caught offending. The punishment, indeed, was mild. But the offender was popular, the offense one never before punished, and being of a nature, too, the boys considered unpunishable, they resented what they thought uncalled for discipline, and "niggur" with a vengeance came to stay. It would be bawled over campus. I would see it on blackboard margins. It would be spelled within my hearing. It was thrust on me in class-room notes. Missives containing it were found beneath my pillow. Letters sent to L——; to be mailed, had this single term "niggur." It was poked at me, in short, from every quarter, and in almost every conceivable way.

I sank under the persecution. O what sense of loneliness and helplessness! One or two of the better disposed boys made advances—from pity, I suppose. My pride rejected them. Earnestly did the teachers try to check the grievance, and bring me into harmony with the college. In vain. Heartsick, I could not rally. True, "niggur" soon died out. But it had made its deep, isolating impression. I shrank from any contact, and conceived a profound aversion towards everything around me. I had no share in the sports. All my recreations were solitary. The Indian clubs I swung alone. If

I played ball, the ball was my own, and the walls my companions. I wore a hunted, strained expression. I would start at little noises, and fly into pieces on every occasion. The slightest provocation, the least annoyance from the boys, would bring forth outbursts of passion. In a word: my temper was transformed. My life was a life apart.

Perfect wretchedness is for the damned alone. There were offsets, or I should have lost my mind. One was anticipation of the Xtmastide, when I would be at home—my dear, dear, happy home. In a letter of this period (a preserved copy is now before me) I tell my Father that "almost one-fourth of the time to Xtmas has gone by already, and only three-fourths more." One-fourth gone and *only three-fourths more!* What pathetic simplicity! What yearning between the lines! I found myself continually turning eastward and looking out towards my home. Whenever I could, I would take a winding walk to the road entrance. Just within stood a giant Spanish oak. Selrachts' was an elevated site. This, its highest point, whence to the east opened a clear and extended view. A seat encircled the oak, and here I would sit alone, and look out towards my home. Eastward lay a succession of cultivated fields. Beyond and beyond in perspective rose the hills—while yet beyond, in the far smoky distance, the outline of the forest summit was thrown upon the horizon. This summit seemed to me the point of division between the dismal region in which I pined a captive, and a fair region beyond, where my home was and my friends. What longing eyes were bent eastward! What thoughts arose of "home again!" I envied the wayfarers eastward, as I caught sight of them on the higher points of the white road-way, that here and there reappeared in its hilly course. O for the day and the hour, I would inwardly exclaim, when this gate would close behind me homeward bound! And great choky lumps would swell in my throat.

Another offset was my self-communings, of nights, in my dormitory cot. The dormitories occupied the fourth story. In the centre of this story was a large hall, sixty feet by fifty, used for theatricals and like purposes. On either side were the domitory attics, each forty by fifty feet, and eight feet high centrally. Great dormer windows admitted light through the sloping ceilings. I slept in the room next the middle hall in the east end. My bed stood nearest the short passage joining the two dormitories on this side, and almost immediately beneath the internal window connected with a small partitioned-off apartment, in which the teacher slept who had charge of this room, and whence, as occasion required, he could look out upon the boys.

At nine, when lights were out and I under cover, began one of the happiest—I mean, least unhappy – portions of the twenty-four hours. The worriments of the day were over. All so calm and peaceful. None to molest or make me afraid. My tormentors, bound in slumbers, lay still and harmless around me. I was free from persecution, and, what was even more, its *apprehension.* It was this apprehension that specially affected me. So sensitive was I to annoyance, that the dread of it kept me all the day long excited more or less and bewildered.

What peace of mind I had this still, dark hour gave. It became my prayer hour. It drew to itself my devotions, and almost invariably brought tears that refreshed, really gladdened me. These devotions were the simple prayers of infancy, taught me by my mother. The central feature (I mean, in my own mind) was the superintendence of angels—a feature the cuts in the "big ha' Bible" had great share in shaping. It was an heir-loom, this Bible, an ancient book, with borders embellished generally in vignette, in some instances filled in with Holbein's Dance of Death, and the prints throughout were copious in angel representation. The volume was lost in the subsequent wreck. But I can see these prints now, every one of them, and vividly—the Angel comforting Hagar, the Angel and Manoah, the Angel appearing to Gideon, the Angel of the Lord smiting the Assyrian hosts, the Angel speaking to Zacharias at the altar of Incense, &c. &c. Of Sunday afternoons, in her low sweet voice, my mother would read passages she thought I might understand, and explain to me the prints. And of evenings, after the prayer at her knee had been said and I was tucked away in my little bed, she would recall these prints, and make use of them to illustrate beautiful stories about the Angels—our own guardian Angel specially, how near this guardian

is, and how dear he should be to us. It delighted
me to hear them. Often have I lain awake dwell-
ing on them, when my mother supposed I was fast
in slumbers, and I would fall asleep encircled by
their sweet influences.

On a supersensitive spirit all this made a profound
impression. Angel superintendence early became
central in my spiritual consciousness.

With advancing years and after my mother's death
the impression began to wax dim. It was now all
vividly recalled. My head would be under cover,
eyes closed, lids repeatedly forced firmly together,
to press out welling tears—physically I was in dense
darkness, yet a great and a burning light seemed
round about me, and protecting Angels appeared
moving in it. Had I thrown the cover, my eyes
would have opened on a heavenly radiance—so it
seemed to me. With many weepings I said my
prayers over and over. I wept, but I was really
happy. It was a tender, sweet hour. All my
thoughts were gentle and loving. I felt severe
towards myself alone. I forgave the wrongs against
me. I put all blame on my own silly weaknesses.
In a state of mind positively ecstatic, I prayed
for my tormentors, that they might bear another
mind towards me—and to the Angels, always to be
about me, protecting me—and fondly believed my
surroundings would improve next day ; and in this
hope at length would pass into sleep—peaceful, profound sleep, yet dreamy at first and confused with
home glimpses and school glimpses and glimpses of
Angels.

Woe is me! I awoke upon a world whose king is Sorrow. This next day was like those before it. My tormentors were at me again. I grew hard and bitter again. Dark clouds hung over me again.

Meanwhile Von Selrachts had a watchful and kind eye. He spoke often and encouragingly. His keen perception must have recognized in my personality something altogether exceptional; for, towards the end of the first month he intimated a visit home, adding that he would write my Father, should I say so. I replied declaring my wish and purpose to make further trial—dying to return, yet unwilling to distress my Father, and piqued, withal, that my weak, troubled heart should be so bare.

But matters grew worse and worse. There was a spell I could not break. I felt, too, my powers of application giving way. Dazed, deadened feelings began creeping over me. I feared the worst, and was on the point of seeking Von Selrachts, to accept his suggestion, when came a letter from my Father calling me home. Von Selrachts had kept him fully informed, I am sure, and my Father saw I must leave.

What transforming power in the suddent advent of a great and unexpected deliverance! A torrent of delight sweep into and purges the soul. Hates, venoms, are no more—expelled through complete occupancy by an opposing sentiment. In a delirium of joy enemies are embraced, deepest wrongs forgiven. It is human nature's summit—for the moment, pure spiritual existence—a glimpse of Heaven itself, where the saints are perfectly good, because they are perfectly happy. As I read the letter a horrid veil fell from before my eyes. The weight on my spirit was gone. A flood of light and joy rolled in. The darkened, disfigured world became fair again. I was transformed, intoxicated, and loved everybody and every thing around me. The sun shone brighter. The birds sang sweeter. The flowers took on another beauty. I mingled with the boys, and greeted them all with smiling confidence. And all the boys, astonished and gratified, seemed turned towards me. I had made no real enemies—thanks to my solitary ways. And when I threw off reserve under the impulse of a powerful sentiment, and extended an open hand, the boys met me more than half way. Some,. perchance, that a rival would be removed. Some, it may be, to make amends for wrongs. Others, from the grace of human nature, since happiness is catching, an echo from those remnants of pure charity still enshrined within the stranded soul. The revolution in my feelings was so complete, that the old college positively seemed dear, and the probability of return even began to take form.

Early next morning I jumped into the stage; the morning after, rolled into L—— to a joyful wind from the driver's horn; and with bounding heart sped on with Cupid to Cloud Cap—alas! to receive into my arms a stricken Father.

CHAPTER III

John Ruffin's swoon excited the liveliest sympathy, and for the moment the appalling character of the loss he had sustained, was forgotten in anxiety for his personal safety. To apply the smelling bottle and dash water into his face, was the work of an instant. There was no rally, however; and they began to think the case serious. A correct opinion; for in falling his head had struck violently the edge of the seat of a solid mahogany chair, causing severe cerebral concussion. He lay profoundly insensible, extremities cold, features ghastly, scarcely breathing. Mrs. Peale took charge, and, directing that the nearest Doctor be sent for post haste, promptly applied the simple remedies her good sense and practical experience suggested—she being an active member of more than one charitable institution, and having had occasion to minister in attacks of this kind. Friction by hand over thorax and upper limbs, cataplasm to abdomen, sinapisms to calves, with hot mustard bottles to feet, presently brought on some reaction. Consciousness returned, and the patient was assisted to his room. But the hot head, white tongue, and flushed turgid face were not reassuring. By this time a neighbor Doctor had arrived. He was soon joined by the family physician from L——. Putting their wise heads together they diagnosed a probable encephalitis—prognonis grave. Whereby the laity may understand that Mr. Ruffin was threatened with brain fever, and recovery in doubt. The M. D.'s were not mistaken. Inflammatory symptoms, of aggravated type, supervened apace—intense pain over the head, fierce delirium, pupils like pins' heads, wild and brilliant look, and a hard pulse rapidly shifting from 60 to 120.

The old time heroics are administered—blood letting and hard purging with croton oil, leeches to temples and mastoid processes following the lancet. That John Ruffin survived was probably due to application of fresh water to the shaved head in the form of a slender and constant stream upon the vertex.

On the third day the stage of collapse set in, with pallor, feeble and flying pulse, muttering stupor, and extreme debility. The physicians watch by the hour. Caps of blistering plaster are now applied to the head, and stimulants and restoratives exhibited.

From the acute attack John Ruffin made a slow recovery, extending through months. With the return of consciousness the sense of his loss was overwhelming, and critical relapses occurred. Almost invariably they were associated with the presence of his son, on whom he would fasten his eyes in the most pitiful way and in tears bewail his condition. So unhappy was the effect that for a period Thomas was compelled to deny himself to his Father's room, save when he slept.

At this juncture the most salutary attentions were those of the Episcopal Minister at L——, a wise and devout man. At the earliest practicable moment he was admitted by direction of the physician, who saw that the patient's suffering and danger were now mainly in mental and spiritual spheres, and more directly within reach of one skilled in the science of the soul. And when John Ruffin railed at the Divine wrath against him, himself done for, and his son of tender years stripped utterly bare, the pastor would reply, that God's judgments are rather to be feared, not discussed—that after all the event might be for his son's benefit—that inherited fortunes have so often proven fatal to youth, at once a temptation, and bar to development—that Thomas would now stand on his own feet, with every incentive to throw the scabbord away—that adverse circumstances would tend to strengthen his character and draw forth his full worth—and that the son might yet provide for the Father even better than the Father had thought to provide for the son.

Conversations in this strain at repeated visitations exerted a soothing tendency. If not reconciled, John Ruffin became somewhat less despairing, and gradually bore his grief with fewer outbreaks. But cruel had been the blow, and the close of the third month saw him a physical and mental wreck, aged and changed beyond the recognition of his nearest friends. His hair and beard, grown long, were of snowy whiteness—his face blanched—frame bent—sight, hearing, memory impaired—intellect permanently weakened. The expression was one of childish imbecility—daft, as the Scotch would say.

Meanwhile, the Peales had gone—Friend Peale, a few days subsequent to the attack, called home by business necessities—Mrs. Peale, several weeks later, when the violence of the attack was over—during which she had been a most assiduous and a most efficient nurse.

The Sanfords, also, had all hurriedly left for New Orleans, almost immediately after the failure—to live there, it was said. They had sent repeated and most tender messages. Had all called, too; but saw none of the family. John Ruffin was denied absolutely to every one, save the nurse; and Thomas could not find it in his heart to meet those criminally responsible, as he thought at that moment, for his Father's ruin. On the eve of departure a heart-broken note came from Amy, saying they, likewise, had lost everything—that her Father was not to blame, having been deceived by the Manager—and bidding Thomas adieu. It smote him, then, that he had refused to see her. This note came in an envelope (a novelty in those days), square and of pinkish hue, and with a monogram formed by A S stamped upon the flap.

It was true, as Amy said. The Sanfords had nothing left but a New Orleans residence, owned by "Aunt Sanford." Later on, Thomas learned indirectly that his Cousin Thomas had died grief-stricken, and that Amy, her health failing in New Orleans, had obtained a position of some kind somewhere up North.

John Ruffin's deplorable condition dragged on through Spring and Summer, and gradually grew worse. The surroundings were a source of constant irritation. He had been an exceptionally kind Master. Between himself and the slaves existed a sincere and strong attachment; and when he would walk out, their manifestations of sympathy, significant though mute (for they had been forbidden to express them), deeply and harmfully affected him. Withal, he became morbidly sensitive to being recognized as having fallen so low, and conceived a violent aversion towards his friends and all who had known him. So the old man shut himself up in his room—saw scarcely any one but Thomas—and appeared verging upon a settled melancholia. The only thought which seemed to soothe, was one suggested by the pastor, that it was divinely ordered Thomas should provide for him. The physicians gave no hope of complete restoration under any circumstances; but thought an absolute change of residence—new faces, new scenes—might possibly arrest progress towards an aggravated dementia, and prolong a helpless, harmless, and measurably happy life.

Poor Thomas! What days and weeks—long, long, weary weeks—of watchings and hopings and sufferings! The loss or fortune did not so deeply

touch him—he knew not then what it was to turn
his back upon Cloud Cap—but his Father's personal
condition. A moving spectacle is that—a strong,
flourishing man suddenly withered and laid low!
How much more, when the victim is a Father worthily
and tenderly loved! The trustful way in which the
old man put himself under his care went straight to
Thomas' heart, and he made a solemn compact with
himself then and there, to give his Father the chance
the physicians held out. But, poor fellow! how
dismal the prospect, now that acute excitements
were over, and the cold facts of the situation stood
out clear! Void of money or what money buys, the
wheels of existence will absolutely cease to move;
and out of an opulent fortune but five hundred dollars
remained, a sum the exemption law allowed. Save
some far off collaterals, too, between whom and
himself intercourse had practically ceased, John
Ruffin was the last representative of his house. His
wife was from a distant state, where her family had
become reduced. None there were on whom Thomas
had any right to call for aid. He himself had no
experience of men or things. In the brass or assurance many esteem the best business current coin, he
was singularly deficient, as already shown. His
entire commercial capital stood in good penmanship
and a complete theoretical knowledge of bookkeeping—the latter a branch of study he had pursued with penchant both under tutors and at Selrachts. A slim stock, truly, to challenge fortune
with. Into his scale, however, can be thrown a pure

heart, and a high and a holy aim, and an impulse towards that broadening of character which the advent of responsibility tends to evolve.

John Ruffin's awful visitation, so sudden and complete, was on every one's tongue, and roused profound sympathy. The pastor and other friends busied themselves in his behalf; and it was their unanimous opinion, that a suitable home could be found only in some one of the many well-conducted charitable institutions in the large cities. They advised Thomas forthwith to institute inquiries; and he was revolving the matter, when came a letter of sympathy from Friend Peale (himself or his wife wrote. regularly every week or two), containing a suggestion in line with the above advice. How opportune, thought Thomas! He's the proper person to address touching a home for my Father—indeed, the very person himself.

So that day he wrote Friend Peale, adding inquiries touching work of some sort for himself. In the kindest of letters Friend Peale replied by the next post, inclosing the last annual report on "The Old Men's Home." He described the institution as being under the control of prominent citizens, and one of the best of its kind, that he himself was a trustee and his wife an active manager, and that his Father would receive every attention; and further assured Thomas that he would be only too glad to do anything he could to secure for him a position, in the event of his becoming a fellow-citizen.

The general character of the report—the rigid

conditions of admission—the restrictions thrown around those admitted—and evident high-tone of the institution—all impressed Thomas favorably. The crowning recommendation was to see the names of Adam Peale and Martha Peale actually down in black and white in the list of trustees and managers. The admission fee—two hundred dollars for those between 60 and 65 (his father had just turned 60), with an additional one hundred dollars, when the applicant resided in another state—nearly consumed their little remnant of five hundred. However, Thomas thought he could surely get work of some sort for himself, and decided at once it was the very place for his Father.

Eagerly seeking the latter and opening the matter, his anticipations were checked by his Father's violently objecting to being in an institution to which Friend Peale stood related, or even in the same city with him. But Thomas reasoned with his Father—assuring him he would never meet either Friend Peale or his wife against his will—that the change was absolutely necessary—that the physicians ordered it—that he *must* consent—and finally the old man became reconciled, submitting to his son, as called to provide for him. So Thomas wrote Friend Peale he would be on within a few days, to confer with him.

Meanwhile, by order of the trustees the Court had appointed, Cloud Cap had been sold under the hammer. The purchaser was a Mr. Kyle, New Orleans merchant and large creditor of Thomas Sanford & Co.

He bought all—plantation, slaves, and personal property; and so quietly was the auction conducted — to avoid harmful effects on John Ruffin—that the latter knew nothing of what was being done. Mr. Kyle, a kind-hearted gentleman and acquaintance of John Ruffin, was so moved by the latter's misfortunes, that he voluntarily proposed to delay formal possession and let everything go on just as usual under the manager, until definite and final arrangements touching John Ruffin's future should be made.

It was the 16th of September, when Thomas left with the testimonials, &c., required by the terms of admission to The Home. Taking the steamboat at L—— he was transferred to a coast line sail at the seaport near the river's mouth, and reached the city without event. A hackman was called, street and number given, and he was driven to the Peale residence. Friend Peale was absent—at Boston on business. Mrs. Peale received him with the warmest demonstrations. Stay was limited; since no one could take his place with his Father. After brief rest, therefore, Mrs. Peale accompanied him to The Home.

The Old Men's Home was a noble charity, one of the glories of the city, and under a name somewhat changed flourishes to-day. Its affairs were guided by a body of trustees, exclusively men, and a board of managers, exclusively women—all representative citizens. The practical administration was entirely in the hands of the ladies, who filled the offices from president down; and the work in its various forms——

admissions and dismissals, purchasing supplies, soliciting aid, providing entertainment, &c., &c.— was portioned out among committees chosen from the board of lady managers.

The building occupied an uptown corner lot by itself—a large rectangular, yellow brick structure. Eastward it aligned with the street. It fronted southward, and from the east and west street stood back fifteen or more yards. It was built about a rotunda with hip roof and sky light. The ground floor of this rotunda made a general sitting room, at whose upper end stood a plain reading stand and parlor organ for religious and like purposes. Galleries ran around the second and third stories, and upon these galleries the rooms of the inmates opened. A handsomely furnished apartment on the first floor, was the committee room. Back, were the kitchen and dining hall. Entrance to the sitting room was through a spacious vestibule. The façade was relieved by a brick wall built out from the central portion of the structure, and terminating in an ornamental gable. From this wall a brick portico projected, with arched openings in the three sides, and battlement roof. The area in front was beautifully set in grass and shrubbery. Diagonally opposite lay a lovely little park. Fine churches and the mansions of the wealthy adorned on every hand this elevation, and altogether it was a locality specially attractive.

With its kindred institution—The Old Women's Home, in another section of the city—The Old Men's

Home met a special want. Found everywhere are
the agéd, the indigent, the helpless, who have seen
better days—too proud to beg, too refined and sensitive to mingle with occupants of the ordinary alms
house. Among these The Home found its patronage.
The strict scrutiny touching both admission and the
admitted, guaranteed, as a class, high grade inmates.

They made an interesting study, these inmates.
Life with some had been uneventful—with others
most varied and most tragic. All were nearing its
close, helpless and alone. The props had been knocked from under. Riches had made for itself wings.
Tender ties had been ruptured. Loving firesides
become a memory. Friends and kindred had gone
early, or children taken before their time. The hand
that would have toiled, the voice to cheer and comfort, had long been still and silent in the grave.
How despairing their lot but for "that most excellent gift of charity!" In The Home they had a
meet resting place, ministered-to by woman's soothing care. Here they found peace—often-times happiness.—Reader, sudden and profound are life's
vicissitudes. Its one certainty is its uncertainty.
Thou thyself mayest one day need such a refuge—
or that dear child upon thy knee, may need it. Let
us commend the noble charity to thy benevolence.

If Thomas was pleased with every thing he saw,
pleasure sprang into joy, when, through Mrs. Peale's
influence, special accommodations were secured for
his Father. John Ruffin's mental state and need of
his son's care really disqualified him for admittance.

But Mrs. Peale was a foremost member of the board.
She represented that no doubt John Ruffin would
soon so improve at The Home, as to dispense with
the services of Thomas, and drew a picture of the
old man's multiplied affliction, that went to the
hearts of the managers. There is, too, a remote possibility that Friend Peale's liberal yearly contribu-
tion and the policy of not displeasing him, had some
weight. So it was arranged that John Ruffin should
have a commodious first floor east room, with private
entrance to the street—that for the present at least,
in his peculiar state of mind, meals should be
served in his room—and that Thomas be allowed
temporarily to occupy the room of nights, at a small
extra charge.

On their way back Thomas represented that his
Father necessarily would have some needs beyond
the accommodations of The Home—that the admittance fee would take more than half of the remnant
of fortune remaining—and that of course he could
not think of bringing his Father on, unless he himself had work for his own support, &c. Mrs. Peale
suggested that he might answer an advertisement;
and, taking up the morning paper on reaching home,
read in the "Help wanted" column: "A bank
bookkeer at 222 North G—— St." She knew little
about that part of the street, she said—thought it
was respectable—a recommendation was its being
not very far from The Home—and proposed that
Thomas call and inquire—adding, that at any rate
'twould do no harm. So a passing 'bus was hailed,

and within twenty minutes, Thomas, accompanied by a servant, alighted at 222 North G—— St.

He read over the door way, "Loan Office." What struck him was the symbol surmounting the sign—one whose significance he did not then understand—that of three golden balls. A symbol, be it known, which the first United States pawnbrokers brought over from England, as the first English pawnbrokers had brought from Lombardy in the sixteenth century, as the coat of arms of their family. For these pawnbrokers were related to the then rising house of the Medici—originally medical men, as the name imports, or rather apothecaries—afterwards renowned for the extraordinary number of statesmen it produced, and its magnificent patronage of literature and art, and by legislative enactment had already been allowed to bear as coat of arms the golden balls that advertised the *pills* of their ancestors.

CHAPTER .IV.

THE PAWNBROKER.

The chief owner and managing head of this establishment (the Loan Office mentioned in the preceding chapter), was Isaac Dalguspin, commonly and jocosely called the *Banker*, as the not unfrequent source of forced loans even to respectable parties in a pinch. Recently, he had purchased the charter privileges of a company composed of benevolent gentlemen, who had attempted to establish a form of the *Mont de Piete*—a movement made in the interest of the poor. Pawnbrokerage in the United States, then, as now, was modeled closely on that in Enggland, with loose methods and under social ban. It's a pity; for the pawn-shop holds a legitimate place in the body politic. It meets a necessary social want—properly conducted, is a form of benevolence. There are crises, when the poor man is sorely pressed for a little money—when he *must* have it, to tide over the exigency, or ruin breaks upon himself and family. His sole recourse is the sign of the three balls, which supplies a peculiar class of borrowing facilities. The pawn-shop is the needy man's Bank.

But through the operation of unworthy laws in unworthy hands, the pawner is skinned in the transaction. The pawn-broker's cupidity is devouring, with his four to six per cent. a month, and *expenses.* In France and on the continent of Europe generally, it is otherwise. The *Mont de Piété* prevails. This institution originated in the fifteenth century in the pious invectives of Francisco di Viterbo. Outraged at the merciless exactions of the usurers— that third power of the middle ages which shared sovereignty with the church and the state, and which Scott has represented in Isaac of York—this barefooted Minorite Friar strode into the market place of Padua, among the tables of the money-changers, and thundered out his anathemas. The result resembled that, when the Master Himself purged the Temple. The usurers grabbed their bags and slunk off. The people prolonged the cry. Wealthy and benevolent citizens took up the cause of the poor, and a *Mont de Piété* was established, with a low interest rate (to cover necessary expenses) for money advanced on the pawner's pledge. Patronized by the church, encouraged by the state, the institution rapidly spread, save in England, so slow to innovate.

The *Mont de Piété* eventually lost its purely pious character. In France, Italy, and elsewhere on the Continent, it is now supported by the funds of the state, and operated under public control. Still, as a vast improvement on the methods of the usurer, as the deadly foe of the old pawn-broker, the institution is essentially charitable. It is thoroughly respectable, too. Transactions with it are totally devoid of furtive features, as much so as entering a bank to have a note changed. Its patrons, for the most part, are the very poor, as may be supposed. Yet men of substance and character, temporarily pressed, do not disdain openly to seek its aid ; and ladies of high life not unfrequently find it convenient. As Summer approaches, they will pawn their fine furs and other winter wear—use the money to swell the outing fund—and in the Fall receive back their valuables, minus the sum advanced and a trifling interest, as well as the ravage of the moth.

In the year 1829, as the municipal records show, a Company of charitably disposed gentlemen introduced into the city we have spoken of, the *Mont de Pieté*, under the name of "The Lombard Association." It continued for a few years. Then wound up. Did not pay. "Lombard" was a handicap. The odor of the pawn shop hung around it repulsively. The Charter, by terms, was transferable, and Dalguspin & Co bought its privileges.; with right to change the name to "Loan Office." There was a provision in the Charter (—it had not been utilized—) for operating a Savings Bank in connection with pawn-brokerage. This Dalguspin put in force, doing business at the old stand. He partitioned off a section of the spacious pawn-shop and fitted it up handsomely, with street entrance, and a sign : "The Wage Earners' Savings Bank." A number of considerations led to the purchase. The discussion connected with the establishment and operation of "The Lombard Association" had raised a hue and cry against pawn-brokers, and it was surmised the City Council would overhaul the whole business, lower percentage, and draw tighter the restrictions. Furthermore, Dalguspin thought he saw in any event better profits in the change.

So far, apparently, events had justified the forecast. Dalguspin nowadays seemed unusually flush. He had made money already at the old business ; for our cities are rich fields for such fellows. The characteristics of American society—fast feverish features, fondness for finery, fickle fluctuating fortunes—all tend powerfully to fill the shelves of the pawn-broker. But the recent boom's bottom was supposed to be connected with the Savings Bank, this being the only visible change in his business, to account for the sudden and marked change in circumstances. The deposits ranged from one to five hundred dollars, and therefor five per cent. certificates at twelve months would be given, the depositors generally being small tradesmen who preferred these certificates to temporary investment in real estate or the public funds. The true source, however, of Dalguspin's being in so full feather, was successful gambling, into which he had been drawn by a crony, with whom he was strangely infatuated, and of whom the reader will hear again, one James Noals.

With the increase of fortune unlooked for changes developed in Dalguspin's bearing and surroundings;

for he appeared spruced up, affected to be somebody, and to the surprise of all who knew him, had bought a mansion, though a bachelor, and supported a style. The purchase, it may be added, was a profitable investment, or probably it would not have been made; though Dalguspin was a real *Banker* now in some sort of sense, and knew no doubt the commercial value of environments.

Thomas looked again at the slip he had cut from the newspaper, to be sure of the number, and entered. A clerk behind the main counter was engaged with one or two shop girls and domestics. It was a large, square, dingy, forbidding looking room, with a very stale odor. A broad screen stood within, immediately before the door-way. Back of the front counter was a great iron safe. All round the room, up to the ceiling, ran series of shelves, in compartments, and more or less filled with packages. Cards here and there hung upon the walls, in conspicuous print, and cautionary: "All transactions strictly private in this office"—"No goods taken from minors, without express consent of parents or guardians"—"If ticket should be lost, party must give bond and security for redemption of goods, &c., &c." Odd looking Bank, thought Thomas to himself. By this time, too, its stale odor began to take effect, and he felt a chill creeping over him. His turn having how come, he replied to the hard featured clerk, saying he had called in answer to the advertisement, and showed the slip. The clerk glanced again at him—then disappeared by a side door—by which door, a moment later, Dalguspin shuffled in.

Thomas drew back in astonishment, so different was Dalguspin from the person he had pictured to himself, as having advertised for a Bank book-keeper. His complexion was the swarthiest—so much so that by those who did not call him the *Banker*, he was individualized as Black Isaac. The nose was sharp and slightly arched. Eyes small and deep sunk. A long somewhat pointed chin. The general expression a combination of hawk and owl—pene-tration and eagerness, with shyness and distrust. The impression on Thomas was anything but pleas-ing. Lavater promptly would have called the face, that of a crafty, designing man, totally devoid of honor.

Dalguspin bent his eyes upon Thomas, and immedi-ately invited him into the *Bank*, the agreeable ap-pearance of which, in contrast with that of the pawn-shop, was inspiriting. In a few moments he had drawn from Thomas a complete history of himself and family—of his Father's former estate, of his present affliction, his object in visiting the city, his relation to Friend Peale, and the difficulty in which the Quaker's absence now placed him. The Pawn-broker's penetration saw before him an open, artless youth, without the experience in bookkeeping he desired, yet in straits, and whom he thought he could easily control and might in more ways than one make useful, and in his own mind determined to take him. They at once proceeded to a discussion of the terms, in arranging which the facility was clearly on Dalguspin's side.

"The ad. has been in but two days," said the usurer, as he rang up the clerk in the pawn-shop —"by ad. I mean advertisement," he remarked parenthetically, answering an inquisitive look from Thomas—"yes, but *two days*, and I've had over a hundred applications."

Thomas' look of surprise assured the Pawn-broker he had made the desired impression. The latter whispered to the clerk, who had now entered, and then asked with hypocritical suavity:

"What wage, my young friend, do you expect?"

"Whatever is fair, replied Thomas. "Something I can live on."

"Ah! Something to live on! That depends. One can live very dear in a city, or on very little—nothing almost—fifty cents a week."

"Young man wants to see you about the ad.," cried out the clerk, popping in his head at the side door.

"Tell the young man to wait," said the Boss.

"What do you pay bookkeepers?" inquired Thomas in a shy sort of way, as if asking the question placed him under an obligation to the usurer.

"Ah! that depends, too. You see you have no practical experience, you tell me, and business men never employ bookkeeps to learn them to keep books," replied Dalguspin, as a mischievous looking little smile at his humorous attempt played over the swarthy features. "What say you to a dollar a week ?"

"A dollar !" exclaimed Thomas. "Why, Mrs. Peale said I should not take less than four dollars a week, to begin with."

"But I throw in a room, remember."

"A room !"

"Yes, I require my bookkeeper—or rather my last clerk—to have a room in the *Bank.*"

"But I'm to occupy my Father's room of nights, you know."

"As I understand you, that arrangement is temporary only. In any event, my young friend, you must have a room of your own. Where will you put your things? Where will you eat? Do you propose to board out? With a room you might board yourself at fifty cents a week, if you chose."

"Could I see the room ?" Thomas inquired.

"It's out of order at present. I assure you it's all right. High up and healthy, and ready furnished. Worth twelve dollars a month, or three dollars a week" (the garret roost would have been dear at one dollar) — "and this, with the one dollar, meets Mistress Peale's terms, eh ?"

"This is for a beginning, then, as I understand, Sir ?" asked Thomas, with symptoms of surrender.

"Of course, my friend," the Pawn-broker unctuously replied. "You must bear in mind that I'm to teach you practical bookkeeping. Certainly, you will be advanced, just as you co-operate and show yourself useful."

Here the head of the pawn-shop clerk popped in again :

"Another young man, Sir, about the ad."

"Let 'another young man' wait, too," the Boss replied in high key, as if annoyed by these interruptions.

Thomas pondered, as, Black Isaac sat with fingers locked and twiddling the thumbs. The former reflected, that a dollar a week would leave him no margin either for his Father, or his own needs. But he would make every effort to please his employer —would be soon advanced, no donbt—a room he must have, he saw—above all, it was the *only* opportunity. So, to the Pawn-broker's question :

"Come, my friend, what do you say ? Others are waiting ——"

He promptly answered :

"I accept the terms."

"*Very* well," said the *Banker*, with marked stress on the adjunct. "You get a place many are seeking, you see. It only remains that you sign the papers."

To Thomas' look of inquiry he replied :

"Yes, my young friend, it is necessary you should give bond in three hundred dollars, to remain with me at least a year."

"I cannot," demurred Thomas, in tones of mingled surprise and disappointment—"I cannot sign papers I do not fully understand, without consulting my friends."

"It's all very plain," rejoined the Pawn-broker

suavely. "You see I'm to learn you the business; and for my services it's proper I should have some hold on the party. I know your word's as good as your bond. But it's city custom, my young friend —it's *business*. And there's no risk whatever—not the least. It's very much of a form. At the end of the term the agreement ceases. You then will have learned all the business—your wages will have risen —the contract expires by limitation—and you will be free, *perfectly* free either to remain with me, or to leave ———"

"Let me speak of this to Mrs. Peale," interjected Thomas, as the Pawn-broker made a momentary pause.

"It's scarcely possible, my dear Sir," came the oily answer. "I am to see a young man presently, to whom I've partially committed myself."

"Could you give me an hour?" Thomas asked.

"I'm to see this party within the hour, and he must have the place, if you don't take it," rejoined Dalguspin, looking at his watch.

The side door again opens, and the head pops in:

"Two more gents about the ad."

"Come in, John," said the *Banker*.

"Yes, Sir," responded the clerk, as he entered and stood just within the doorway.

"Shut that door."

John obeyed, with hand upon the knob.

"If many more come, John, you'll scarcely have room to hold them all," said the usurer, with that mischievous little smile of his. "Tell these young

men," he continued, in lowered, confidential tone,
"I am engaged. They can return an hour hence."

"Yes, Sir," responded John, as he quickly disappeared. And then many voices were heard in the
next room, and much moving about and shuffling
of feet, and rapid opening and closing of the front
door; and John—applying the point of the left
thumb to the extremity of the nose and vibrating
the fingers, while he stepped it a tiptoe in saucy
style—retired from another successful exhibition of
the training he had got from the Pawn-broker.
(John, by the way, was thinking of setting up shop
for himself).

Meanwhile, Thomas was in a profound study.
The sole thing he was in any sense fitted for, was
bookkeeping—his knowledge of this, theoretical
only—he could get no position without experience,
it appeared—and this experience he could obtain
right here. The place, too, must have some special
advantages, he thought, so very many were seeking
it. When would a chance like this offer again?
And it was Hobson's choice, he further reflected—
this or none. The state of his purse would not
allow another visit to the city on such an errand.

The Pawn-broker saw the scales wavering toward
his side, and the moment ripe for a *coup de grace*,
and remarked:

"222 is not far from The Home. *That's* a consideration."

Thomas looked up at the speaker, and then
looked down again, as the latter went on:

"And, young man, as you've caught my fancy, I'll begin advancement right now, and raise the wage fifty cents, making it a dollar and a half a week."

Thomas was captured. The indentures (copies whereof Black Isaac kept ready for clerks, having had difficulty in retaining them) were brought forth. Thomas read over the contract. It was smoothly worded ; and, perceiving no objection, he affixed his signature—then accompanied Dalguspin to the office of a magistrate hard by and made affidavit—next, the paper was taken to the Record office and recorded—and the transaction, making him an indentured clerk, was complete.

On the way back to the Peales,' Thomas indulged in reflections altogether of a self-satisfying character. He had secured a position and settled the matter of his Father's coming, and all by himself, too. In a year he'd be master of a calling, with control of the market, in a sense, and could look round for a better place, if need be. Meanwhile, he could squeeze out a living, with a little margin for his Father, he hoped.

Mrs. Peale's first glance read good news in his eyes, and she saluted him all in smiles. When Thomas told her he had gotten a place, she expressed her gratification most warmly. When she heard it was with a real Banker, she was positively delighted. When he mentioned the terms, she checked up somewhat, and considered it a bargain for the Banker, unless the room was much better than he had occasion for. When he told her he had bound himself for twelve months to a stranger, and showed his copy of the indenture, she opened wide her eyes. When she read in the bond the name of Dal-guspin, she paused, looked grave, and spoke the name aloud deprecatingly—then, reassured, re-marked, that she knew by hearsay of one by that name, but there were others no doubt of the same name in the city. When she asked for descriptions, to identify, and Thomas spoke of the sign with its strange devise of three golden balls, suddenly and very visibly her face darkened. Yet for a moment only. She was aware of the impression she was making. She saw the guileless youth had been caught. She remembered, though, having heard her good man speak of Dalguspin's recent sudden rise of fortune, and his being connected with some moneyed institution of creditable character, if she was not mistaken. Possibly the hole might not be as deep and dark as her fears imagined. She would let her good man explain, and would herself put the best face upon the inevitable. If other considera-tions drew her towards Thomas Ruffin, now penni-less and more than orphaned, they were deepened at the spectacle of this ingenuous youth taken in on so pious a mission by a crafty usurer. A mother over an afflicted child, could not have manifested more tender sympathies. So the good woman brightened up and redoubled her attentions. She spoke to Thomas encouragingly—promised to have Friend Peale write at once—and advised that his Father be brought on without delay.

The effect on Thomas was cheering. He thanked Mrs. Peale for her kindness again and again—bade her inform the President of the receiving committee, that arrangements were complete for his Father's coming—and left that afternoon for home with a heart far lighter than when he entered the city.

Within the second week of his arrival he received from Friend Peale the following letter:

Sept. —— 183 ——

"Dear Thomas:

I am just back. Sorry, sorry, sorry, missed seeing thee! Martha has told me all, and I write without a moment's delay.

Deeply do I regret thee felt compelled to bind thyself to a total stranger. But the thing's done. I have seen the papers at the Record office, and there is no escape. It is an unfortunate step, Thomas, I am bound to say; yet I beg of thee not to be unduly troubled. Thee was confronted by difficulties, I know; and it may end well, after all.

It is my plain duty to speak without reserve of the man to whom thou art bound. Thee must know every circumstance before the service begins.

Dalguspin has been a licensed pawn-broker and professional usurer, and thee knows what that means. I can say *has been;* for a year and more ago he purchased—rather, was mainly instrumental in purchasing—the charter rights of what was known in this city as The Lombard Association, under which he now operates a Savings Bank, continuing pawn-brokerage as regulated by the terms of the charter.

As chief of the pawn-brokers, Dalguspin has been notorious in this city, without position or influence, prominent only as first among a low class of dealers, accounted shrewd, supposed to have more or less money, lived secluded in his pawn-shop, and, as it not unfrequently happened that genteel parties, under temporary pressure and without available commercial securities, applied to him for loans, he was jestingly known among business men as the *Banker*—a title he singularly affects.

The bad odor of the pawn-shop we all know. Almost universally it is run by unworthy men, who are hardened again by constant contact with unfortunates, outcasts, and the vicious. I cannot say that Dalguspin has been above his class and the tendencies of the calling. By hook or by crook he drives a trade with every one, as he did with thee. I remember his figuring in some questionable transactions. But the law, I believe, has never reached him.

I speak of Dalguspin particularly, as he was. Within the past eighteen months a marked change has occurred—outwardly, at least. It began with the purchase of the Lombard Association Charter. That institution was in the hands of representative citizens and thoroughly worthy; and doubtless an element of respectability passed over to the business under its new name of "Loan Office" and "Wage Earners' Savings Bank."

I can say, too, it's rumored, that Dalguspin has at his back certain substantial citizens, who have faith in his ability to make the enterprise successful. Secret aid from such a source, while it shows on the part of these citizens due regard for their reputation, must be considered somewhat lifting to Dalguspin, who has had no reputation. In fact, he has felt flattered, and been led to improve his surroundings, and give evidence of a wealth which it had not been thought he was possessor of. For nowadays he dresses well—is seen upon the street—has made valuable investments—and occupies a residence on an avenue with regulation outfit.

I know him. That is, we speak in passing—no more. I hope change in the moral status commonly given him, has been as radical as in these outward things.

These, Thomas, are the short and simple annals of his character.

Now, I know, my son, all this will greatly shock thee. But the shock would have been greater and serious, had thee come hither without information. In my anxiety to state the case fully, I may have overstated it. And yet, it may in some way be all for the best. Who knows? Certainly, the twelve months will soon pass, and thee may retire without disadvantage—possibly with gains. It all depends on thyself, and I feel sure thee will not be wanting. Dalguspin will employ thee in the *Bank*, I suppose. The work will scarcely be heavy. One thing thee must guard against—don't let him use thee for unworthy or dishonorable ends. I have an impression of street rumors charging him with having gotten

his employees into trouble, or attempted to do so.
Be absolutely clean; and should Dalguspin make
improper advances, thee would not only have just
ground for leaving, but of sustaining legal action
against him. I trust there is little cause for apprehension. Let us hope the tricks Dalguspin may
have been given to in other days, he would be above
in these, now that he is somewhat of a real *Banker*.

My dear son, I've felt it my bounden duty to tell
thee all this. But there is something I am absolutely unable to tell thee—the depth of the sympathy
and affection Martha and I have towards thy Father
and thyself. The former I have known for years.
His affliction is daily before me. It touches me as
that of a brother. Bring him on at once. At The
Home everything shall be done for him. And for
thyself, my dear son, remember that we shall be
near to thee here in every way, and that I am ready
to stand full handed behind thee.

Martha sends a loving message; and may the God
of all counsel and comfort abide with thee at all
times and in all places.

ADAM PEALE."

As Thomas read this communication his heart
sank within him. He was so stunned and chilled by
the first lines, that the warmth and cheer of the last
made no impression, and he threw the letter from
him in despair. But he reflected. A second reading was not so cold and dismal. A third, and light
glimmered. And when for the fourth time he read
it collectedly, the letter was all brightened up by

the kind-hearted Quaker's closing sentiments, like the evening clouds by the setting Sun's effulgent rays.

His resolution was taken. The arrangements for leaving, not of an elaborate character, were already under way. They were now speedily completed, and the next day, at 10 A. M., was decided upon for the departure.

A personal word here touching Thomas Ruffin: Within the past eight months decided change had come over him. He still carried sensibility on his sleeve—was still notably shy and retiring. But a sense of responsibility had exerted a tendency to broaden and establish him, evidently. Grief, too, had settled on his brow. Deep it was; yet the circumstances of his Father's twin affliction obviated in a degree sudden shock from either. While life hung in the balance, his attention was distracted from the temporal loss, and its magnitude approached dimly from a distance, as it were. At the same time, the dethronement of reason grew upon him gradually, the subject of hope and fear through watching, weary weeks and weeks.

His personal appearance was engaging. The dark brown eyes were full and tender. An apparent weight of responsibility upon delicate shoulders, roused sympathy. In its general expression the countenance was pensive, and the smile that often played over it, one of singular sweetness.

The next day would be the last at Cloud Cap! Thomas could scarce realize it. Other matters, weighty and pressing, had kept him in such a whirl, he had not given this thought consideration. But the hour of severance from scenes so full of the happiest associations, had really come. He rose early and walked forth. The storm of the equinox had passed the evening before—of unusual severity. For forty-eight hours it blew great guns, and discharged floods, leaving in its wake clear, bracing weather. It was a fine autumnal morning, towards the close of September—the atmosphere so fresh and pure. Just the gentlest ripple of air played by starts through the trees, a sear and yellow leaf here and there falling before it. The sun was half hour high, sharply outlined in the slightly hazy horizon. His light was lessened, yet sufficient to deck the dewy grass that sparkled again in the slanting rays like stretches of brilliants. "Ilka blade had its drap," and dipped with a "diamond in its head."

Thomas sought for adieu the fields and the woods of his rambles, the scenes of sylvan sport and pleasure. It had been long since he had visited them—such was the pressure. They appeared to him to have voices, and greeted him on every hand. Here in this thicket he was wont to set his partridge traps. The space he had cleared was all bare, save some scattered slats, remnants of a wreck, and Bob White hard by was piping cheerily. Down there at the branch his dams would be built and the flutter wheels run. The flood of the equinox had swept every vestige away, and the gurgling stream seemed to be laughing in its liberty. He entered a wood.

It was full of sweet memories ; for this was Amy's favorite walk. Here, beneath that ancient spreading oak, was the rustic seat his hand had made for her. Yonder were the carnations, from a child his favorite flower, that Amy had given him ; and beyond, in the border himself had prepared, was the rose her own hands had planted, now a splendid Bon Silene ; for the gardener knew it and had given his special care. Its last, brilliant, carmine blooms were fading, yet still loading the dewy air with "Sabean odors." Where was Amy now ? An orphan, and earning her bread among strangers, he had heard ! Did she think of him ? Would they ever meet again? What changes ! What changes ! he murmured. Sorrow is king here !

As he turned to retrace his steps, an upper whirl of air caught for a moment a growth of lofty pines before him. Their summits swayed, and with that peculiar weird and wailing sough this flora gives, when its needles are swept by the breeze. It seemed to Thomas a nod and sigh of farewell, and was a spark to the train of his emotions. The flood of feeling gave way that had been gathering. He stood and wept. Then hastened back with lighter heart. The baggage had all been sent on. Everything was in readiness. At nine his Father, bidding adieu to none, entered a close carriage—was driven rapidly to L.— went aboard the boat—and made an easy, inexpensive, uneventful journey to the city, where his and his son's fortunes will be told in the chapters following.

CHAPTER V.

NEW HOMES.

The November morning opens · dark and surly.
The wind had settled in the North. Leaden lowering clouds stretch over the heavens—a dismal vault,
belted along the horizon by bluish fringe. Milk
carts rumbled noisily over frozen cobbles. Few seek
the streets. Early errand women step briskly,
shawled and hooded, and workmen trudge along to
their tasks muffling great coats close about the
neck. By nine the storm breaks. Cold, cold, cold!
Blow, blow, blow! And the snow is coming down
thick and fast in whirls and zigzags and curling
sheets from wind-swept housetops. By' noon the
storm had passed, leaving the day perfectly fair.
Three inches of snow had fallen, the first of the season. A rising temperature follows the passing of
the cloud. The atmosphere grows foggy, and
through the snow-patched branches of the park trees
the eye may dare November's sun, sweeping low
above the southern horizon.

The afternoon of this day John Ruffin and Son
reached the city. It was Thomas' first impression

6

of a snow scene. He had witnessed occasional flakes of snow. He had never seen before the whole earth spread over by a mantle of pure white—to him a most striking and a most beautiful revelation. A cab was called, and they were taken at once to The Home.

At this particular time the institution was under the executive control of the board of lady managers. The superintendent had been uniformly of the other sex. But the last masculine representative did not get on well with the inmates. Finally, he was dismissed; and while the managers were looking round for a successor, they placed in charge, under their immediate supervision, the housekeeper, Catherine Sullivan—or Miss Kitty, as she was commonly called.

Miss Kitty was a genuine, unhewn, worthy Irishwoman, with the richest brogue—fair, fat, and forty —or, to run it on the p's, pretty, plump, and pleasing—rough and resolute of spirit, yet kindly withal. In the chance opportunities from time to time afforded, she had displayed executive talent; and when given this new position, as a temporary expedient, managed the old men as cleverly as she did the economies of the institution.

As already mentioned, Mrs. Peale had secured for John Ruffin certain special privileges at The Home; and her good will she further manifested by herself furnishing his room. It was a large, commodious, first floor apartment, rather off by itself, with two inner doors; one connected with a lavatory and

bath—the other, with a vestibule; and a private external entrance, besides, opening immediately on the
north-and-south street. The appointments were
plain, but neat. An art square took the place of a
carpet, purposely chosen, to be readily removed and
shaken. On the left was a bureau. Near this a
stand with a clock. On the right was the bed, and
under it a cot, rolled out of nights for the use of
Thomas. The stove was a heater, but with arrangements for plain cooking, if need be. And there
were chairs and sofa, &c., &c. All simple, but in
every way genteel—by no means luxurious, and yet
what wealth, with severe taste, might choose—and
so of a character to spare the occupant unpleasant
contrasts.

The physicians at L—— had impressed upon
Thomas the absolute necessity of his Father's having
manual employment of some kind, to occupy and
relieve the mind. What it should be was now a
most serious problem. Happily, his Father himself
solved it, and spontaneously. From the beginning,
when the question of removal to the city began to be
discussed, John Ruffin repeatedly had expressed his
wish and purpose to do something to help Thomas get
along. At first no attention was paid to the notion.
Thomas, however, soon saw it was set in his Father's
mind, and encouraged it, as in line with the physicians' injunction. The old man would dwell and
dwell upon the idea. It came to possess him, this
notion of doing something to help along. And no
sooner had he become settled at The Home, than it

took shape, when he declared that something should be *bottoming chairs.* It was a shock to Thomas— probably, because associated with negro life. But he reflected it was the only thing his Father could do—certainly, for the present, at least. And it was a final consideration, that his Father, who long and secretly had been cherishing the notion, was rigidly bent towards it and absolute in the expression of his purpose, to do this particular work.

So, another problem arose: How would he get patrons? This, too, presently received solution, through the agency of one Sandy Johnson.

Sandy Johnson was a curly haired, bullet headed, freckled faced Scotchman, with yellow locks and zanthous temperament. Sandy was a man *sui gene-ris.* When sentiments of an agreeable character were addressed to him, he had a peculiar way, all his own, of accompanying the sentiment with a sympathetic motion of lips, eyes, and features gener- ally—the most noticeable movement being a quick side to side play of the head. He was clean shaven, save a full, bushy, overhanging moustache that had become sufficiently saturated with nicotine, and had brushed acquaintance with soup and such like often enough, to justify the use of the individual com- munion cup. In earlier life he had been a resident of L—— where he enjoyed quite a reputation for making puns and rhymes, as well as boots, his nor- mal vocation. In one of Friend Peale's business visits to L—— a point he cultivated as being a dis- tributing centre for an extensive back country with a rich trade—the jolly Quaker happened to make Sandy's acquaintance through the medium of a ripped boot. He was attracted by the Scotchman's ready humor— made inquiries touching his character—learnt from Sandy himself he was not succeeding as he would wish—and the upshot was, that, upon Friend Peale's representation in a correspondence following, Sandy packed up awls, pegs, &c., to set up shop in the Quaker's city. That he did not prosper at first was his own fault very probably. In the ordinary Scotch thrift he may not have been deficient. But his humor and jovial turn drew around him here, as before at L——, improvident currents, and "busted" building associations did not help along. When he lost his good wife, Sue, he lost his financier; and even with Sue's careful management, it often happened that ends would not meet, and he was fain to seek the pawn shop of Dalguspin—against whom, by the way, he harbored a grudge for certain alleged sharp dealings; though in truth he had partially righted wrongs by such under work and over charge on boots, as would pass Dalguspin's scrutiny. However, Sandy at this time was doing much better. He had a snug home of his own; had paid off debts—had put by something, too—and if reports were to be credited, was casting sheep's eyes at Mistress Kitty, the housekeeper at The Home.

Really Sandy Johnson possessed abilities much above his station. He had a shrewd and lively intelligence—was a very respectable improvisatore—and excellent company, as may be supposed. When he opened his mouth, ten to one but apt saws and jingling lines would drop out. Friend Peale was very fond of him. In truth there was intimacy, as far as difference in social position allowed. Sandy remembered Thomas, as a child, but had left L—— before Thomas was old enough to remember *him*. John Ruffin he knew well—had cut leather for the family—had heard through Friend Peale the recent history of his old townsman; and if thereat his ready sympathies were roused, they took fire when told how Thomas had been entrapped by Dalguspin.

Sandy, you may be sure, was on the watch for Thomas' arrival, and at the earliest moment sought him out. The latter was taken captive at once by the interest manifested by the warm-hearted Scotch-man, and his racy conversation; and at the first inter-view brought up the matter of his Father's projected work, and the difficulty he feared touching patrons. Sandy's 'cuteness was equal to the occasion. He himself would supply the chairs—Thomas could give him (Sandy) the half dollar (the price John Ruffin had settled on)—he (Sandy) would give it to his Father for the work—his Father would give it to Thomas—Thomas again would give it to him (Sandy), to be given in turn again to his Father, &c., &c., and so the half dollar be made to run in a circle. And as for chairs, if he could not command a sufficient number, what was easier than to rip a bottom, and have the same chair travel round the circle before the half dollar?

Thomas considered the proposed arrangement the

identical thing itself, but for the fear lest his Father
might recognize his old acquaintance. Sandy felt
confident, however, he had so changed John Ruffin
would never know him—yet would be cautious and
go disguised, if necessary; and so parted from
Thomas with the chair question solved, and each
wonderfully pleased with the other.

John Ruffin soon settled down comfortably and
satisfactorily at The Home. He liked his room—
liked the location ; was disposed to like everything.
One change he made in the appointments of the room.
Mrs. Peale had had prints hung. These John Ruffin
removed, replacing them with four cuts of his own
and with which he held daily communings, cuts
representative of Cloud Cap scenes—here one of the
mansion, and here a cotton field scene, and here a
rice field, and here a print of the sugar mill.
Shucks were provided, and he went to work dili-
gently upon a trial chair, to revive and perfect skill
in the handicraft.

The Peales Thomas never mentioned to him.
They expressed the strongest desire to see their old
friend, without his knowledge, and Thomas promised that at an early day, when his Father would be
in the Park, or under some other circumstances, he
would try to gratify them.

The servant specially detailed to wait upon John
Ruffin—to tidy his room, answer his bell, bring the
meals, in short to look after all his wants—was one
Sabina. That Sabina was an old-time Virginia
darkie, black as the ace of spades, was all the more

agreeable to the Southern planter, and she had been selected purposely with reference to such an effect.

Sabina perhaps had more sense than her appearance and manner would seem to indicate; for she was cock-eyed and looked at you with one organ only, accompanied by a certain twisting of the head as if endeavoring to force the fellow-organ into position—would go staring, gaping about, like any provincial in a city—and had a way, often without any apparent or at least adequate cause, of breaking out into vacant guffaws, amusing, at times startling in their effects.

Thomas—who gave to his Father the purest and deepest affection, all that a dutiful mind can conceive—remained with him the whole of the first week, looking after every want, and rejoiced to see him so well satisfied. John Ruffin's impressions were new, and, being new, were salutary. Scenes and environments were entirely changed. He was surrounded by strangers, yet strangers whose attentions were sympathetic and tender. He had been a master and a law to slaves. He was now living by rule and under authority, even though an authority most considerately exercised. All this so far lifted him from old conditions with which his losses and afflictions were associated. In a new sphere, these losses, in a measure, were lost sight of, and betterment set in. A link to the past was Sabina—yet not a harmful link, rather otherwise; since her negro character and John Ruffin's Southern ways were in harmony.

Sabina had been told his history, and pointedly enjoined not to regard anything he might say or do out of the way. By nature an amiable creature, John Ruffin became really attached to her, and when from habit he would assume the tones and bearing of a master, forgetting his circumstances, and at times threatened her doings, and even attempted punishment, Sabina would only stare and roll her eyes, and retreat good humoredly in a chorus of guffaws.

The institution had its regular visitors—we mean unofficial visitors—all representative of religion, more or less—some formally so, as members of religious orders—others individually. John Ruffin point blank refused to see any of them. One, however, persevered and finally gained admittance by means of a little chair she carried bundled up, to be bottomed. Sabina, it is thought, furnished the hint of the chair. She gave the name of Sister Jessica. Dressed in deep black, with the heavy veil in every instance worn down all the while, disguising the features completely, apparently she was a religieuse. To John Ruffin's inquiry as to her business, she answered, that having known sorrow herself, she visited those in distress. Is that all? he asked. No, she replied. She would have a chair bottomed. The following week she called again for the chair, and insisted on paying the full dollar for a half price job. The visits—often with a little chair— were continued; and while the ample wage established an immediate interest in his visitor, her personality grew upon John Ruffin rapidly. The visits were generally made just before candle light at Saturday's eventide, and John Ruffin soon found himself looking forward to them with pleasing anticipations. The exceeding kindliness of tone and manner, the inexpressible tenderness, the care she took to find out and to gratify his fancies in the minutest particticular, the flowers he loved which she invariably brought—all combined in a most happy effect.

An early request from John Ruffin was to beg that she would remove the veil and let him look upon her face. She declined, saying she was bound by a vow to appear under such conditions of apparel, and checked all attempts to draw forth any portion of her history. It was sometime before Thomas met Sister Jessica, her visits being at an hour, when he was at the "Bank." But his Father spoke of her so constantly. "Jessie," or "my little angel," or "my little Sister," or some other term of endearment (he rarely called her Sister Jessica) was so often on his lips—and the influence upon his Father of this ministering spirit so palpable, that a special interest in her was inevitable.

Thomas made inquiries of Miss Kitty, and was informed that the lady had visited TheHome before his Father came—that she saw other inmates—that she had orders to admit her outside of regulation hours—and that that was all she knew about Sister Jessica. Curiosity led Thomas to go further and

question Sabina, and to his inquiry what *she* might
know the darkie made answer, introducing it with
the roll of eyes and the stare and the guffaw with
which she commonly enlivened the expression of
her sentiments :

"I doesn't know nuthin at all, honey."

So Thomas and his Father could gather no more
than that Sister Jessica was Sister Jessica, and that
her visits of mercy or vocation grew out of some
affliction, grievous and peculiar it must have been,
that had befallen her. This settled, curiosity
ceased, and the visitations were taken as routine
matter.

The Sister so ingratiated herself, that John Ruffin
finally became confidential, and, under pledge of
secrecy, imparted to her, in all its details and over
and over again, the story of his own affliction—how
rich he had been—what a lovely home he had had at
Cloud Cap—how he had lost it all—how embittered
he had been against the Sanfords—how he had
learnt his cousin was innocent—how grieved he was
for the sorrows that had stricken his family—how
often he thought upon his little Amy—how she had
been to him as a daughter—how she would bring to
him every season the first yellow Jessamine and
Moss bud, his favorite flowers, &c., &c., &c.

It was from hints in these conversations that
Sister Jessica learned John Ruffin's fancies and was
able to gratify them. She found, for example, that
the Moss Rose was a favorite flower, and in almost

every bouquet she brought, some variety of the Moss was present. It struck Thomas with surprise. From cultivating it for John Ruffin, the Moss became a favorite with Amy herself, and, under the circumstances, Thomas had given this rose a study. He knew the entire list, the dwarf, the cupped, the full blown flower—all the best species, touching form and color, from the crimson Luxembourg to the pure white Comtesse de Murinais. He knew, too, the Moss was a Spring bloomer, flowering at Cloud Cap in May. But here his Father's visitor was supplying beautiful specimens in Winter. He had never heard of the Moss as a perennial. The flower had tender associations, and he would seek information the first opportunity from his Father's veiled friend. Meanwhile, he made free use of her gifts and almost daily carried a Moss bud as a boutonniere.

The arrangement was for Thomas to begin work the week following his arrival. Meanwhile, he took the necessary steps for occupying the room at the *Bank*. He had already seen it, having called the second day after reaching the city, and by the close of the week had partially recovered from the shock its general appearance presented. It was on the third floor, a low-pitched, 12 by 12, half front attic. The back attic was filled up with household rubbish, whence apparently had been selected the outfit for the front apartment. A dormer window, opening eastward, was about the sole intrinsic comfort connected with the room; for Thomas, of early Winter mornings, would stand at this window, and catch on his head the warm sunshine and feel better—the sun shone so warm and good upon him. The ceiling which once had been whitewashed, was dingy and dirty. The walls, with dark paper, showed cracks and bulgings. For wardrobe a corner was curtained off. There was a single bed, and an ancient bureau (one of the drawers out of order and unserviceable), and a small pine table for eating and writing, with an old moth-eaten worsted cover—two windsor chairs—and a washstand, which a bungler had smeared with varnish holding such an excess of turpentine that in warm weather everything stuck fast upon it. The wash-bowl was cracked, and, as a whole, looked so infiltrated and uninviting, that Thomas bought a bright tin basin; and while in the tin-shop purchased some tin spoons at a half penny each. He provided, too, an oil lamp, with attachments affording capacity for cooking to the extent of drawing a cup of tea, &c., and the moth-eaten table-cloth he discarded for sheets of clean paper. Heating was by a small coal stove, which smoked most annoyingly, when the wind was on the chimney; and a rickety coal box, with a peck of coal, stood near.

On the walls hung an ancient dusty cut of a girl in a garden watching a humming bird at a flower— an advertising card—a horse-shoe suspended by a faded ribbon —and some queer looking, put-away, sallow prints (of ancestors, perhaps) in oval frames.

John Ruffin expressed a warm desire to call on the
Banker, before Thomas went to work, to thank him
for his kindness, and to see his son's room with his
own eyes. But Thomas persuaded him against it
all. His Father must not know the location—must
not even pass by 222 North G. St., lest he see the
golden balls. He represented it would be better,
later on, to see the *Banker* at his residence; and that
he need not be concerned touching his room. That
it was high and healthy, with beautiful sun light,
and walls all hung with pictures, &c. So John Ruffin was obliged to content himself with fancyings.
He dwelt on the peculiar name "Dalguspin," and
pictured to himself a foreign looking personage, of
noble and benevolent aspect, presiding over vast
money affairs in a stately building—in one of whose
luxurious apartments his dear son was domiciled.

As has been said, Dalguspin was the head both of
Bank and of pawn-shop. Shrewd and of exceptional working capacity, he had the affairs of each at
his finger ends. "John" was clerk in the Shop
with an assistant. He received goods, cast interest,
computed storage charges, conducted forfeiture
sales, &c., &c. Dalguspin was assessor and cashier.
A long experience enabled him to give swift and
accurate valuations touching those thousand and
one different sorts of things offered, that make an
established pawn-shop a remarkable museum. A
private back door communicated between *Bank* and
Shop, and at the ring of his number, Dalguspin

would shuffle in and dispose of the matter at a glance. The *Bank's* executive staff stood in Dalguspin, President and Treasurer—Thomas Ruffin, clerk—and William, the watchman. Thomas, under pressure, was to get a lift from John; and it was expected, that, in a Shop exigency, he was to take John's place, or give the latter a return lift. There was the usual finance committee, with the President at its head, which nominally controlled the investments. Practically, Dalguspin had affairs in his individual hands. ⸳

CHAPTER VI.

The Monday came, when Thomas was to com-
mence work. It was one of those typical November days significant of weather change. The morning opened hazy and lowering. The temperature
rose. The clouds thickened and moved lazily from
the South West. The atmosphere was charged with
a penetrating dampness. By noon a light quiet rain
was falling. As evening drew on the wind shifted
and blew cold from the North—the clouds rifted towards the Western horizon—and the Sun, on the eve
of setting, burst forth, illuminating with his level
rays many a wall and window, and filling all the
West with floods of crimson glory! Could it be an
augury of his career, thought Thomas to himself,
as he caught the sun-set from the Bank's window—
this contrast between the opening and the close of
the day?

Thomas received his Father's blessing, that Monday morning, and was at his desk by times. The
situation was clear to him in all its objectionable—
yes, ugly—yes, risky features. But the indenture's

run would be short. He resolved to be true both to himself and to his employer.

Dalguspin occupied the early hours in general instructions. The *Bank* opened at 10, and from that moment till long after dark Thomas' hands were full with the various books, &c—that is to say: Depositors' Credits, Depositors' Debits, Paying out and Receiving moneys, Receipt-Book, Ledger, Casting Interest, &c., &c.

John Ruffin had been awaiting his son with unspeakable anxiety. All that live long day he had been on his knees, or with hand and heart upraised. In what agony of prayer did he beseech God to be with his son—to make him faithful and successful—to grant him favor before his employer—and strength of body to stand up! He could not eat. Night came. He could not sleep. It was 9 p. m.! What! what! had happened! Presently he heard a step, and he knew it. O what relief! What a calming of the spirit! How joyfully he received him back! And when Thomas told him he had come out all right, what tears of rapture were shed!

Next day, early, Thomas was at work again. He hit his nails with the hammer of Thor. So active was he, "caught on" so readily, and was so amiable and winning withal, so complaisant and ready to yield to Dalguspin's wishes, in short so different from the clerks Dalguspin was accustomed to, that the *Banker* saw he had won a prize, with large capacity for *usefulness*, and began, in various little ways,

8

to show his appreciation.   As an instance: Not unfrequently there was night work at the Shop, and
with Black Isaac it was a hard and fast rule to require the clerk employed last to sleep in the building ; yet he volunteered permission to Thomas to be
two nights off, Thursday night and Sunday's, in lieu
of the one Sunday night, as had been agreed upon.
Then, in speaking to him alone, he would often call
him "Tammie," or "our Tammie," the name, as he
learnt, by which his Father addressed him ; and
hinted, moreover, that at an early day he should
have more money.   All this greatly stimulated
Thomas, who had already set up a high standard of
duty, and he exerted himself far beyond the reasonable limit of his raw, undisciplined powers.—Be wise,
young man.   Over work is a noble folly.   Labor
judiciously, and so bear life's burden with strength
and joy.

In this way of mutual satisfaction, matters went
on for some weeks far into December.

But suddenly a change came over Dalguspin.   He
looked sunk, was silent, and disposed, without cause,
to be cross.   Apparently, something had happened.
It was really so.   The early portion of 1837 is memorable for the wildest speculation, and Noals, this
time, had been bitten fatally.   With cotton at ten
cents, and all the outlooks, as he felt sure, most
favorable for a rapid rise, this speculator bought,
through his New York broker, four thousand bales,
giving a note for $140,000 at ninety days with the
cotton as collateral, and the residue in cash.   Of

this cash, Dalguspin advanced personally $35,000, raised on mortgages—Npals $10,000—and the balance ($15,000) Black Isaac "borrowed" from the *Bank*, supplying the shortage by forging notes on certain of the Bank's patrons. The notes, he knew, would pass the finance committee, even should an examination be made; since none of the committee were cognizant of the signature of these patrons, and they would not take the trouble to test them. And though aware that the district Examiner, one Edward Stone, no doubt *would* test them, yet this rigid functionary was not expected on his rounds for some months. Stone, by the way, was a recent appointee. Dalguspin never had met him. Knew him only by report and correspondence.

The cotton note matured December 20th. Against all expectation, cotton had dropped at that date 'to seven cents. Three months later, by a remarkable fluctuation, it rose to seventeen cents, the highest point for 1837. But it was then too late, and Dalguspin was swamped. No wonder the man felt blue; or that he began looking round for chances at money by hook or by crook, after his old methods.

It was not long before an opportunity presented itself. One Cameron, well known to Dalguspin, a man of means, but suddenly needing a hundred dollars on the spot, ran into the *Bank* one day and executed a sight note for the sum. A week later Cameron was stricken by apoplexy and died unconscious within a few hours. Here was a chance. So by a chemical process discovered and known only to himself, Dalguspin effectually removes "hundred" from the note's face, and, adept in counterfeiting hand-writing, replaces it with "thousand," and annexes a cipher to the figures. What could be easier, he thought?

But Cameron's executor became suspicious. There were memoranda to show the amount borrowed was $100, and other circumstances pointing towards forgery, a law suit was threatened. Matters looked serious. Should they reach a crisis, a witness would be necessary, or the devil might be to play, and Dalguspin hoped and thought he had one in Thomas, who was present on the occasion, and no doubt recollected his paying money over to Cameron. But Thomas needed some coaching.

The morning, therefore, following the threat of suit (it was Saturday morning), Dalguspin came down to the "Bank," and, with a manner unusally suave, said to Thomas:

"Don't you remember last Thursday week, about half-past 10, a large, fat, red-faced, clean shaven man came into the _Bank_ and had a conversation with me?"

"Yes, Sir," Thomas replied. "I remember him distinctly."

"That man's name was Cameron."

"Yes, Sir. I heard you call him so."

"Very well, Tammie—very well—you remember him distinctly, you say, and you heard me call him Mr. Cameron, you say.

"Yes, Sir."

"Very well. Mr. Cameron died the week following, and he owed me by note a thousand dollars."

"Indeed !"

"Yes, Tammie—one thousand dollars. You will
remember that, Tammie ?"

"Yes, Sir."

"Very well—very well. Now the executor threatens to go back on the note, and I may have to sue,
to get my money."

"I hope not."

"You can help me, Tammie, if I should be forced
to law him. Cameron executed this note in your presence" (handing Thomas the note). "You see the
writing and the figures—one thousand."

"Yes, Sir," Thomas answered, handing back the
note.

"You saw me paying him money."

"Yes, Sir. I remember that very well."

"And I tell you, Tammie, it was a thousand dollars I paid him. You'll swear to that, if necessary ?"
interrogated the Pawn-broker, as he bent upon the
youth his deep-set glittering eyes.

"Yes, Sir. I will. Certainly."

"Tammie," said Dalguspin effusively, approaching the young man and taking his hand. "You're
no gilly. A jury'll believe anything you say. You
face is honesty itself. Here's an X" (handing a ten
dollar bill). "You deserve it, Tammie."

Thomas reflected a moment, and then offered back
the ten dollars :

"Mr. Dalguspin, I can't see why I should take

your money for doing what is so plain and simple."

"No! no!" exclaimed Black Isaac, raising his hand deprecatingly against the proffered bill. "It's justly yours, for extra work any how."

"If you put it on that ground, I suppose I may keep, it, and, indeed, Mr. Dalguspin, I thank you for the kindness."

"You're a trump, Tammie, and deserve more, and I hope soon to do more for you. I'm thinking of getting some one in your place and making you my private secretary and putting all my personal affairs into your hands. You'll have less to do and more pay, and can be every night with your Father—eh? It'll be a snap, Tammie."

"You're very kind, indeed, Sir," answered Thomas, with a countenance expressive both of the surprise and the gratification he felt at the very unusual proceedings on the part of Dalguspin.

"Co-operate with me, Tammie, and you'll have the stuff. That's all I can say, and that's enough," replied Dalguspin, giving vent to one of his low little laughs—"he! he! he!"—as he recognized the jingle he had made. "You've promised," he continued, "to swear that you saw Cameron enter the Bank that Thursday ———"

"Yes, Sir."

"That your attention was drawn by his manner of entrance ———"

"Yes, Sir."

"That he was a large, fat, red-faced, clean-shaven

man, and you could not be mistaken as to his identity ———"

"Yes, Sir."

"That you distinctly heard me call him 'Cameron' ———"

"Yes, Sir."

"Very well! very well! Tammie.—And that you saw me pay over to him one thousand dollars."

"No, Mr. Dalguspin, I did not say that."

"What!" ejaculated the Pawn-broker.

"I said, Sir, I'd swear that you told me you paid him a thousand dollars."

"The devil you did!" Dalguspin exclaimed, with a changing countenance. "You don't propose to make me a liar, my young man, do you?"

"No, Sir, I do not."

"Why can't you believe, Thomas, what I say?"

"I am ready to believe it."

"You see here the note drawn in Cameron's own hand for $1000. You saw me paying him money— ten one hundred dollar bills. Can't you believe it?"

"I have no reason, Mr. Dalguspin, not to believe what you say."

"Then, can't you swear, with this note before your eyes, and my words which, you say, you believe, in your ears, that you saw me pay Cameron $1000. Take care, Tammie," Dalguspin went on, dropping the bluster for a low and significant tone, *"it'll benefit me, and benefit you, too."*

"I can swear only to what I know, that you said you paid Mr. Cameron $1000," Thomas replied in a rising and decided inflection, as the Pawn broker's drift broke upon him.

"You're a fool, Thomas Ruffin," growled Dalguspin, losing self-control and his face turning as red as his swarthy countenance would admit. "You shall repent of this, Sirrah! Remember the indentures do not specify your wage. I can starve you and your old Father," he continued, advancing towards Thomas, as he spoke, his eyes snapping and forefinger shaking an angry menace.

Thomas Ruffin was one of those natures not uncommonly recognized, who ordinarily may be timid and shrinking, but with a reserve of genuine spirit making wholly unexpected displays in the presence of real danger or under great provocation. He now rose trembling with emotion and white as a sheet, yet resolute to act in the face of such an assault upon his deep sense of right and his filial love, and met Dalguspin's eyes with a gaze so firm and fixed, that the latter stopped—then he spoke in low deliberate tone:

"Mr. Dalguspin, I understand it all. I've been warned against such attempts. I will do what's right, and I do not fear your threat." He paused a moment, then continued: "I've been instructed by my friends, and, if I chose, I could break the contract for what you've done, and"—he paused again, then added—"could bring you to justice, besides."

Black Isaac was thunderstruck. He had failed to take the measure of this slender, modest youth.

All at once he found himself "in a hole," and scrambled out the best he could.

"Thomas," he cried, with a change of voice and manner to fit the turn, "it's just a put up job—all a fib. Some of my clerks have proven knaves, and it's my rule to test new ones. You'll *do* Thomas—you're pure gold," he continued, turning hastily towards the back entrance to the Pawn-shop, as the ring of his number called him thither, very much to his relief, we dare say. "I'll try to reward you for this," he added, turning towards Thomas on reaching the door.

As the door closed behind him, he turned towards the room, just left, with faces and low curses and divers thrusts and sweeps of the finger, to represent apparently the stabs and cuttings he would be glad to do, or intended to do, to somebody.

"Yes," he muttered, "he gets the better of me by ten dollars, besides. Yes, I'll try to reward you for this."

The affair left Thomas in the unhappiest frame of mind. Dalguspin's latter words were all pretense, he felt. That it was a deliberate attempt to use him criminally, that Dalguspin was still a bad man, and that he had incurred his enmity, he did not at all doubt. What should he do? Might not the usurer seek revenge? Very likely. There was something peculiar, Thomas thought, in the tone of the words: "I'll try to reward you for this." And might he not be able to entrap him in some way he could not avoid? There was danger in remaining. On the other hand, should he take legal steps and break the contract, could he keep the trouble from his Father? Must his Father not discover that something had happened? And would he not be affected by it and his improving condition checked? There would be hazard in leaving, or even making the attempt. And might he not find difficulty, too, in getting the kind of work he could do? Friend Peale temporarily was out of the city. There was no one with whom to counsel judiciously. The poor fellow was in great trouble—distracted and without a guide.

Dalguspin's bearing during the day, was much as usual. Not a word was said outside of current business. The morning incident was not even alluded to, and the usurer's manner of adieu, as he left for home, the same as it had been.

When Thomas entered his room that Saturday evening how different his circumstances and feelings from those with which he had left it that Saturday morning! He had risen at half-past 4, and, refreshed by sound sleep, began tidying his room humming snatches of song. The garret roost he kept clean and orderly, and actually was becoming attached to it. How happy the faculty of adaptation! The prints and very walls seemed companions. They had heard his prayers and sighings, and seen his tears. Affairs, too, were now getting into better shape. His Father was improving. His own health was stronger. Dalguspin was appreciative. The Peales, encouraging. Of the remnant of fortune, a few dollars were still in store for emergencies. The skies all looked brighter; and he went about preparing the simple morning meal with a grateful and a hopeful heart.

What a change on his return to it in the evening! The wind was on the chimney and the stove smoked. Gloom everywhere—in the room—round his heart—and out over the prospect. With no spirit to prepare food, he forced a remnant of the morning's meal; and the atmosphere having now become absolutely vitiated by smoke and products of combustion from an oil lamp, he raised the sash to purify the room, and sought the street. Square after square he sped along, and returned to his room in no better frame of mind. Neither did the bed bring rest. All through the night he turned and tossed in broken sleep—rose early and aweary—and went forth for relief. It was Sunday morning. The heavens were shrouded, the fog was dense—sympathetic weather, raw, damp, and thick. Thomas walked rapidly, and his long stride soon brought him within the precincts of a noble out-lying Park, of stream and lake and woodland and lawn yet green. At an hour so early, and in such weather and locality, and on this particular day, few were stirring, save the frogs. It was, indeed, a fine frog morning, and these merry musicians were much in evidence. The air was so fresh in the Park. It struck Thomas with tonic influence. His blood, too, was up from exercise. He felt better; and began to think better of his circumstances. One thing he could say, that his hands

were clean—that "the ungodly have laid a snare for
me, yet have I swerved not from Thy command-
ments." And had he not a wise friend in Adam
Peale, whom he would see perhaps to-morrow? The
difficulties did not now seem to him altogether so
formidable. He'd take courage and try to forge
through. And he felt that he would. And all at
once there came to him a lifting of the spirit and a
confidence. The weather, too, apparently was in
sympathy; for it was now perceptibly improving.
As Thomas faced eastward, on the return, he would
catch, every step or two, glimpses of the Sun's disk.
Anon, a ray struggled through a rift. The fog was
lifting. All around was brightening ; and by the
time he reached his door, the mist had all rolled off,
and a genial December Sun poured light and warmth
from a cloudless sky.

"An omen!" cried Thomas.

That Sunday and Sunday night Thomas passed
with his Father in a cheerful mood, as if nothing
had happened. Next day he saw Friend Peale, who
became enthusiastic over his conduct. He advised
Thomas to let things rest, for the present at least;
but to keep close watch. That while he scarcely
doubted Dalguspin's evil mind, it was possible he
had made no misrepresentation. In any event it
was not certain he could prove his case; and, should
he fail, his position would be so much the more un-
comfortable—not taking into account the probability of the affair's reaching his Father and affecting
him injuriously.

Under these circumstances, matters went on at the *Bank* pretty much as before. The cloud over Dalguspin appeared to be deepening. He continued moody and meditative—spoke little—looked woebegone—and almost daily was in retired conference with a stranger, whose name Thomas afterwards learnt was Noals.

December almost had passed, a busy month, with increased work for Thomas. Xtmas was drawing near—happy season to the young—pensive to the old —to Thomas full of sweetest memories. The festival was a week off, and the impulse it imparted conspicuous to eye and ear in every direction. Such crowds and bustle and jams on the streets and in the shops! Such groaning counters! Such garish windows! Every body busy, busy, busy—buying or selling or sight-seeing! Such a joyous, buoyant, expectant spirit in the air! Faces, everywhere, so bright and anticipative! This mighty Xtmas throb of a great city, congesting all the arteries of trade, and sending a stir into every degree and condition of life, as though the world were born again and advancing afresh on its course, was something new and striking to Thomas. Speaking of the impression to the Peales, they told him he must be out Xtmas Eve at candle-light—that the markets and thoroughfares and merry marauders would be another revelation.

Dec. 24th, 7 p. m., Thomas was at his desk, finishing up the day's work, when a confused roar from the direction of the market, two blocks off, fell upon his ear. He remembered the Peales' suggestion,

and, closing the ledger, hurried forth to witness his
first city Xtmas Eve. A few minutes walk brought
him to the precincts of the market, where Xtmas
trees in great stacks were being disposed of to bustling buyers, and mountebanks were haranguing, and
toy-peddlers exhibiting their jumping monkeys and
marching mannikins, &c., &c. Another step, and
he was within the market proper, celebrated where-
ever known, and now in its glory for the chiefest
holiday of the year. The vendors were all in the
freshest and whitest aprons and overalls, as well as
the heartiest humor. The stalls, the cleanest and
the tidiest, ablaze with lights, and decked profusely
with evergreens; and the array and artistic arrangement of viands of every description, and the thous-
and-and-one other commodities vended here, was for
new eyes a sight to see. The regulation Turkey was
conspicuously in evidence, presented on all sides—
of every kind, form, age, and gender—turkey *fera*,
turkey *domestica*, turkey dressed, turkey half-
dressed, turkey undressed, as well as turkey distressed (in over full coops). Great bustling, wedg-
ing throngs greeted the jovial vendors, pushing and
nudging and jostling along good-naturedly with
hearts and hampers full of Xtmas cheer, all laughing or greeting or bargaining or chaffering—a babel
of voices, whose level was pierced almost incessantly
by the shrill soliciting cries of the market-men. It
was a stirring scene—Xtmas Eve on its gastronomic
side.

Thomas entered the market near midway and

slowly worked on eastward, attracted by the mighty din which came from that quarter, and rose far above even the hubbub immediately around him. Reaching the eastern limit of the open shed-built market-house, he saw something. All down the street leading up to it, as far as he could descry, till a curve cut off the view, on side walk and from curb to curb, was a dense, hurly-burly, uproarious mass of merry-makers, revealed by the lamps and the lanterns innumerable. Thomas struck an eastward current, and was borne along into the thickest of the whirl. The most pronounced feature was the ceaseless and awful noise that gathered from hosts of throats and extemporized agencies. The tin horn was omnipresent, from the twenty incher to the twenty footer (borne on a line of shoulders). Dinner bells and cow bells were clanging. The watchman's sharp rattle would be answered back by ear-splitting college yells. Tin pans were drumming, and there were cheers and shouts and peals of laughter, and blowing of fists and of fingers, and cat calls, and cock crowings, and dog barkings—altogether making a mighty sound, loud enough and long enough and discordant enough to rouse the seven sleepers.

Masks, too, were much in evidence, and the wax nose, and caricatures, and dominoes, and white dittoes, and what else God only knows. Here was a party of fellows with white stove pipe hats two feet high, fiercely bewhiskered, overcoats turned inside out, in lock-step, and bawling a bacchanal. And here a body of collegiates, of foot-ball fame, thrown into a V and cleaving a passage. And here a set of youngsters who had caught a docile fat man, and were bearing him aloft to the shouts of the crowd, &c., &c., &c., &c. It was a rushing, furious outpour of jollity. But every one seemed good-natured, and the Blue Coats on this special occasion kept hands off. Xtmas Eve on its merry side, thought Thomas.

He was not, however, *en rapport.* Merry, merry, indeed, had the season been at Cloud Cap and at L——. But merriment was secondary and subdued, and through it all the Prince of Peace was distinctly visible. Here his features appeared lost. Even had it been otherwise, personal recollections and painful contrasts were unavoidable, and Thomas, bred in a simple spiritual way and dissatisfied, escaped into an alley.. A few steps brought him to the parallel street. It was a thoroughfare, but now deserted; for all had been drawn into the whirlpool of revelry behind him. The solitude was grateful. As he stood a moment listening to the uproar, a number of women hurried by, one after the other, and all in the same direction. From some cause (was it the attraction of gravity? or force of example? or occult magnetic influence? or psycological sympathy? or may be a good angel's hand?) he followed at a little distance, turning as they turned, though rather out of the way to his lodgings. As he went, others and others joined, and Thomas became interested as to the outcome. Three squares off they

reached the Cathedral gate. Many from every
quarter were going in, and with them he passed into
the venerable temple, and took a seat in the nave
just within the circle of the dome. Though one of
the city's special attractions, never before had he
visited this sanctuary; for it represented a worship
to which not only was he a stranger, but against
which by breeding he was prejudiced. Still, he
held his seat, and with a sense of growing satisfaction. The sacred chancel lamp, with fitful red flame,
symbol of the Blood shed, brought the altar into
relief sufficiently to reveal a wealth of Xtmas flower
and evergreen. Back, the apse was darksome, and
its fresco paintings barely distinguishable amidst
the cedar festoonings and decorations. This was
Thomas' first view, as he looked out before him;
and the sweet sympathetic Xtmas-tide impression
made, went on gathering fullness and force, as other
features of the scene grew into his consciousness.
The imposing edifice, its size and proportions—the
noble dome—the striking frescoes encircling its base
—the dim religious light—the reverential silence,
broken only by the cautious step of the incomers or
outgoers, or passers to and from the confessionals—
the apparent devotion of the worshippers, intent at
book or prayer or communings, as if absorbed in
introspection and conscious of but one Presence—all
these influences pointing upward, wrought an impression in complete harmony with a spirit bowed
by memories of other days—a chastened, soothing
impression, deep and full. Now and then a far off

murmur from the revel-rout, would be heard. It seemed to Thomas from a world way below. Here was another world, with another spirit, serene, hallowed, inspiring. And as he rose presently to leave, with yet another view of a city's Xtmas Eve, he said within himself, as did Jacob of old, "Surely, the Lord is in this place . . . . and this is none other than the house of God."

Meanwhile, the weather had grown cooler, the breeze had risen, the clouds had all fled, and eastward in the heavens the stars, in unusual combination and admirable for size and radiance, presented a scene that no one, with any sense of the grand and the beautiful—though no star-gazer like Thomas— could behold without emotion. The kingly Jupiter, this night a most singularly splendid eastward star, was the central feature. Fiery Mars, at its perihelion and in opposition, led the way before him. Castor and Pollux in the Twins followed in his train, and magnificent Orion with dazzling white Sirius were attendants—the apparent elect among the starry host, those stupendous and glorious worlds that make perchance "the many mansions in His Father's house." It was upon an open Thomas entered, as he left the sanctuary, and this resplendent *"Star in the East,"* set in "living sapphires," caught and held his eye. He stood and gazed upon it, and the Xtmas-tide associations and sentiment deepened and widened still.

The young man sought his lodgings. The hour was late, His eyes were heavy. The scenes he had just witnessed, faded and faded out at sleep's approach; 'but anon, in other form, the train of thought vividly revived them. For behold! he dreamed. And again it was a joyous Xtmas-tide at Cloud Cap. And again he stood by Amy's side, cutting the cedar twigs she was binding into wreaths for the Xtmas altar.

CHAPTER VII.

The door-bell rang (3 p. m.) at Dalguspin's up-town residence. It was answered by a man-servant—something over twenty, one would have judged—with a bearing apparently above the position he was occupying—and whose bright general appearance gave every indication of his knowing a hawk from a hand-saw.

Robert Small (the valet's name) had entered Black Isaac's service under peculiar circumstances. On a certain street a certain day his steps were arrested by a violent altercation between two men—one, old and feeble looking—the other, a young vigorous fellow. The latter was about to commit an assault, when Robert spoke up. He knew nothing touching the merits of the controversy, but instinctively interposed to protect the agéd man. The fellow struck Robert. Robert knocked him down. The fellow rose with a dirk in hand and made for Robert, whereupon a ball from the latter's pistol broke the fellow's right arm. Arrest followed —then a trial. There were extenuating circumstances, and Robert got off with three months' imprisonment and fine of one hundred dollars.

The old man was Black Isaac. His assailant, an honest fellow whom the Pawn-broker had tricked in a money transaction. Naturally, Black Isaac was drawn towards his defender. He visited him in prison, and, needing a · head-servant, proposed to Robert, at the close of the prison-term, to pay the fine, if he would work it out in his service—a proposal Robert was not slow to accept.

The visitor was Noals—of whom the reader has heard before, incidentally. Noals was a ready-witted, comical sort of a man. In earlier days he had been a comedian of local celebrity in an amateur company—and was still an inveterate wag, making light of everything, cut out for low comedy, and, had he held to the stage, unquestionably would have risen a bright, particular star. He dealt in real estate. Speculation in this field had brought him money—which, however, passed from him readily through the channel of a free and easy life. They had brought him, too, something else—a fancy for speculation in other and less secure directions. Cotton then was a gambling rage. Noals took a hand and at first was fortunate. He drew Black Isaac into it, and made for him some brilliant hits, until finally, as we have seen, he was hit back.

Noals' personel was peculiar. He was a fattish dumpy kind of man—clean-shaven, save some patches of beard in sheltered spots passed over by the razor in its morning round, and a remarkably noticeable tuft of long thin hair on the chin. The cutaway coat, besides, with skirt all too short, seemed shorter still from a persistence to wriggle up towards the neck; so that he may be said to have been individualized, anteriorly by a *goatee*—posteriorly by a *coatee.*

In the last venture himself was involved, as well as the Pawn-broker; and he now came to press on Black Isaac (over whom, as we have said, he exercised great influence,) a •desperate remedy. The Pawn-broker was "at home" and immediately received his visitor (who had called by appointment) in a private apartment.

"It's an awful fix! awful! awful!" broke out Black Isaac the moment the door closed and before his guest had time to seat himself; "yet I can't realize it, Noals. I can't realize I'm *dead broke,* Noals—that this house and all these comforts are really mine no longer. I know it's so; but I'm insensible to it, Jimmie. It dazes me, deadens me, Jimmie—like those sudden and fatal wrenchings of the body, we hear of, which take from the victim the power to feel."

"Come! come! Dalguspin. Real men look into the face even facts like these, and cast about for a way out."

"A way out and be hanged!"

"A way out and be saved, say I."

"My own money's all gone," bewailed Black Isaac, as he paced the room wringing his hands and gesticulating in bitterness of spirit—"the Bank's fifteen thousand are gone—my office will go—my character will go! Poverty, misery, dishonor hang over Dalguspin! Oh! this damnation luck of yours. *Can* there be a way out, except along a pistol's barrel?"

"Pos-si-bly," was Noals' slow and emphatic rejoinder.

The Pawn-broker stopped—bent his miserable eyes upon his visitor a moment—then spoke:

"James Noals, are you jesting or not?"

"I'll eat my old hat, if I ain't in dead earnest."

"What do you suggest, then?" Black Isaac asked in a way which seemed to imply that no suggestion could be effective.

"Now look here—are there any *funds* you could use for a time—funds sufficient to lift the mortgages and settle our personal losses?"

The reply came short and snappy:

"None."

"Think again, Dalguspin. No *f-u-n-d-s* you could lay hands on?" asked Noals, dropping his voice to a significant whisper. (—By the way, some one has remarked upon the singular fact, that the voice, when dropped, should make less noise than when it is raised).

The Pawn-broker paused a moment, reflectively:

"I know of none but the *Bank's*."

"Why not lay hand on these?"

"What! Steal and skip?"

"Neither."

"To take the *Bank's* funds and be caught, not stealing!"

"No more stealing, than to take the *Bank's* funds
for private spec., is stealing. You meant to replace
the money then. You would mean to replace it
now."

Black Isaac paused again, with eyes upon the
floor and left forefinger tapping the nether lip.

"How would tracks be covered?" he presently
asked.

"It might be arranged to have the *Bank* robbed."

"Robbed! You said there was to be no stealing."

"The robbery would be a blind."

"A blind! Away with riddles, Noals! Explain
yourself!"

"Suppose, then, Dalguspin, that, under disguise,
I should employ a man, a proper man, a right sort
of a man, may be a cracksman, to do the job. Suppose I were to go to him and say: For certain reasons it is desirable a certain Bank apparently should
be robbed. Suppose I should tell him that, on a
certain night at a certain hour, he would find every
thing to his hand, the private watchman away, and
access to the *Bank* and to the Safe easy—that he was
to do his part with drag and jimmy and jackscrew,
and leave every mark of a burglary—of a genuine
break-in and blow-open. Suppose I were to tell him
he would find in the Safe, say, $500 or $1000—and
ask him, whether, for this sum, he would undertake
the job. Suppose I should seriously suggest all this.
What would you think of it, Dalguspin?"

The Pawn-broker made no answer, but sat absorbed, and Noals went on:

"''Twould be good pay and little risk, with no motive to squeal. No suspicion would attach to *you*. No one knows you've been speculating. I would make it a condition that the man at once leave the country, or this part of it, and he would understand, that, should he cause or attempt trouble, revenge would pursue him to the earth's ends.—What would you think of such an arrangement?''

The Pawn-broker still sat silent and absorbed.

"Carry it out, Dalguspin, and your fortune is saved—your character is saved—the *Bank* could be reorganized—and you could bend your energies to raise a pile sufficient to replace *every dollar* of this borrowed money. What say you to it?''

"It must be thought upon, Noals. Call here at 10 to-night.''

Noals took a cigar from the table, applied a match, and retired. The Pawn-broker rang up Robert, and giving instructions that he be kept absolutely undisturbed, closed and locked the door upon himself.

The door bell again rang and Mrs. Peale was received. She had called for a word with her good man Adam, who, at this hour, was to speak to Black Isaac in behalf of Thomas Ruffin. On the plea of hard times the Pawn-broker had cut his clerk's slender wage, and Thomas (who would not lessen what he had been accustomed to spare to his Father) was actually in want. Friend Peale offered and even pressed assistance. But Thomas knew the kind-hearted Quaker had met recently with business losses and refused the help.

Mrs. Peale, an excitable little woman, always

bustling, and now partly out of breath from her walk, glanced around the vacant room—then turned upon Robert with the snappy query :

"Where's Adam ?"

"I hope in heaven, Madam," Robert replied solemnly and with a puzzled look, not knowing what else to say to the wholly unexpected and unapprehended interrogation.

"Does thee say he's gone, my Adam ?" cried Mrs. Peale, startled and ready to weep.

"No ! no ! no ! Madam ! I thought you meant the first man, Mrs. Peale."

"Nay, nay, I mean my old man," rejoined the now smiling woman.

"A thousand pardons, Mrs. Peale.—What a blunder !" Robert ejaculated to himself—"how could I know 'Adam' was in his name ?"—Then aloud : "Your husband is not here, Madam."

"Then I'll wait a bit. He *was* to be here at this hour," (looking at her watch), "to speak with Dalguspin for Thomas Ruffin."

"Thomas Ruffin, Madam !"

"Yea. Why does thee ask so ? Does thee not know who Thomas Ruffin be ?"

"No, Madam."

"He's clerk in Dalguspin's *Bank*."

"He is ?"

. "Yea. Thee should know *that*, I think."

"Why should I, Madam ?"

"Headman in the *Banker's* house should know something of the *Banker's Bank*, I think."

"I have never seen the *Bank*, Madam, nor do I know anyone in it, save Monsieur Dalguspin. Bank and Court-house I shun on principle."

"And wherefore?"

"As likely inlets to the jail."

"Thee does!" rejoined the amused Mrs. Peale.

"Yes, Madam. 'Twas a father's counsel."

"Thee may be a wise son of a wise Father," Mrs. Peale remarked reflectively.— "Well, I can tell thee," she added, "that Thomas Ruffin is clerk with thy master. We feel great interest in him. He is son to an old friend of ours, now at The Old Men's Home, poor John Ruffin!"

"John Ruffin!"

"Yea. Whose else son could he be? I was at Cloud Cap—"

"Ah! The bell, I believe," Robert interrupted, as he assumed a listening attitude. "Excuse me, Madam."

Robert retires to answer the bell. A moment later re-enters, and remarks:

"You seem warmly interested in John Ruffin, Mrs. Peale."

"Yea. He's an old friend. I was at Cloud Cap, his lovely home, when the news came."

"What news, Madam?"

"That he had lost *every cent,* of his fortune, poor man! It came in the twinkling of an eye. And what a change! What a change! Never shall I forget it! Oh! so sudden, so complete, all the circumstances so tender and affecting! John Ruffin fell, as if from a shot. For weeks I nursed him at death's

door; and, when his body recovered, his mind was
gone !''

"Have a glass of water, Mrs. Peale. You look
fatigued.

"I am not so fatigued. Yet I will thank thee."

Robert turned to the buffet, and, while blowing
his nose and fumbling, accidentally and most unfortunately poured from the whiskey decanter and
offered the glass. Mrs. Peale tasted with a face and
a sputter, and returned the glass indignantly :

"Thee can spare the liquor for thine own use."

"Excuse me, Madam, do excuse me, I pray," apol-
ogized Robert, confounded and abashed by the error.
"Really, it's unpardonable. My mind was off at
the moment, and the decanters, you see, are just
alike, and the liquor is water-color."

Robert awkwardly replaces the glass on the tray,
spilling part of the contents, at which he remarks :

"I take pride in my service, Madam, and the blunder really unman's me."

Turning now to the buffet, he pours a glass from
the water decanter and offers to Mrs. Peale. Receiving back the glass, he busies himself a moment
at the buffet, to recover from his confusion; then
turns and observes :

"And John Ruffin's at The Old Men's Home, you
say, Madam ?"

"Yea—and his sole stay his son Thomas."

"He has a son, then ?"

"Yea—and *such* a son ! Oh ! it's awful sad, the old
man's lot ! I fear he can't do anything at all, but

pray. He's just like a child, and hath no kin to
love him or take care of him, but this young son.
And he's such a dear, good son! He works so hard
to get his Father little extras to which he has been
accustomed, and so help him to forget his poverty.
And he touches up his room for him, and reads to
him, and walks out with him every day, and is so
tender and encouraging towards him, and looks
after him just like a little mother, and is just too
nice for any thing, I can tell thee. Yea, yea—John
Ruffin knows what it is to have a son, I can tell
thee."

"Good for the old man! Madam."

"But Dalguspin, for shame! is rough upon the
youth."

"Pity! pity! Mrs. Peale."

"Yea. Thy master's grown a hard man. Years
ago, when I first knew him, he was kindly disposed."

"Years ago!"

"Yea—when he began running the Pawn-shop.
He had redeeming qualities then and was ever ready
to lend; but age has made him close and cruel."

"Why doesn't the young man leave?"

"Oh! he can't. He's an indentured clerk.—But
Adam's to be here, to speak for him to Dalguspin.
And will you please give him this?" (handing a
note). "I thought I might miss Adam, and wrote a
line. It may help Thomas. I don't want Adam to
forget a certain thing."

"Certainly, Mrs. Peale," Robert answered, as he
received the note and ushered out the Quaker lady.

CHAPTER VIII.

THE PAWN-SHOP.

In whose stale atmosphere the reader shall not be long detained.

It may be observed, that, while the Pawn-broker and Noals were wickedly conferring and plotting, Thomas Ruffin was having his bowels of compassion moved by scenes among the unfortunate; for on the same day and at the very same hour, when Black Isaac received Noals at his residence, as recorded in the chapter preceding, Thomas for the first time took his turn in the Pawn-Shop, as clerk or receiver. John's assistant was ill, and John himself, a young expert, this day filled the Boss's place as appraiser in the rear apartment. The Bank closed at 3 p. m., the Pawn-Shop generally at 7; and on these occasions, when Thomas gave John a lift, the former was expected to finish up at night the afternoon work of the *Bank*—balancing cash, posting to the ledger, notifying note-debtors of approaching maturity, &c., &c.

As has been stated, the charter name and sign of the establishment was "Loan Office," and it was conducted on the general principles of the Mont de Pieté; but the repute which the latter institution held abroad, had not been drawn towards it. The offensive odor of the old Pawn-Shop still prevailed, and its patrons were of the same low and debased character. True, that now and then those of real respectability, and even of wealth, for the moment embarrassed, sought its aid; but the great mass of customers were the working poor, the spendthrifts, the roués, the debauchees, distributed among laborers, orphans, widows, shop-girls, domestics, students, soldiers, &c.

Business at the Pawn-Shop was now brisk; for it was the middle of January. During summer many of the poor laboring class seek the country. Those remaining in the city find employment, and expenses are light. The season, too, is healthier, and, were it not for rum and idleness, the Pawn-Shop in summes time practically would be deserted. With cold weather expenses increase—more food is needed—often there is sickness—crowds flock in from the country and the shelves of the Shop begin filling up.

But at this juncture a potent special cause was operating. It was the closing days of Jackson's second administration, when experimental finance, rash meddling with the currency, the nation's life blood, had brought about a state of affairs, which resulted a few months later, as thoughtful men foresaw, in the historic panic and crash of 1837 that emphasized the commencement of Van Buren's term of office. Two years before, the United States Bank

had been allowed to expire by limitation. Its down-
fall was followed by a multitude of state banks,
emitting floods of issue. Speculation and overtrad-
ing ran riot on the swell of inflation. The gold and
silver of the country, wholly inadequate for redemption purposes, rose to a premium and disappeared
from view—save where borrowed at two to three per
cent.' a month, to carry all sorts of the wildest
schemes. Shinplasters went on depreciating, and
the sufferers, first and deepest, were the poor. The
laborer saw "his bag of meal and peck of coal going
up in price, and the rag money received for the
week's wage going down." It was the day for the
Pawn-broker.

Black Isaac's absence had closed for an hour the
door of the Pawn-Shop. When Thomas opened it
at 3, a more than usual number pressed in—for the
most part women. Never before had he so confronted these unfortunates. As liable any day to
be called upon to give John a lift, he had been instructed in the routine duties of the Shop; but now
for the first time was he officially brought face to
face with its wretched patrons. And if to one of
generous and refined sensibilities, under the most
pleasing personal conditions, the spectacle was moving, the present surroundings of Thomas Ruffin all
tended to deepen the spectacle's influence. He was
a kind of sufferer himself—beset by circumstances
of a nature to draw forth sympathy for sufferers.
He knew he had incurred Black Isaac's enmity.
There was a painful sense of having an evil eye upon

him and of being insecure. He had a constant fear of having some web of malice secretly spun around him; yet saw no immediate way fairly open by which to withdraw from the danger. And, withal it was that hour of special nervous depression (with very many), 3 to 4 in the afternoon, when sympathies perhaps are more easily touched, or at least the gloomy aspects of misfortune appear still more gloomy.

The applicants filed in and took seats in the order of entrance. It was a rule to serve them in like order. So Thomas beckoned, and the first in the row came forward to the counter—a pale, weak-eyed, hollow-cheeked woman—and offered a pair of bed sheets. The quality was fair, and the sheets in a state of good preservation, and worth, in the money of the period, fully three to four dollars. Thomas pinned on a check with number, date, description of goods, &c., and passed in the bundle to John for appraisement, as the woman reseated herself. A moment later John returned the bundle, with a note of valuation; and Thomas, calling out the number, stated that the goods were rated at three-fourths of a dollar, and a two-thirds loan would be a half dollar. The poor woman cried out at the smallness of the sum, and the cry was taken up and repeated in a low but impressive way by all those present, so great is the sympathy among these unfortunates. At the same time the woman advanced and besought for more, pleading her wretchedness, that her husband was down sick and could not work, her own

strength broken, and the little children had eaten
the last loaf. The evident reality of the woman's
poverty and solicitude would have affected a heart
less tender than Thomas Ruffin's. He thought, too,
the valuation was below even a pawn-broker's standard, and was disposed to refer the case again to
John. But what was the use, he reflected. John
was a close cutter, he knew—a hardened fellow, with
the spirit of a true pawn-broker, who is pitiless
and always decides these matters as his own interests dictate. He simply replied, therefore, that it
was her privilege to refuse the valuation. The woman shook her head in silence, and, coming up to
the counter to close the contract, presented a grocer's
receipt for identification. Whereupon her ticket
was made out and given her with the money, and so
she departed.

"Next!" cried Thomas, and the call was responded
to by a much younger looking woman whose whole
shabby-genteel appearance suggested one who had
known better days. She came forward modestly,
and with that smile on her wan features which ofttimes masks a fullness of sorrow. Her well-worn
dress of black was the plainest, yet scrupulously
neat and clean—her eyes large, watery, and lustrous
—the blue veins shown distinct over the pale shrunk-
en face—and the body was wasted and weak, so weak
that the jaws, in repose, hung slightly apart. The
evident signs of a fatal disease, and the refined,
modest, lady-like air, could not fail to rouse at once
unusual sympathy and interest. Thomas took down

the bundle called for by the ticket, and, observing
the pawn had been renewed for the fifteenth time,
felt curious to see it and peered into the package.
It was a dimity petticoat, and, as the young woman
caught a glimpse of it, unobserved she brushed away
a tear. The material was superfine, and the fabric,
with border richly embroidered, could not have cost
under an eagle. It had been valued at three dollars,
with a three-fourths loan upon it of two and a quarter dollars.

"I see it has had fifteen renewals," remarked
Thomas.

"Yes, Sir," she replied with a smile.

"Why don't you redeem it?"

"Because I am too poor, Sir."

"Wish to renew again?"

"Yes, Sir."

"You know that every renewal carries a tax,"
said Thomas, with a growing interest roused by the
young woman's looks and bearing.

"Yes, Sir, I do."

"And the sum of the taxes will soon equal the
valuation."

"Yes," she answered, as her pale countenance began to grow yet paler and she became visibly agitated, "but I've never known the day, Sir, when I
could pay down at once the full ransom money."

"Why not let it go then?"

"Oh! Sir!" she cried, bursting into tears, "it is
the last relic of my Mother!"

It was a scene even for the Pawn-Shop. The usu-

ally dull, self-communing pawners present, attracted
by the colloquy, were now wide awake and eagerly
interested. Thomas himself, fresh in this business,
was deeply moved and could scarce withhold his
own tears. He paused a moment. The filial affection of the poor creature, sobbing as if her heart
would break before him, touched the tenderest spot
in his breast, and, obeying an impulse quite out of
character with the Shop, he dived into his pocket,
drew forth the scanty purse, and counting down the
two and a quarter dollars, dropped the sum into the
till, saying as he did so :

"Well, my good woman, I will redeem it for you"—
at the same time handing her the treasure.

A cry of admiration rose from the sad-eyed, blasé
company. As for the young woman herself, she
gazed a moment at Thomas in mute astonishment.
Then, attempting to speak her thanks, broke down
at every effort; and Thomas, to end the trying scene
and not trusting himself to speak, waved her out,
with delight and gratitude beaming upon her countenance.

The rest were served without noteworthy incident.
By 7 the work was over and the door closed. From
the atmosphere of the Pawn-Shop, tainted by many
an ancient odor-bearing bundle, the transition to
the *Bank* was agreeable enough. Late was the hour
that saw its unfinished afternoon work done. Yet
Thomas did not fail to walk over to The Home to
bid his Father good night—a sacred daily duty never
omitted.

On the way, as he ran over the course of the day, the Shop scene was conspicuous. His generosity had stripped him, with not enough left to meet the scant needs of to-morrow. But there were no regrets. He felt better for what he had done. And as for "to-morrow," it was not the first time he had trusted it.

The night was clear and cold, with the wind settled in the North, and the stars, as usual (for Thomas was a confirmed star-gazer, it has been noted), drew his attention. They shone magnificently. Ruddy Procyon and Betelyeuse beamed like rubies near the zenith. Jupiter ruled resplendent in the western sky. In the southern hemisphere, far below the bands of Orion, Sirius' white light glowed with unrivaled lustre. How beautiful, thought he, are the lights of heaven! How vast, how wonderful, how glorious these lights! And what, then, must "the *Father* of lights" not be!

CHAPTER IX.

" Rather than not accomplish my Revenge,
Just or unjust, I would the world unhinge."
— *Waller*.

There was nothing in Noals' suggestion itself (to take the *Bank's* funds and mask the theft by an apparent burglary), to which in any sense Black Isaac was opposed, if thought to be necessary or conducive to his interests. A prospect of the destruction of the evidences of debt due the *Bank*, with more than sufficient cash to replace his personal loss, was something, indeed. The moral quality of the mode, comparatively nothing. In truth he felt surprise that the scheme had not occurred to himself. The sole points for consideration were : Could a suitable agent be found, and the degree of the risk of discovery. Upon these points Black Isaac sat in his private room and long pondered. The result was satisfactory, seemingly; for his face and manner gradually assumed a less cheerless aspect. He took tea with far more relish than for weeks past—smoked his Narghilé with unusual zest— and, by the time Noals returned, was positively in a degree of good humor. The fact was that the Pawnbroker, readily catching at Noals' suggestion,

had developed himself a complete scheme of robbery, with agents chosen and details all arranged.

Noals was back on the hour, and to his interrogation :

"Well, Sir?"

Black Isaac replied in apparent opposition :

"It's collecting pigeon's milk, Jimmie Noals. You
advise the impossible."

"Mistaken, Dalguspin!"

"Your scheme's desperate, Jimmie."

"So's the situation. I'll eat my old hat" (Noals
was as ready to swear by the old hat, as a Turk by
his beard), "if it can't be done, Dalguspin. I say
we can work it. I say we pull a strong team. We
can 'smite the gates of brass and break the bars of
iron in sunder.' "

"Quoting Scripture! He! he! he! I'd as soon
expect to see Angels' wings sprout from the backs
of politicians."

"Needn't note what I quote. To the main point,
Dalguspin : What say you to it, if it *is* desperate ?"

"That it lacks an accomplice."

"The dickens! An accomplice! Are you crazy?
Wouldn't it complicate and add to the hazard ?"

"Probably. But wouldn't it strengthen the notion of burglary?

"Probably. But where could a fit one be found,
when we haven't got yet the burglar himself ?"

"I can name him."

"Who ?"

"Thomas Ruffin, my clerk."

Noals arched his eyebrows and gave a shrug.

"I mean an *involuntary* accomplice, mind you—
one we can make to appear so, Jimmie."

"Ah!—that young man 'Tammie' I've heard you
call him—that pet of yours—that most amiable and
most excellent clerk! Ah! yes—*involuntary* puts
another face on it. It's hardly probable he'd be a
voluntary helper."

"Couldn't a money-roll be secreted in old Ruffin's
room at The Home, to be found there at the proper
moment? Twelve month ago he was rich. Lost his
pile and's gone crazy. Poor now—very poor—nothing at all but Son's pay; and I could cut that and
put him in straits. There's the motive, you see.
Full yesterday—to-day, hungering and thirsting.
Pinched by want, with the memory of riches yet
fresh and green. Poverty's a curse, Jimmie—isn't
it? And for him who has had wealth, to shrink at
once into its fittings—ah me! ah me!—is a hard and
a painful task. There's the motive, Jimmie."

Prior to his sounding Dalguspin, as related in a
preceding chapter, Noals had formed in his own
mind a distinct scheme of robbery; but, for the present, held it back. While each had done things more
or less "crooked," and while Noals placed a high
estimate on the Pawn-broker's villainous and vin-
dictive capacity, the latter had never gone as far as
this hint he had thrown out to him, and it was plain
wisdom not to divulge the scheme, unless Black
Isaac should become committed to the idea. He
now perceived that not only had the instigation found

lodgment in the Pawn-broker's mind, but had developed there into a scheme of his own, and Noals realized the necessity, as well as the policy, of giving his scheme consideration at the least. With this end in view, he put the question :

"You think the old one could be handled easily ?"

"Crazy and deaf. No trouble."

"Crazy from losing his pile, I believe ?"

"Yes—a bad case, very bad. A dear deceiving cousin tricked him into a shaky Cotton House down South."

"Generous soul! What are we for, Dalguspin, but to help each other !" exclaimed Noals with an air of lofty sentiment.

"The break was too broad, or the purse was too narrow, and a week after signing the firm John Ruffin found himself without a red."

"Sad sequel to benevolence. But there's another world, Dalguspin," observed Noals, pointing and looking heavenward with an affectation of piety as complete as it was comical.

"Certainly, Jimmie Noals, certainly—he! he! he !" responded the Pawn-broker, irresistibly amused. "Comedian in a role of tragedy."

"One can but follow his bent."

"A joke, Noals, will be your last gasp in this world; and your best hope in the next———"

"To humor old Nick into gentle treatment. I dare say," Noals interjected. "Well, every man to his making. Now, how about your Tammie ?"

"*Extrinsically*, *intrinsically*, and *personally*, he fills the bill."

"Humph! Explanations, I take it, are in order."

"Well, *extrinsically*, he's a stranger here—no acquaintances, no friends, no pulls, you see."

"So.--And *intrinsically ?*"

"He's a very gentle sort of somebody—gentle, Noals, as the dear ladies."

"Who are often dear deceivers, I can tell you. Wasn't Epaminandas the bravest, yet the gentlest of men ?"

"Confound your philology and hair-splitting. I'll say, then, that *intrinsically*, he's a very *timid* sort of somebody."

"So."

"And, *personally*, I hate the youth. He won't co-operate in my little schemes, you see. I've told you about one of 'em."

"I remember. The block-head! To refuse an opening like that! He *is* a green one, or I'll eat the old hat."

"I tried him,. and hang it! he told me, for my pains, that he'd mistaken my character! And even threatened to law me !"

"The blackguard !"

"I've never before had a clerk to make a fool of me and force me to eat my words, and I've vowed not to forget it. My age will not put up with the codlin's slap, Jimmie."

"The blatherskite !"

"So pious, you know. Such a good, conscientious young man, you know.

"Why haven't you dismissed the rascal?"

"Waiting to get even; and here's the chance."

"Yes, yes," replied Noals, who saw no objection to the Pawn-broker's suggestion, "verily, a kind Providence has preserved him to our hand. If *he* won't co-operate with you, *we'll* co-operate with Providence, and I'll devour the ancient chapeau, if 'Tammie' doesn't prove a first class silent partner."

"Very good—very good!"

"And now, Dalguspin, having supplied the tail, suppose you try for the head and name the burglar himself?"

"Suppose I do?"

"Well!"

"He will be you."

"Sir, you are complimentary."

"Now, now, Jimmie, do pray don't take me for a Simple Simon. Can't I see all you've said has been a feeler, and that your scheme has been formed around your own self? Otherwise, it's a folly and no sane man could propose it. You're the very person, Noals. Risk then would be nil. Squealing would be shut out. The burglar, too, should personate William, the watchman, and who so fit for this as yourself. You're about his age and make and size. You know him well—his voice, his limp, his manner. Your mimic powers could re-produce him to a T. All you want is the watchman's garb and a full gray beard, aids easily supplied. Withal, Jimmie, we should remember the scheme has a moral side, and isn't it the proper thing *he* should stand forth to repair the loss, whose damnation luck caused it?"

"Ah! Dalguspin, you can see very far, if you can't see quite through a mill-stone. Suppose I *should* have had myself in view—suppose I *should* be willing to go in—one thing's certain and sure : *I must have the necessary help.* That's a point I'm bound to score for myself."

"Help multiplies risk, Jimmie. The scheme doesn't call for help. Cracksman's skill is not required. The keys and all, you've said, would be to hand, the private watchman away, and access to Bank and Safe smooth, without a hindrance. What need for help? The job's most easy—thus : Watch Thomas from the street. By ten he should be through the extra work that night and awaiting Will's return from my house, where I would be detaining him on biz. That's your moment. Enter with duplicate key, while Thomas is within the 'cage.' The *Bank's* light's dim, and as you limp along, like Will, outside the 'cage,' call to him in Will's low tone : 'Mr. Thomas, you can leave now ;' and then make for the rear office. That Thomas should delay or show suspicion, is most unlikely. If he *should*, at pistol's point gag and nipper him. With keys in hand, a moment will then suffice to open Safe, wrench drawers, scatter their contents, and out, with all the marks of burglary behind. There's but a youth to deal with, Noals. Can't you deal with him alone?

You're far larger, and there's much in size, as you
will feel, when you get a wife bigger than yourself."

"Dalguspin, the second, sober thought says nay.
That fellow Thomas may defy the pistol's point. ·
Manners like his often mask a heart of steel.
Haven't I told you that Epami——"

"No, no, Noals," broke in Black Isaac. "No
more of 'Epami;' it's all about 'our Tammie.'
Thomas Ruffin defy the pistol's point! he! he! he!"

"Yes—and then to floor and fix him, neatly and
without alarm, would need another's aid."

"*Two* men, to floor and fix Thomas Ruffin! he!
he! he!"

"Besides : Will, the Watchman, may return too
soon, or loungers may imperil the exits. There *must*
be some one on guard outside, to hold the Watchman
in a chat, if need be, and give me warning how best
to leave, whether by front or rear. If cracksmen,
whose art we are simulating——"

"Simulating!" again broke in Black Isaac, with
his low little laugh. "Good, Jimmie!"

"Yes, Sir! yes, Sir! I say *simulating;* for

We're simply *borrowing* money in a certain way,
   As many an honest man has done, and is doing to-day—"

"True! true! Jimmie," interjected the Pawn-
broker. "He! he! he!"

"If cracksmen never single handed boss a job
like this, hasn't a novice greater need of aid! How
answer *that* argument?"

O I don't believe in argument, Noals."

"In what then?"

"Intuitions, Sir; and one tells me it's time to drink."—Dalguspin rings.

"Whiskey and cigars, Robert."

Robert retires, and directly re-enters with the "things." Noals pours a glass, and, sniffing it, remarks :

"Good liquor this, Dalguspin."

"What's better than Old Rapp in its teens ?"

"Why, Old Rapp in my gills, to be sure," responded Noals, as he drained the glass.

"Trim, fine fellow Robert seems to be," observed Noals, as the servant-man retires.

"Yes—he's a character. Educated, intelligent, gentlemanly—handy, witty, spunky. You know how I got him."

"I remember. A sort o' Sam Weller, he."

"Yes—but I'm getting afraid of him."

"Why ?"

"O it seems he's a butt cut of original sin—such a dare-devil, from his own account—been every where and in all kinds of scrapes—done the Wild West, and took a hand in adventure of every sort— worked sailor's passage to South America, and after roaming up and down and across that continent, turned up in Mexico and Texas, and must have been a regular 'fighting Bob' at San Jacinto; for he shows scars from a dozen wounds received, he says, in that battle; and altogether I'm half afraid I've got a Cow-boy or Bandit, watching for an opportunity."

"You've spoken to me somewhat of Bob's life before, and do you know while I've been revolving our scheme, I've been thinking of him as a possible confed?"

"Robert! Gracious me! Why, Robert is about to leave! His special service to me is over, and, with a roving spirit still, he intends, just as soon as I can fill his place, to take the road again."

"That much the better, Dalguspin, for our purpose. By jingo! events are so shaping to our hand, that our scheme begins to look like a special providence."

"Robert a confed! Well, well! That's to be thought on, too, Noals. If he could be induced to leave the country!" added Black Isaac reflectively.

"Anyhow, disguised as a cracksman, let me sound him and report."

The Pawn-broker pauses to reply:

"But use every care, Jimmie, and decide nothing till you see me."

"Certainly. Depend on me. Disguises and tricks are somewhat in my line. I'd lay a wager I could gammon even your own sharp eyes."

"I've no money now to try luck with. If I had, I'd up with it against so luckless a fellow as thou."

"Egad! the Banker shows a short memory. He forgets the hits, and that himself, too, pressed this latter venture; and if it has miscarried, haven't I shown how we may recoup? But to biz: Touching Bob, I should really like to be sure, Dalguspin, since I need a practiced hand, that he has been all the dare-devil he makes claim to."

"We can but take his word."

"Aha! Eat my old hat, but I have it," exclaimed Noals after a moment's thought.

"What ?"

"A way to test him."

"How ?"

"You say he has been in Texas ?"

"Yes."

"And a Cow-boy ?"

"So he states."

"Well—there's no Cow-boy who can't give the Texas Yell. *That* I'll swear to; and I know the Yell, besides. I heard it once, and never shall forget it."

"Yes, yes—I see, I see. We'll try Robert."

The Pawn-broker rings and Robert enters. At a motion from the former, Robert takes up the waiter and is in the act of leaving with the "things," when Black Isaac observes, as if accidentally :

"Here, Robert, a moment. There's a little favor you must do us."

"Yes, Sir," replied Robert, turning and replacing the waiter on the table.

"You say you've been in Texas ?"

"Yes, Sir."

"Among the Cow-boys ?"

"Yes, Sir."

"And a Cow-boy yourself, I believe you told me ?"

"Yes, Sir."

"Now, Robert, the Texas Yell is something we've often heard of, yet never heard. Let us have one, a real *good* one, Robert."

Robert made ready, stooping and twisting his body, and gave forth a loud, a long, a wild, wierd whoop. Whereupon Noals cried out:

"Very well done! A genuine Texas Yell."

"And I think, by George, it has waked up h—ll," exclaimed Black Isaac, as a great noise outside smote his ear.

"All the household are on us pell-mell," chimed in Robert. And they all, indeed, came bursting in, the housekeeper with pistol, cook with carving-knife, scullion with broom-stick, &c., &c., and all shouting together:

"Gracious Heavens! What was *that?* Thought they were murdering you!"

"No! no!" the Pawn-broker reassured them. "Robert is acting the Cow-boy. No danger, no danger—except to Robert's lungs. He! he! he! Whoop it up again, Robert."

And again the fearful yell shook the chamber; and Noals winked hard at the Pawn-broker, as much as to say:

"*He'll do.*"

CHAPTER X.

The indenture binding Thomas Ruffin to Dalguspin, included no definite terms touching pay, the
clause relating thereto stating simply that "the second party aforesaid, in consideration of inexperi-
ence, agrees that his salary shall depend on the
character of the services rendered." The wily
Pawn-broker explained, to Thomas' satisfaction at
the time, that to an ambitious young man a contin-
gent salary of this sort, was much to be preferred
to a fixed sum. So far, therefore, Thomas was under the thumb of the Pawnbroker, and the latter
began to bear down. On the plea of financial pressure he had cut the wage to the extent of a half
dollar, making it one dollar per week.

Thomas spoke of the matter to Friend Peale, but
his sensitiveness refused a revelation of his real
condition. Friend Peale knew, as he thought, that
Thomas could not be living on one dollar per week,
leaving out of view the little extras he provided
his Father, and supposed he must have some

source of means unknown to him—an opinion in which he was confirmed by Thomas' refusing the aid he more than once offered. He did not press inquiry touching his means ; for it was a topic which the shrinking Thomas seemed to wish to avoid. But one thing he plainly perceived, that Thomas was out of sorts, a prey to some secret disturbing influence of recent origin, apparently. Whatever might be the cause or causes, in one direction he felt there was certainty, that Dalguspin was treating him most unjustly, and the warm-hearted Quaker, for the second time, sought out the *Banker* and remonstrated. Black Isaac replied that he was learning the young man bookkeeping, and that he was getting the worth of his services. And when Friend Peale reminded him of the encomiums he had bestowed on Thomas at the beginning, and that he did not now allege a lowered efficiency, Black Isaac's reply was so unsatisfactory, that the indignant Quaker gave him a very sharp piece of his mind.

The fact was that Thomas Ruffin was in want. Of his expenses he kept a most exact detailed account, and actually reduced the per diem for food to less than 12 cents. With bread (he would cut the loaf into just ten slices) at five cents, sugar at four cents, eggs at eighteen, butter at twenty, a package of corn starch at five, and milk at four cents a pint, the outlay (exact to the fraction of a cent) for a certain day, veritably taken as an average from the diary preserved in his family, was as follows :

BREAKFAST.

1 boiled egg,	-	-	-	1 1-2 cts.	
2 slices of bread,	-	-	1	"	
½ ounce butter.	-	-	5-8	"	

Cup of content { 1 gill milk, - - 1 cent }
 { 1 ounce sugar, - - 1-4 } 1 1-4   4 3-8 cts.

DINNER.

Custard { 1 egg, - - - 1 1-2 cts. }
 { 1 gill milk, . - - 1 " }
 { 1 spoonful corn starch, 1-4 " } 3 cts.
 { 1 onnce sugar, - - 1-4 " }

2 slices bread,	-	-	-	1 "	
1-2 ounce butter,	-	-	-	5-8	4 3-8 cts.

SUPPER.

Cup of content { 1 gill milk, - - 1 cent }
 { 1 ounce sugar, - - 1-4 " } 1 1-4 cts.

1 slice bread,	-	-	-	1-2 "	
1-4 ounce butter	-	-	-	5-16 "	2 1-16 cts

11 1-16 cts.

While the fact is unquestionable that Thomas Ruffin actually did support himself on such a mite, it should be added that he did not fall at once to these figures. Experimenting he found he could subsist on less and less, and finally got down to the above— the infinitesimal, one might say—and discovered he could live and labor.—Americans should note the fact, nation of spendthrifts and dyspeptics, as well as of tourists. We eat from habit, not from need, and by the matured body in moderate exercise, small, indeed, is the amount of food required.

In this discipline of pabulum Thomas' main stay was the special loaf he used, bought of one Arthur— touching whom it may be said, that if his bakery had one aspect, its products had quite another. The former was a narrow, short, old-fashioned, neglected- looking, three-story brick affair, squatting betwixt two towering modern structures, with the upper

stories for a domicile, the basement for the bakers
and the ovens, and the front first floor apartment for
the Shop—a little, dingy, uninviting room, 24 by 15
feet. Here, however, the dark features end. All
the rest is bright. Arthur's Shop was famous. He
had a great run of high-class customers, used the
best material, employed the best bakers, and sold
over the counters unequalled loaves, at the hands,
too, of employees, it can be added, exceptionally
engaging. These were two ladies whose physical
characteristics differed considerably. For if one
suggested rather a spear than a dumpling, the other
suggested rather a dumpling than a spear. But
each was so genteel in appearance, and so thoroughly lady-like and obliging, and the delivery so gracious, that the fine loaves from their hands really
acquired an additional attraction.

The loaf Thomas had been recommended to buy,
and which he did buy; a rare loaf in those days, a
loaf difficult to make well, and whose excellency
was one of Arthur's prides, was the Bran loaf, giving
the full force of the wheat berry. He soon came to
prefer it to any other bread, in the matter of taste
even, the bite was so substantial and satisfactory;
and it proved the young man's salvation. Without
its bowel-regulating and tissue-forming and all round
supporting qualities, the relentless fast, it is almost
certain, must have ended disastrously.

But, to be sure, Arthur's shelves and counters held
other good things. There were crullers so rich and
brown—and there were cakes, of every size and shape

and shade and variety, from the penny-pound, up—
and there were pies of all sorts, from master hands,
fresh every day, plump and full-measured, and filling the little room with dainty, toothsome odors.

But all this Thomas had to pass by. It involved
effort, no doubt. In his circumstances it was, without question, a serious matter, this passing of Arthur,
so to speak.—Dear reader, please allow the setting
down of a thought occurring to us just here, and for
which we assume full responsibility, that the passing of Arthur *was* serious—whether it be Sir Bedi-
vere with strained and tearful eye watching from
the crag's summit the dusky barge on its way to the
"happy island-valley of Avilion, where the wind
lies deep-meadowed," till the black hull becomes a
vanishing point on the mere—or the fasting Thomas
in the aroma of this famed pastry Shop, and unable
to go beyond the tantalizings of the eye and the
nose.

There was one indulgence, however, Thomas Ruffin
occasionally permitted himself. He would sometimes
be in the Shop about 11 a. m., the hour when the
dusty baker boy was accustomed to bring up from
below the great trays of hot buns, with the currents
all sticking out of them like so many tempting little
black eyes. They were not dear, yet fine—two for
a penny—and Thomas now and then would buy.

One other little indulgence must be mentioned.
On market days (it will be remembered there was a
famous market near the *Bank*) Thomas would watch
his chance to step out a moment for a glass of fresh

country butter-milk—that is, as often as he could spare a penny. The market man he patronized was one Smith, acquaintance with whose goods he made under these circumstances :

In one of his first visits to the market his attention was drawn by a huckster soliciting for asparagus—or "grass," as usually called by the market men. His cries were especially shrill and assertive, and the vegetable itself had an interest of its own; for asparagus had been both a famous growth and a favorite dish at Cloud Cap. Thinking it odd to see it offered in Winter, he stopped; and to his inquiry, the huckster replied, that it was cut from hot house force beds, and then went on shouting his cries :

"Sparagrass! Sparagrass! Come up, Ladies and Gentlemen, and see Dr. Dorsey's celebrated, O. K., A No. 1, perfection Sparagrass—

Raised under the glass—
Best of its class—
Good for lad and lass—"

(and then with a wink at Thomas' ear)

"To make the humors pass."

"Got it from old Smith over there," said the huckster, replying with a grin to Thomas' amused expression. Thomas glanced "over there," and seeing an uncommon press :

"What means that ?" he asked of the huckster.

"That old Smith sells a genuine article."

And so Thomas found out. For, if Smith was capable of palming off for his own Dean Swift's triplet (with some variation), he undoubtedly sold high grade goods 'at first hand, and had a great reputation.

Smith was an old-fashioned countryman of drawling speech, who thrice a week drove to the city, and bracing the front wheels of his great wagon on the curb-stones outside the market-house, with tongue tied up and team tethered at the side, from the wagon's rear, stretched out on supporting poles an extended canvas, with ample wings, beneath which were arranged the tables, with their snowy coverings, displaying baskets of the cleanest eggs, and ripe luscious fruits, and churns—all scrubbed till they shown again—of ice cold milk and butter-milk, and tubs of smear-case, and pails of the nicest butter prints, and, in season, great freezers of ice cream, &c., &c. Though aided by wife and stalwart son-in-law and two helps, to serve the constant throng was all that Smith could do. He slipped money into his purse, Smith did; and would slip himself—too often, it is feared—into a little groggery near by, the old man's only fault. Smith soon learned to know his customer, and at sight of Thomas began to prepare for him. A deep and ample old-styled tumbler three-fourths filled with fresh country butter-milk, into this a gill of sweet cream, and, on warm days, a lump of ice—ye gods! what a drink it was to Thomas! And all for a penny!

These were the solitary self-indulgences, if they can be called so, Thomas Ruffin permitted himself. The ordinary recreations of young men, even the most self-restrained, of course were all closed out-

The many little individual wants, outside of bare subsistence—really often in the nature of necessaries —were all closed out. True, there was the one dollar Sister Jessica brought for the chair (and it came in most opportunely); but it was a dollar and no more. True, there was the sum of seventeen dollars (out of the orignal five hundred) to his credit in the Savings Bank (not Dalguspin's, by the way); but he had resolved wisely not to touch this, save under the extremest circumstances, the most dire necessity. True, Friend Peale (as has been said) repeatedly pressed upon him aid; but he could not accept what he saw no way of returning—from one, too, who, as Thomas knew, had just sustained business losses. No doubt his sensitiveness here carried him too far; since Friend Peale was well able to bear the losses. But Thomas chose his path. And truly the young man was put to it.

To such a regimen and circumstances the physical organism must ultimately have yielded; and Thomas knew and felt it. But, a few months would see the end of service to Black Isaac. And Friend Peale already had in view for him more than one position where pay and surroundings would be of another sort. If all this was encouraging, Thomas drew further support from a sense of supreme duty done to his Father. There were many little wants The Home did not supply his Father—many little extras that gave his Father pleasure. For instance, frequently he would ask Thomas for small coin, to give, he said, to the "poor beggars" he would meet in the

Park, or on his walks (for he was beginning now to make short strolls by himself). To answer these and other little demands, Thomas at first drew upon the bank reserve, hoping soon to merit such an increase of pay as to be able to answer them from this latter source. When the pay was docked and the bank reserve had sunk below the safety point, to less than a score of dollars, none of these supplies would Thomas cut off, though it brought his own subsistence nigh to the vanishing point. To have done so would have roused suspicion in his Father's mind and almost inevitably unmasked his position and circumstances. His Father's enjoyments, too, were so few and simple, and bore so materially on the progress of improvement. He *could not* deprive him of any, the least, of these. Had he not been the tenderest, the most loving of fathers? Through all the years gone by, had he not yearned over him, the centre of all his thought, solicitude, and activities? And in the day of darkness, with no light in his eyes, save as he looked up to him so trustfully for support and care, shall not affection's debt be paid to the uttermost farthing? Yes, yes—joyfully will he take hungerings and thirstings and whatever besides, to add aught of ease to his Father's lot.

What gave Thomas concern was the fear he should be unable to conceal from his Father the actual state of affairs. He watched himself and made it a point never to appear otherwise than cheerful in his Father's presence. Over-worked and under-fed as he was, the dear fellow kept a bright face. Whatever depress-

ing influences might exist, whether drawn from apprehension touching Dalguspin, or from a straightened living, or any other condition or circumstance,
he did not allow an outward manifestation. Often
he would carry to The Home bills from the *Bank*
and count them over evasively, as it were, yet so
that his Father would see them and feel that he was
not wanting funds.

There was one direction, however, in which little
innocent deceptions of this sort were impracticable.
There was no method for concealing the tangible
results of rigorous and continued fasting. His by
no means was a fattening regimen. He showed none
of that physical degeneration known as corpulency,
so common a blotch on this high civilization of ours,
whereof many of us are getting tired. Evidently
his body was losing weight—his cheeks becoming
hollowed and paler; and there were no means of disguising it from the searching observation which his
Father's supreme affection and morbid apprehensions constantly maintained over him. As he feared, the first symptom of a change John Ruffin was
quick to notice and anxiously remark upon. Thomas
tried to laugh it off. In vain. His Father grew
more and more disquieted. The change, as it went
on, appeared all the more marked to John Ruffin,
because he saw Thomas fairly but once a week, Sunday. There was another circumstance, too, that
seemed peculiar to his Father, and, in connection
with the thinning process, deepened anxiety. As
has been stated in this narrative, Thomas passed

Thursday night with his Father and invariably shared his Father's supper, as he did all the Sunday meals (—it may be observed, that, on these occasions, Sabina, whose warm friendship Thomas had secured, was sure to smuggle on the plates extra portions—); and what seemed of late so strange to John Ruffin, was, that Thomas—though the latter endeavored to control himself and be on guard against unusual and suspicious action—should get at the food with such eagerness. The old gentleman wondered. He never had seen his soon eat so before. And here he was, too, with such an appetite, getting thinner and thinner! Thomas could see his Father's growing distress of mind—which by cheerfulness of demeanor and in every other way, he sought vainly to allay. At length, there came one day a burst of lamentation from John Ruffin, that his son was diseased and must have treatment.

Thomas declared such a thing would be absurd— that his Father was entirely mistaken—that his health was all right; and, to confirm the statement, fell upon an expedient that proved a boomerang. On the way to The Home one Thursday night, bethinking himself how it would please his Father to appear in the hue as well as with the substance of health, he vigorously applied to his face new fallen snow (a recipe for pallor, as he had been told), and entered his Father's room with cheeks as red as cherries. John Ruffin at first did not know what to make of it. He gazed at Thomas in mute astonishment. Then became frightened and broke out into wailings, declar-

ing Thomas had a fever and that a Doctor must be sent
for. Thomas entreated his Father, explaining that
the flush was the natural result of cold (and in truth
it was a wintry night), and no cause whatever for
alarm. John Ruffin appeared to be satisfied. But
when presently the brilliant bloom passed off, and
reaction left the cheeks paler than before, he began
to make a great to do again; and again was Thomas
obliged to entreat and explain how it was all the
effect of cold and reaction, and asked his Father how
he could reconcile ill health with his uniform cheerfulness of spirit.

John Ruffin finally concluded that all the trouble
lay at the root of overwork; and Thomas promised,
that, if matters did not go on to his satisfaction, he
would give up his position at the *Bank* in a month
or so—that other positions just as good, if not better,
had been offered him already, and would continue to
be open to him any moment he might choose to accept them—having in mind Friend Peale's good
offices in his behalf. This had a quieting effect.
Meanwhile, John Ruffin's opinion of the *Banker*
rapidly changed. In fact, a sentiment of animosity
began to take root.

The personal attentions Thomas gave his Father
were of the most devoted character. During the
day, at meal hours, he would often, though with
great inconvenience, run over to The Home a moment; and every evening he made it a point to bid
his Father good night. It was a sacred duty, he felt,
and never omitted, however late the hour that saw

his release from work, and whatever might be the state of the weather. And whenever he foresaw that duties at the *Bank* would detain him beyond the usual time, he took the precaution to convey, or have conveyed, to his Father word to that effect, to avoid the distressing anxiety which he knew his Father, in his peculiar state of mind, would be sure to feel. And John Ruffin always would have a light at the window, to let Thomas know he was expecting him, either up or abed. On these occasions, when Thomas came in early and the weather was pleasant, he would walk out with his Father, at first generally in the Park or Square near by, and then further and further forth, as his Father's health and strength showed signs of improvement.

His life was solitary and manifested on its upper plane, as a *duty* first, not a pleasure, not a gain. Work at the desk and attentions to his Father absorbed every moment. And amidst these duties— disquieting his life with its uncertainties—there was a burning *thought* constant in his mind. That affection does not fade under the influence of absence, was clear in his case. The thought was of Amy Sanford. It was a deepening, as well as a constant, thought. Where could she be? What was she doing? he would be asking himself repeatedly. He knew she was an orphan and moneyless, and that, on the score of health, she had left New Orleans and gone North, to fill a position of some sort. He had had a notion that she might be in this very city, since she had attended school here. But her name was not in the directory, and Friend Peale could give no information. Over and again had he written to the address of her Grandmother (Aunt Sanford), without replies. Was *she* dead, too? He had sent letters, likewise, to the surviving members of the late House of Thomas Sanford & Co., but all in vain. Heart-heavy he suspended the search for want of a clue. The thought of Amy, however, still grew. The location of the school where his cousin had studied, was one of the first inquiries he made of Friend Peale after reaching the city; and invariably in his walks, whenever he could possibly make them suburban, he would take in this school and linger near it. Nor scarcely would a day pass and not see him take out the little silver locket with the Moss bud, that she had given him. Of nights, too, many a time would he wake with the locket in his hand and dwell fondly upon its memories.

So come and go the days, completely filled. Rarely did he visit even the Peale residence. No time for it. Often, however, he saw the hearty Quaker who felt and manifested the warmest interest in him. Every day or so Friend Peale would drop in at the *Bank* about dusk, after Black Isaac had left. It was the hour, too, for Sandy Johnson's frequent visits, and often would the three be together. Beyond these Thomas Ruffin knew no one socially, it may be said. He held converse with few—was in the world, not of it, as it were. Much was he by himself, communing with himself, weighing present responsibilities and how to meet them, and so led on and on to revolving the further and deeper problems of life. It was a lifting influence to Thomas, who thus followed, if afar off, those illustrious spirits that have gathered power in seclusion. The silent communings of Manresa ennobled St. Ignatius; and was it not from the cloisters of Citeaux and Clairvaux that St. Bernard drew the strength that made him the oracle of christendom? Great souls are formed in solitude.

CHAPTER XI.

A DISCOVERY.

It was Thursday, to John Ruffin one of the two bright days of the week. Thomas was to be with him that night. All day long he had worked hard to finish a chair for Sandy Johnson. The Shoemaker was to call for it that evening. Pressed for time he had refused to allow Sabina to "do" his room at the usual morning hour. Towards the afternoon's close the chair was finished, and to relieve his cramped body the old gentleman walked out, notwithstanding the lowering weather. Scarcely had he gone, when Sister Jessica called. She left flowers, saying she might call again, on her way back before dark, if the weather permitted. Miss Kitty, finding John Ruffin out, hurried up Sabina to make use of the chance to "do" the room, and not knowing how long he had been gone, and fearing his return before the room was done, or properly done, especially since of late he had been complaining—causelessly, no doubt—about his room, she presently followed Sabina, to stimulate her work.

"Dust up, Sabina, dust up," she said with an

11

accent somewhat of reprimand, as she entered the
room and found Sabina had not been as brisk as she
might have been.

"Yes'm, Miss Kitty, I *is* dustin' up, an' de dus' is
all up my nose, too," replied Sabina, dusting vigorously, and confirming her nasal declaration by a
succession of very violent reports and sneezings.

Miss Kitty stood a moment in a degree of astonishment at these remarkable explosions, remarkable
even for Sabina—then observed :

"If ye'd been doin' yer duty, ye'd been through,
and yer nose would niver be a dust-hole."

"Yes'm, Miss Kitty," Sabina responded, energetically plying the brush, and accompanying the stimulated duty with one of her peculiar and expressive
guffaws.

"Misther Ruffin's been spaking about his room."

"Yes'm, Miss Kitty."

"Dust up well, Sabina," repeated the Housekeeper, but in a softened and encouraging tone, as
she turned towards the door, retiring after the simil-
itude of good wine, that leaves a pleasant farewell
on the lips.

"Yes'm, Miss Kitty, yes'm," was the iterated assurance of the negress, as she dusted away with yet
quickened vigor and renewed guffaws; for apparently
she was so abundantly stocked with these explosives,
that a very little effort brought forth, as it were, an
involuntary discharge.

Sabina having reconnoitered the door and finding
Miss Kitty was not watching outside, for the moment

ceased "doing" and dusting, to examine the pictures. She had heard and she really felt the story of John Ruffin's life, and both himself and Thomas had a warm place in her heart. She could see they had been "grand folks" as she termed it. An air of gentle blood was manifest in Thomas, and his Father, even in his present afflicted condition, gave abund-ant evidence of the high strung Southern gentleman of the old regime. Then, too, the unusual consid-eration shown John Ruffin through the Peale influ-ence—the spacious room assigned him, the peculiar privileges allowed—naturally tended to advance the Ruffins further in Sabina's estimation. She consid-ered The Home distinguished by their presence, and herself honored as being the servant especially in charge. In rendering service she was ever ready and most amiable, and John Ruffin, as before has been intimated, became really attached to her. These pictures on the walls he had explained to Sabina from time to time, and, as representative of his past life, they possessed for her an irresistible attraction. While "doing" the room, day after day, she never seemed to tire of examining them, with a running comment enlivened by the guffaws with which it was her wont to emphasise her opinions and sentiments; and this particular day did not prove an exception, though the work had been so hurried up.

"Dese picturs, dey tells me," she said, looking up, "is where de ol' man lived way down Souf. Dey calls dis"—examining the first print—"'Cloud Cap. Don't see any cloud, only house"—a guffaw pointing her criticism. "Mighty fine house, though, in de trees an' flowers.—An' dis"—examining the second print—"dey says, is his cotton patch. Sakes alive! how de niggurs is a pickin' ob de cotton!"—a pealing guffaw, enough to have brought back Miss Kitty, signalizing her amusement. "An' dis"—third print —"is de rice patch.—An' dis"—fourth print—"de sugar mill.—So rich! so rich! an' now here at de, Home, gone crazy an' a bottomin' cheers! Lord ha' mercy! No money, no sense, no nuthin' ter help him, but he son Thomas, an' him so tender like! Trouble, trouble, dey tells me, made him go crazy. My! my! my! dis worl'! dis worl'!

Dat shoemaker, Sandy Johnson, brings dis here cheer here"—dusting the chair as she speaks—"to be bottomed. An' I heerd 'm say Mr. Thomas buys dese ol' cheers at auction-house, an' den gits Sandy Johnson ter bring 'm here, an' den gives de money ter Sandy ter pay for de bottom, an' den Sandy he give Mr. Thomas' money ter Mr. Ruffin, jes' ter 'muse him like an' make him think he's helpin' ter git along. I'm buyin' shucks fur him all de time, an' all de time, day an' night, he's a twistin' and a twistin' de splits, 'cause he say, he wants ter help Mr. Thomas to git along. Sandy Johnson say he knowed him at de ol' home, but he won't let him fin' it out, 'cause he say, he don't like ter see he ol' friends. Funny!" she added, as another guffaw roundly asserted her sense of the whimsical.

While indulging in these reflections, Sabina was

busy all the time dusting and tidying the room. As she turned to the table the flowers Sister Jessica had just left, attracted attention. She had discovered that almost every posy contained, among others, a certain kind of flower, and had found out, by inquiry of Miss Kitty and others, that this flower was the Moss Rose, She had noticed, further, that Thomas Ruffin all the while would be wearing these Mosses. Now, by no manner of means was Sabina an intellectual character, yet was she not without some faculty of reason, and having put the above facts together she had drawn a significant conclusion touching the supposed relations of Thomas and Sister Jessica. A pleasing conclusion to her it was; for the Sister, too, had won the negro woman by the gracious consideration she invariably showed her. The latter had a fixed notion that a voice so sweet and a manner so gentle could belong only to a charming young lady; and, knowing nothing touching the celibate vows of sisterhood, the profane opinion had gotten into her noddle that "Miss Jessie" (as she designated her, after John Ruffin's manner of address; for she had declared, sealing the declaration with a decided guffaw, that "dis here nigger ain't a gwine fur ter call *dat* Lady—*Sister*") ought to be, in Sabina's vernacular, somebody's jularkie.

"I'll *bet* dat sweet Miss Jessie brought dese," was Sabina's emphatically expressed opinion, as she placed the duster on the table to examine the flowers.

"She's allus bringin' flowers. An' I b'lieve Mr. Thomas is makin' up ter her, I does"—with

one of her amorous guffaws, as low and tender
and bewitching as she could make that mode of expression. "Looks so to *me*. Dare is one flower allus
in her bunch, *Moss Roses*. Here it be"—examining flowers. "Dat mus' be *her* flower. An' den I
see Mr. Thomas, all de time now, wid Moss Roses
in he button-hole. Looks ter *me* like he's gwine to
set up to her"—saluting the iterated sentiment with
another guffaw of the same tender sort of character.

"Dis'll do, I reckons," Sabina remarked, survey-
ing the room and feeling satisfied with the results of
broom and duster.

It was directly after her leaving that Thomas Ruffin
came in, by the private entrance. The flowers immediately caught his eye, and he knew Sister Jessica
had called. Her last posy had particularly attracted
him, containing, as it did, a full blown Luxembourg
Moss and a Comtesse de Murinais Moss bud, most
beautiful specimens of the choicest varieties, the
former a brilliant carmine, the latter pure white—
blooms so exceptionally lovely and with associations
so dear, that Thomas had composed some lines upon
them. He noticed, too, that this posy included certain exact similitudes of those in the last—that is, a
full-blown Luxembourg and a Comtesse de Murinais
bud, and, having transferred them to a button-hole,
he was engaged on a note to his Father, telling him
he had stepped over to say extra work would make
him two hours late, when Sabina entered and announced "Miss Jessie" in the receiving room.

If a surprise to Thomas—Saturday uniformly had

been the Sister's visiting day—it was an agreeable
one, and Thomas then and there decided to take half
an hour from his desk, and seize the opportunity, so
long and so much desired, of meeting this Sister.
He requested Sabina, therefore, to ask her in.

She entered. Thomas introduced himself. The
Sister glanced around for John Ruffin, when Thomas
informed her his Father had walked out, that he
must certainly be back presently, and asked her to
please be seated and wait a few moments—particularly as he wished himself to speak to her. He did
not offer his hand, having heard it was against custom, if not against a rule, for a religeuse to receive
the hand of a man. In subdued tone the Sister
spoke of its being late and time's pressing, and could ,
give him, she said, a few moments only, taking, as.
she spoke, a seat apart and in silence. The bearing
of man towards woman, as essentially distinguished
from that of man towards man, is marked by a peculiar softness, a delicacy and a reserve, which is
sexual and inherent; and if before men Thomas
Ruffin was a retiring character, much more was he
thus, under ordinary conditions, in the presence of
women. Yet his behavior on this occasion was comparatively free. The circumstances were exceptional. His Father had spoken of Sister Jessica so
often and so lovingly, and her kindnesses towards
him had been so manifold and thoughtful and salutary, and he had cherished himself so deep a sentiment of gratitude, that not only did she seem to him
to be no stranger, but a bond was felt to exist be-

tween them. Besides, in a religeuse the notion of sex
is replaced by that of the institution. And the
topics, too, whereon he wished to speak were ener-
gizing.

"Sister Jessica," said Thomas, opening the conversation, "you've been kind, indeed, to my Father."

He paused a moment, and the Sister responded to
the implied expression of thanks by a slight incli-
nation of the head.

"My Father seems more patient and contented,
since he has known you. It delights him to see you,
and I wish to let you know how deeply grateful I
am for your most kind attentions."

The Sister again bowed in response.

"I notice," said Thomas, after another brief pause,
"that your posies always have Moss Roses."

The Sister again replied in a bow.

"It's my Father's favorite, as you've found out,
and for myself has dear associations on other grounds,
besides. I cultivated it at our old home. I am
somewhat read, too, in its literature, and as a bloomer
only knew it as having a short season in the Spring;
and it has appeared strange to me to see the flowers
in Winter."

The Sister not replying to the implied interrogation, Thomas put the direct question:

"Will you please explain this, Sister Jessica?"

"They are furnished," she answered, in a low tone,
"by a friend, an experienced florist. Fecundating
Moss Roses with the pollen of the ever blooming
sorts, he produces a group of perpetual Mosses; and

the nursery and force bed give the Winter bloom."

"And yet the blooms in the crossing do not appear to have lost any of the peculiar beauty which marks the Moss."

"The florist, though a young man, is an expert in the cultivation of this particular rose."

"They must be costly," remarked Thomas.

"Our friend has become interested in their purpose, and furnishes them without price."

"He is very kind, certainly."

There was another brief pause, and then Thomas observed:

"I see among the flowers to-day the same varieties of the Moss as in the last bouquet, and in the same stage of growth."

The Sister bowed her acquiescence.

"And I appropriated them, with My Father's permission, as you see I've done these."

The Sister again inclined her head in silence.

"Indeed, they are lovely flowers, and as I looked down on their beauty the other day and thought upon their memories, I composed some lines, and—"

Thomas paused in the sentence, as if bethinking himself of the propriety of what he was about to say.

"You've been so faithful and so kind, Sister Jessica, in bringing these Mosses, I will repeat the lines," he modestly said, "should you care to hear them."

"Certainly," came the low reply; and Thomas gave the lines, extending with his left hand the

lapel of the coat and looking down on the boutonniere as he spoke :

> If among flowers the *Rose* is the queen,
> The *Moss* is the queen.rose. And here are seen
> The *queens* of the Moss. A Luxembourger this,
> Flowering out in crimson loveliness ;
>   And this bud a Comtesse de Murinais.
> It has no equal—nothing can eclipse
> This rose-bud, bursting from its mossy lips.
> Its freshness, sweetness, and lovely hue,
> Of youth and beauty make exponent true ;
> And theme has been for poetry and art.
> Withal—it lends a point to Cupid's dart,
> And speaks a tender language to the heart,
>   The language of—Love confessed.

"Thank you," gently spoke the Sister ; and
Thomas went on :

"I wear, Sister Jessica, a Moss Rose all the
while," disengaging, as he spoke, a small silver
locket, held about his neck by a delicate chain of
the same metal. "I'm sure my Father has spoken
to you about my Cousin, Amy Sanford. We grew
up together, and at our last parting she gave me
this locket, holding a Moss bud from the bush we
had planted together, in the days when sunshine
was all about us."

Thomas' emotion began to be embarrassing and he
stopped a moment for self-control. During the
pause the Sister, having occasion to use her hand-
kerchief, drew forth with it a paper which fell from
her pocket to the floor, unobserved either by herself or by Thomas ; for it was the close of a dark
evening, nor had the lamp been lighted.

"Amy," Thomas went on without break or pause, in a headlong impetuous way strangely unlike him, kindling with the theme, "was very dear to us and her family shared the misfortunes of ours and she's now an orphan too as I've heard and earning her bread somewhere up North and I've had a notion she was probably in this city for she attended school here but my searchings have been all in vain and a near friend of mine a leading citizen here can give me no tidings and I've written and written to New Orleans to get her address from her Grand-mother and my own Aunt who is living or was living there but I've not been able—"

Borne on by a swell of feeling Thomas was speaking with rapid energy, when, confused by the consciousness of his warmth and egotism, he suddenly stopped short, with an apology:

"You must excuse me, Sister, for speaking so of myself. . These personal matters are nothing to you. But you can understand now my interest in Moss Roses."

The Sister rose, saying it was late, and bid Thomas adieu.

Thomas drew a chair to a window and had finished the note to his. Father (whose absence, by the way, did not give him concern, as John Ruffin often now in favorable weather sat late in the Park of evenings), when he noticed a paper on the floor near where the Sister had been sitting. He picked it up. It was an envelope, square and of pinkish hue, unsealed, folded once upon itself, and containing something. What it contained, however, was not material to Thomas. His gaze was riveted on the envelope, which he turned over and over and examined in the more excited manner. Then he rushed to a trunk of his, kept in his Father's room and holding some of his most valued things, and took out an envelope which he carefully compared with the other., They seemed identical. Evidently Thomas was greatly excited, breathing rapidly with lips apart, and color coming and going. He was still contrasting the envelopes, when the door was rapped, and to his response Sister Jessica re-entered.

"Did I drop a paper here containing money?" she asked with hurry in her manner.

"Yes, Sister. Please be seated."

"My time is limited, and the limit has been passed."

"But I *must* speak, Sister Jessica," replied Thomas with a trembling voice, scarce able to control the excitement under which he was laboring. "Pray be seated, if but for a moment."

The Sister took a chair near the door where she had been standing.

"Sister Jessica," said Thomas, holding up the envelopes, one in either hand, "the envolepe, you must know, is both novel and rare, and is it possible, by mere chance, these should be the self-same in size, in shape, in color, and in the monagram of A. S.; for I can make out the letters, I think, on yours, though the impression be worn? This you dropped here. And the other contains the last note to me from Amy

Sanford. She *must* be in this city, as I have suspected; or you must know something about her.'"

The Sister did not reply immediately, and Thomas
implored her :

"Sister Jessica, why do you not speak ? I *must*
know the truth."

"Mr. Ruffin," came the reply in a low, deliberate
voice, "if there has been a discovery, in my view the
circumstances under which it has been made, should
go far, at the least, to bind a man of honor to respect
the wish of the party interested. If you will pledge
your word absolutely to reveal to none what I shall
have said, I will speak. Otherwise my lips are
closed, and moreover my visits to your Father must
cease."

There was nothing for Thomas to do but to give
the pledge, and the Sister continued :

"Yes—Amy Sanford is in this city, and wishes to
remain unknown. I was with her in a long illness
at a Church Home. We became close friends, and
her giving me, as a novelty, a number of these bits
of paper has been the means of disclosing her. Singular are the ways of Providence !"

The Sister paused—then went on :

"She confided to me her history. It was to gratify
her most vehement desire that I began these visits to
your Father. She it is who furnishes the flowers
and the chair and the pay. In all I have done for
him I have acted under her direction and as her
representative. I can say no more now. To-morrow
you will receive a letter,"

"Let me ask," said Thomas who had been listening with rapt attention, "how my Cousin is faring?"

"At present her circumstances are peculiar. I can
say she is among the friends she has made, and is.
well—save in so far as the sorrows of your house
and her own, weigh upon her.

But I say no more. It is beyond my time limit
and the weather threatens. You must neither follow
nor inquire about me. Remember the pledge. By
next mail will come a letter."

With these words the Sister, receiving the envelope, bade Thomas adieu.

All in a quiver Thomas hastened back to the *Bank*.
He had fasted that day with more rigor than usual,
in anticipation of having supper with his Father,
and, before renewing work, ran stumbling up stairs
to his room, to draw a cup of tea. His feelings can
better be imagined than described.

Amy in this city (so ran his thoughts)! I knew it!
I knew it! I had the strongest conviction she was
somewhere near. I have read in a book of innate attractions and antipathies, and it seemed to me I could
feel my Cousin's presence!—But why should Amy
live hidden? And from me, least of all? And
how happens it that Friend Peale knows nothing
about her? Strange! Passing strange! But there's
to be a letter!—And what can Amy be doing? And
who are these friends she has made and with whom
she is living? And who is this florist friend that
furnishes without price the costly flowers? And his
face clouded as the thought obtruded: And what

might not possibly be his relations to Amy? No, no, he reassured himself, the well-born Amy Sanford cannot be thinking of a florist. Amy cannot have forgotten *us*. She is well, the Sister says, except that our sorrows, with her own, weigh upon her. Surely her heart is towards us! How can it be otherwise! There is mystery, but out of it would come light and joy, and thrills would flash through and through him.

He struck a light. He always felt better, when night set in and the lamp brightened his dark little room. It cast a spell, as it were, upon its defects, and he could no longer look out and have invidious contrasts forced on him. His room now seemed to be uncommonly bright, and the little clock on the shelf more sympathetic than usual. The clock and himself had become really good friends. Of nights he would lie awake so often and listen to its tick, and it seemed to be talking to him kindly. It appeared now to tick clearer and brisker than ever, as though speaking to him with renewed encouragement. He drew the tea and drank the cup of cheer all lifted up. The theatre of life seemed suddenly to be expanding around him—new motives presenting—new springs of action developing—and he went down to his desk with a most hearty good-will.

CHAPTER XII.

Though the evening was dark and lowering, it was uncommonly mild, and, as Thomas had said, his Father had been sitting and walking in the Square or Park near by—a favorite resort. It was after 6, when he returned to his room with a small cat'o nine tails in his hand. Since his affliction he had become as afraid of dogs as an Indian, and, when in the Park, it was his fancy to carry a cat, rather than a cane, to frighten them off.

Sabina was on hand, to trim and light the lamp, mend the fire, bring fresh water, &c. He read Thomas' note, with a mutter of reproach against the *Banker* for overburdening his son—was very sorry to have missed seeing "Sister Jessie"—and would have supper, when Thomas came in.

Presently Sabina returned, to say that Sandy Johnson had called. He had come, by agreement, for his chair, the third he had brought to be bottomed. The visits connected with the first two and with the bringing of this one, had been very short, Sandy fearing recognition. Finding he had little to fear, he purposely prolonged the present visit, to observe John Ruffin more closely and satisfactorily; and this he desired to do as well on his old townsman's account, as on that of Thomas Ruffin's, to whom he had become strongly attached.

These chairs of Sandy's, with those Sister Jessica brought, occupied all of John Ruffin's handicraft time. He worked only when he felt disposed; and, besides, over the work itself exercised the most patient and exacting particularity. It was found no easy matter to get just the proper kind of husk or shuck (as the covering of the corn-ear is called throughout the South). The northern article is much below the southern in its pliant, fine-grained, silk-like quality; and this latter John Ruffin made the standard. Then, he would use only the second or third shuck leaf from the ear. Then, the splits must all be of a precise width by a definite individual measurement. Then, they would have to be dampened or lie in water just so many minutes. And then, again, the least flaw in the twist would require an untwisting back and correction, it being not an unfrequent thing for him to rip up the fine work of a half or even a whole bottom, to correct an irregularity or unevenness in an early twist that had been overlooked. When the chair finally left his hand approved, you may be sure the seat was a model of close, smooth, neat workmanship.

John Ruffin would buy shucks often in small lots, the cost being a song ("not worth shucks" is a com-

mon southern expression for worthlessness). Sabina
generally was the purchasing agent, and frequently
he would tax severely her good nature, as well as
that of Miss Kitty, by requiring her to fetch him
samples from livery-stable or mat or mattress fac-
tory in distant sections of the city. Sabina being
but an indifferent judge, not a few of her purchases
were thrown away entirely, with a round scolding
for her stupidity—to all of which the negro woman
would respond with a respectful guffaw.

Sabina's announcement of Sandy's having called,
was followed, a moment later, by the entrance of
Sandy, who, as he came in, placed his Scotch cap on
the top of the bureau near the door.

"What d'you want?" asked John Ruffin queru-
lously, forgetting who his visitor was. It may be
his well-being and his humor had not been improved
by the stay in the damp evening atmosphere of the
Park. More likely, his feelings were ruffled by the
injustice of the *Banker* in imposing extra work
upon Thomas, and keeping him two hours beyond
time, late in the night. Probably, each cause was
operating. At any rate, highly irascible evidently
he was; and in this state of mind he had forgotten
that Sabina had announced Sandy Johnson a moment
before.

"Me chair, Sir," responded Sandy in a hearty way.

"Oh-h! it's you—Johnson—the shoemaker. There
it is."

"It's gude wark," remarked Sandy, examining the
chair admiringly. "Ye hae mad it look sae braw, I

scarce wud ken me auld restin' piece. And here's
the money"—handing a silver dollar.

Sandy seated himself in his chair and regarded his
old townsman with tender interest, while the latter
—notwithstanding Sandy's being a customer—looked amazed at his stay, and asked sharply :

"What do you want *now ?*"

"Me change, Sir. I gied ye a dollar, Sir."

"O-h !" John Ruffin responded, and then began
fumbling in his pocket—brought out the dollar—
looked hard at it a moment, as if collecting his
thoughts—went to the bureau— fumbled in the upper
drawer, placing part of the contents on top of bureau
upon Sandy's cap—found a half dollar—replaced
contents of drawer, Sandy's cap being among them—
handed the half dollar to Sandy—and resuming seat,
asked with an added emphasis, as Sandy still remained chaired :

"What d'you want NOW ?"

"Me cap, Sir. When ye pat back the things, me
cap gaed in, too."

"Oh-h !" exclaimed John Ruffin, after a moment's
reflection. Then he went to the bureau, and, having
fumbled in the drawer, got Sandy's cap and gave it
to him. Then took his seat, and, thoroughly worried at Sandy's prolonged stay, asked almost fiercely:

"What d'you want NOW ?"

"To rest a bit, if ye please," replied Sandy in the
pleasantest way.

A pause followed, during which Sandy took from
the table the cat o' nine tails,and regarded it curi-
ously.

"A cat! What's the cat for, Sir?"

"Troublesome fellows."

"Ha! ha! ha! Iver use it, Sir?"

"On dogs—sometimes."

"Mony troublesome dogs aboot, Sir?"

"Yes—some on four legs," snappishly replied John Ruffin, from whose clouded reason would come now and then unlooked for flashes of bright intelligence.

"Ha! ha! ha!" was Sandy's greeting of the sally, just as Sabina entered in her bustling way, and with a sample shuck in hand.

"O Mr. Ruffin!"—Sabina paused at her intrusion, as she recognized Sandy's presence.

"What now, Sabina?"

"Dare's a man here as what's got shucks, an' yer axed me fur ter git some ter day fur yer."

"Well—bring 'em in, Sabina."

"Bring 'em in!" (with a great guffaw). "La! Mr. Ruffin, dey's a cart-load!"

"A cart-load!"

"Yes, Mr. Ruffin, a *good* cart-load."

"A cart load of shucks, you fool!"

"Yes, Mr. Ruffin," rejoined Sabina glibly, in happy oblivion of the old gentleman's opinion of her stolidity; "an' where does yer want 'em ter stay!"

"In the cart, Sabina."

Sabina paused in reflection—then queried naively:

"An' where does yer want de cart to stay?"

"Behind the horse, Sabina."

Sabina again paused in the endeavor to take in

John Ruffin's disposition of the shucks, and had started another query:

"An' where does yer want—," when John Ruffin vigorously broke in:

"And I want *you*, you black goose, to stay out of this room."

"Ha! ha! ha!" roared Sandy; and for volume of effort Sabina was not behind the jovial Scot in a rousing guffaw, ending in a very high key, as she sailed from the apartment.

The Sabina episode had not abated John Ruffin's impatience at the shoemaker's unwarrantable stay in spite of broad hints. He was so nettled that he had a thought of calling in assistance, to have him put out. Taking in hand an unfinished chair he began twisting away at the splits, every moment or so glancing nervously at the clock. Presently he remarked, with significant look at the time piece:

"It's getting late."

"But ye'll let a customer rest his auld banes. I work vera' hard, Sir."

"I work hard, too"—twisting energetically—"and like to work by myself, too."

Sandy passed the hint by, and, recalling the patrimony he had squandered in early life, remarked (he knew he was venturing on risky ground, yet was desirous of prolonging the conversation as far as he could):

"Like mony ithers, I hae seen better days, Sir."

John Ruffin gave him a suspicious glance; yet Sandy ventured on:

"Aince I hed cash and to spare, but like mony ithers I gaed doon, and hed a warsle wi' want, Sir."

Suddenly John Ruffin turned upon Sandy a searching look, followed up by a query, and the latter for a moment thought he was gone.

"Do you know anything about *me?*"

"I ken ye do gude wark on chairs," came the ready reply.

There was a change of manner—perhaps the tie of kindred misfortune came up—as John Ruffin added after a pause :

"All gone? Nothing at all now?"

"Na, na—I canna say juist that. I hae a wee sum pat awa' in a Bank."

And with the word "Bank" came rushing to John Ruffin's mental front the relations of Thomas and Dalguspin, which all the while had been the basic thought and source of his acrimony.

"A Bank!" he exclaimed, ceasing work and rousing in the direction we have indicated. "*What* Bank ?"

"Dalguspin's—Do ye ken ony thing aboot it?"

"*Bad* Bank! *Work 'em to death!*"

"Ah—but I hae a young freend in that *Bank*, Sir, and pat me money thar, because he's thar."

"Who is he?" John Ruffin asked earnestly ; for he was now all awake. Possibly it might be "Tammie," he thought. (Thomas had informed his Father there were two other clerks in the *establishment*, John and his assistant in the Pawn-Shop).

"Aweel, aweel, I canna gie fu' eenformation. I

hae tried to find oot the young mon, but he keeps his ain counsel."

"*Who is he?*"—with increasing emphasis.

"A gude customer o' mine, Sir. He brings to the shop his ain shoone and his Father's, and a mair winsome, weel bred, weel spoken young mon, ye may sarch amang a million for, but canna find him."

"WHO IS HE, I say?"—in excited tones.

"Wha is he? Why, he's a new clark in the Bank, Sir—cam frae the South—and is a gentleman, Sir, a *born* gentleman. *That's* wha he is, Sir."

"BUT WHAT'S HIS NAME?"—showing great excitement.

"Weel, noo, ye hae me fast," replied Sandy with provoking composure. "I canna gie a' his name. I ken the first part only."

"My God! man, *WHATS'S THAT?*" almost screamed John Ruffin, and rising as he spoke.

"Tammas they ca' him at the *Bank*, Sir, and I ken him as Mr. Tammas."

At the mention of "Thomas," John Ruffin at once calmed down, and a low, inward, happy laugh was seen to move his frame.

"I maun gang," remarked Sandy, rising.

"No, no, no! Stay! stay!" objected the old gentleman, approaching Sandy and affectionately placing an opposing hand on his shoulder.

"It's gettin' late," Sandy said, glancing at the clock.

"No, no, no, Mr. ——, Mr.——" (trying to recall the name of Johnson) "Mr. Shoemaker. It's not

late, and the wind blows cold.　Don't you hear it?
Stay and warm yourself."

Lovingly he pressed Sandy back into his seat.
Next, drew his own chair close to Sandy's; and as
the latter answered the questions he asked about
"Tammie," John Ruffin paused, seriatim, to take it
all in.　The praises Sandy so freely bestowed upon
his son were sweeter than honey and the honey
comb.　Ripples of inward joy played over his frame
and broke in smiles upon his face.　Sandy exerted
himself to the utmost to humor him, and took vast
delight in being the means of imparting delight to
his old townsman's heart.

"You say your young friend is named 'Tammie!'"

"Ay, ay, Sir.　'Mr. Tammas,' I ca' him."

"You say your 'Tammie' is a nice young man?"

"In a' me born days I hae niver seen ane half sae
nice.　He taks me heart, Sir."

"Is your 'Tammie' tall or low?"

"Tall and slender like."

"How does your 'Tammie' talk?"

"Whan ye start him, he talks right alang.　Gin
ye *is* sae modest, he hes gude larnin', and talks
juist like a bookie, gin ye tak him right."

"What kind of eyes has your 'Tammie?'"

"Nae lassie hes sweeter—dark brown tender een,
a sparklin', whan he lifts 'em, wi' inteelligence and
feelin'."

"What kind of hair has your 'Tammie?'"

"Ah! his hair, indeed, Sir! It's auburn, a lovely
auburn."

"And is it soft and wavy?"

"Ay, ay, thar ye hae it, Sir. It's soft as silk, and wavy like, and whan bright light's on it, shines wi' changing color, like a settlin' sea, touchit by a settin' sun."

"Does your 'Tammie'—?"

"But I maun gang. It's late," said Sandy, rising and interrupting.

"No-o, no-o! It's not so late," dissuaded John Ruffin, rising with Sandy.

"Na, na—I maunna stay. Time for honest fouk to be abed."

"Well—I'm glad, glad you've been here, Mr.— Mr.—Mr. Shoemaker. God bless you and your friend 'Tammie,' too."

"The same to ye, Sir. And as for Mr. Tammas, why he may draw on me to the last dollar."

"Now, why don't you say *to the last breath?*"

"Ha! ha! ha! Ay, ay, to the last breath, too, Sir," Sandy responded; and closing thus a conversation in a tune quite different from that with which it had begun, the warm-hearted, ready-witted Scot shouldered his chair and left.

John Ruffin drew the dollar from his pocket— looked at it reflectively—then opened a bureau drawer—took out powder and a piece of flannel— and, as he rubbed up the coin, treated himself to a soliloquy:

"He didn't know he was talking to Tammie's Father. I wouldn't tell him"—with a little chuckle at his acuteness. "I didn't want to hear false praise. If he'd known I'm Tammie's Father, he might've given me blarney. But he didn't know it" —another little chuckle.—"Dear, *dear* Tammie. He's all the man said and a thousand times more. I'll make this dollar bright for him. 'Tisn't much, but I must help Tammie. I used to think he'd never catch on, and kept heaping up a pile, to take care of Tammie; but now Tammie's taking care of me. It's most time he was here"—looking up at the clock. But not seeing clearly the figures on its face, he had risen from the chair for a nearer view, when Sabina rushed in after the obstreperous fashion not uncommon with her, even when comparative trifles were in question:

"Mr. Ruffin! Mr. Ruffin! Oh! Mr. Ruffin!"

"What! What! What!" cried John Ruffin in great alarm.

"Mr. Ruffin!" exclaimed Sabina, with both hands up and shaking all over as though palsied, *"your Tommie's in a fit!"*

"My God! Woman! my God! Where's the child?"

"La! Mr. Ruffin!"—with a great guffaw. "Sakes alive! don't do so. It's Tom Cat you pet so. Dey wants you to cut its tail fur de fit."

"The cat's tail!" gasped John Ruffin, with feelings outraged and panting from shock—"the cat's tail! you confounded black huzzy! I'll give *you* fits with this cat o' nine tails;" and, seizing the cat, he made for Sabina, who fled screaming and guffawing from the room.

CHAPTER XIII.

"The kindest and the happiest pair."—*Cowper.*

Dalguspin was right. His keen eyes saw through it all. Noals really had concocted the scheme, with himself at its centre. But it stood little more than frame work, until the Pawn-broker's malignant fertility supplied details and gave it flesh and blood. Noals at first had simply acquiesced in these details temporarily; but upon reflection realized their utility. So, it was a well satisfied pair. The prospect all around seemed improving. Black Isaac was cheerful, even happy, over the outlook; and Noals so elated, that it would have been surprising, if his irrepressible bent towards joking had not discovered on the scheme points for its expression.

It was not so easy to get a favorable opportunity for finally sounding Robert. We say *finally;* for prior to hinting to Dalguspin the scheme of robbery, Noals, in cracksman's guise and with an eye to a confederate, had approached Robert. Some time elapsed before it could be done. The first intimation in this direction to Black Isaac, was Robert's announcement, early one Monday morning, of his intention to leave the following Thursday—that he wished to see something of the old world—and that a way had just opened to him to secure an ocean passage. During the day the Pawn-broker received a note from Noals, that he would call at 8 p. m. Noals was strictly on time, and a lively conversation followed in harmony with the satisfactory state of affairs.

"Have you seen Robert?" asked the Pawn-broker, as Noals and himself became closeted in the little private home office, with its antique centre table holding whiskies and waters (hot and cold), and the rest of the outfit for grog and toddy.

"Yes—the *cracksman* has seen him, and—what's more—got him. Eat my old hat, if he ain't a good one. An ocean ticket and £100 in gold, half in hand, the rest the moment of my exit from the Bank—this secures him."

"You should have seen me, before going so far. That was the distinct agreement made in this room."

"But I understood you then as intimating, and in that street talk last Saturday as expressing, a willingness Robert should be got, could he be led at once to leave the country. The fact is, Dalguspin, I really didn't know where to stop. It was a good opportunity, and opportunities don't come every day, and the fellow seemed so eager and gave evidence, too, of being such a trump, that the whole matter was disclosed and bargain struck, almost before I knew it."

"Let it be. He's the only ally I'd consent to have,

since he goes abroad. I saw your hand this morning, when Robert asked leave to quit my service Thursday, designing, so he said, to sail for England."

"And you accommodated him?"

"Of course—But we're too loud, Jimmie. We should whisper these things."

"Whist!" Noals suddenly exclaimed, as he looked startled towards the door.

"What?"

"I'm certain I heard sounds like muffled footfalls," Noals replied, dropping his voice.

They both looked towards the door and listened intently. Presently Dalguspin tip-toed to the door and listened. Then opened the door suddenly—but saw nothing. Resuming his seat, he rang up Robert.

"What noise was that in the hall just now?"

"I dont't know, Sir, unless it was Gowrie" (a Scotch collie). "He is in the house."

"Put Gowrie out, and observe my wish that we be not disturbed.—'Twas nothing"(to Noals, as the door closed on Robert). "But softly, softly, Jimmie. We've been too lively over business so solemn. A sharp ear at the key-hole might have gotten clean away with us.—Now for details: Does Robert know of the part the clerk's to be made to play?"

"He does."

"All will say, of course, the cracksman had duplicate keys, and the surmise will be they were made from impressions got either from the Watchman, or the clerk. Suspicion must fall upon the latter, in the way I suggested."

"You mean through the hidden money?"

"I do."

It should be remarked, that, if the Pawn-broker's malignant mind towards Thomas Ruffin, had been aroused by the latter's conduct in connection with the "doctoring" of Cameron's note, the sentiment of hate, thus formed, became subject to a constant process of stimulation from another cause. In a moral sense Black Isaac's clerks had been uniformly of the slippery sort, more or less; and if he had not led them into acts palpably or legally criminal, they were not insensible to his suggestions touching peccadilloes. On the contrary, the conduct of Thomas Ruffin was as straight in its course as the arrow from the bow of an archer. He could not be turned aside a jot towards aught savoring of crookedness, however Black Isaac might allege precedent or custom. At first this character, with amiability and industry for attendants, charmed the Pawn-broker. It was something new and interesting—a fresh and novel flower of agreeable fragrance. But when once Thomas had given occasion to Black Isaac to turn against him, the latter's character, contrasting so pointedly with his, became a source of perpetual irritation. The air of high and honorable breeding unconsciously manifest—the transparent honesty that the Pawn-broker could not budge—the spirituelle presence, almost feminine in its delicacy—all this was the very opposite to the hard, old, moss-grown sinner, and kept forcing on the latter a sense of inferiority and of insult—so to speak. Like the

opposite poles of a magnet, their characters repelled
each other. Black Isaac's hate grew and rankled,
and he now chuckled over the thought, that a day
of reckoning had come. It is a Nemesis of our own
conjuring, that we come really to hate those we
desire to hate—to see blackness in those we wish to
be black, though they be white as the driven snow.

With the advent of the *scheme*, however, his outward conduct craftily changed. His bearing became civil. He restored the half dollar to the wage.
Friend Peale knew and could swear the young man
was pressed. That was enough, he thought. And
he intimated to Thomas there was betterment in
store.

"It's all arranged with Bob," said Noals in reply
to the Pawnbroker. "It's his own special job. He's
well up in such tricks, he tells me. In disguise furnished by the *cracksman*, at 8 that evening Bob is
to see old Ruffin in his room at The Home, and
watch a chance to thrust between the mattresses a
roll of bills. 'Tis done most easily. Bob can twist
to his will the daft old fellow."

"The rascal! I've been a fearing him, that he
would trick or harm me in some way. But here he
is proving our right bower. Man proposes, Noals,
but God disposes."

"Most well spoken. Verily, we seem singled out
for a series of special providences.—We must be
ready, Dalguspin, for our parts at the finalé. The
rendezvous is so near the Bank, that I can doff disguise and be on hand as Jimmie Noals, when the

watchman rushes forth with outcries. I'll join him and we'll make for your house. Then for The Old Men's Home. The clerk will be accused of complicity . He'll deny of course. Search will be made —the money roll found—and the clerk arrested. The *cracksman* has warned Bob to be at home on duty as soon as possible—twenty minutes, say—after the event. See that he goes with us to The Home. The scene will chime in with his humor."

"We'll be on hand.—Here, Noals, take these"— drawing keys from pocket—"keys to front door and Safe. Get duplicates; but, mind, don't have'm *made.* Might give a clew, you know. Match 'em and cut and file yourself to a fit. I'll try them for you. Match 'em down at Kirk's, Jimmie. You'll find there all sorts of keys,"

"Except a *turnkey !*" Noals remarked with due gravity.

"He! he! he! *And the key of wedlock !*" put in the Pawn-broker,

"Ha! ha! ha! *And the key to the situation!*" Noals again fired off.

"He! he! he! And *whiskey!*" fired back the Pawn-broker, taking the cap.

"Ah-h-h! if you haven't struck a *key* note, I'll eat the old hat. It's a reminder. Let me try that key. Fits so nicely."

Noals mixes a bumper of grog—sips—smacks lips –and, holding the glass aloft, apostrophizes the liquor, as he looks at it cunningly :

"W-h-i-s-*k-e-y !* the key . of keys! Used, not

abused, it's the very *power of the keys* itself, admitting troubled souls to a paradise of content !"

"Bravo ! bravo ! Try it again," said Black Isaac, as Noals returned to the table the emptied glass. "*I* don't drink now, Jimmie—kidneys touched—sworn off—once did, though, hard as the chap Jack Randolph told about in that last speech of his here."

"Poor Jack ! The country has lost the prince of speakers.—How about the chap ? I don't remember."

"Got up every morning a whiskey barrel, and went to bed at night a barrel of whiskey."

"Ha ! ha ! ha ! Yes, yes.—You're jolly, Dalguspin, jolly, old fellow. You feel better."

"Sh-h-h-h ! Soft ! soft ! Less noise, or we may have noise outside.—Yes, I feel better, now it's all arranged, and the prospect clears up. Remember, too, Jimmie, there's another key, the rear-door key. You may need it in making exit. As I told you Saturday, I gave mine to the clerk some time ago ; but I'll have another to-day."

"Very well. Still, let Bob get the key. The *cracksman* has given Bob this other special job, to test his skill and fidelity. Disguised and representing a Pen and Ink Pedlar, Bob is to see young Ruffin Wednesday eve at the Bank, to get an impression of this key. He may fail. So hold yours in reserve. But the *cracksman* knows somewhat of Bob's preparation and goes it strong on Bobby Boy, too; for if he doesn't *do* a job to tickle *you*, my old hat I'll *chew w-w*—bands, lining, and all."

13

The Pawn-broker saluted Noals' humor, and then remarked :

"By the way, Noals, I've never seen you in your disguises. Bring 'em over. You can try on here behind bolted doors. I'd like to note your bearing and see how you would do."

"*All* right. I'll be back anon.—Courage up, Dalguspin. No danger, no danger; for Bob goes abroad, and *we* shall hang well together."

"If we don't, by George ! we hang separately."

"Ha ! ha ! ha ! Now, you stole that."

"All the same—it comes in pat."

"Comes *from* Pat., too—Pat Henry. Ha ! ha ! ha !"

Upon Noals' departure Black Isaac sat a space in thought. Then rang up Robert.

"You're to leave soon, Robert."

"Yes, Sir."

"You once raised your arm to protect me, and you've been faithful in my house. I'm not unmindful, Robert, and wish to give you a parting counsel."

"Thank you, Sir."

"You must stop roving, Robert. You *will* before long, and settle down to business of some sort; and then, whatever it be, Robert, *stick* to it. My counsel lies in that word *Stick*. It doesn't matter so much what the business is. The point is to stick. Lots in business, but few stickers. They change to this or to that, or live loosened from the biz.—don't stick to it. And I believe in sticking, not only to things and ideas, but to men, too. Yes, Robert, stick to men, too—stick both to your friends and to your enemies.

And, again, Robert—learn how to *use* men. I began with nothing and have made my thousands— and honestly, too, Robert—by *sticking,* and knowing how to use those around me and getting them to *co-operate.* Yes, 'co-operate' is the word. I have a clerk now who started out well enough, but will not work with me, I find. He's a fellow I can't use. I've tried him and he won't lift the end of his little finger. Why, here lately one word from him would have made me a cool thousand, but he wouldn't co-operate, you see; and I've turned the fellow down, and evil will get him yet. My clerks are my slaves, Robert. Every one in his turn. *I* had to slave it once. I'm on top now, and the grass shan't grow under my clerks' feet. I've no use for any about me who ain't ready to co-operate, and whom I can't get to help me carry out my schemes. Yes, Robert, when you set up in business be a *sticker* and know how to *use 'em,* and you'll win.

"Ah! there's Noals"—door bell has rung. "Jimmie's brisk. Receive him, Robert."

A moment later Robert returned and presented a card. As the *Banker* read it dismay sat upon his countenance.

"Clear away these things, Robert, and admit the gentleman."

"Edward Stone!" exclaimed Black Isaac, as Robert disappeared—"connected with the Boston Bank we deal with, and Bank Inspector for this district! At this time, too! Fiends of the Pit! What luck!"

Presently Mr. Stone entered, a nervous, choleric

looking man, with deep red hair and beard and sandy eyebrows—hard of hearing—worked fingers and snapped eyelids, when talking—rapped out short sentences—and, with nose up in the air, gave abundant indication of an arrogant and highly irritable character.

"I am, indeed, happy to meet you, Mr. Stone," said Black Isaac, coming forward smirking and bowing, and with the address he could command on such occasions, at the same time extending his hand, which the visitor received stiffly on his finger tips. "Allow me your hat and cane, Mr. Stone"—offering to take them.

"No, thanks," was the short reply.

"Have a chair, Mr. Stone."

"No, thanks. Stay but a moment," again came the curt snappy answer.

Dalguspin was rather chilled by the Inspector's manner, but mindful of his function, again unctiously addressed him:

"We know each other, Mr. Stone, *per literam*"— Black Isaac had committed to memory one or two classical phrases for use on special occasions—"but I've never before had the pleasure of grasping your hand, Sir"—Stone bending forward in the effort to hear.

"Glad to see you"—Stone's supercilious manner administering to the sentiment a black eye. "By the bye, per lit*eras* is better Latin than per lit*eram*" —a scholarly remark, though grossly rude.

The Pawn-broker colored up, as much as his

swarthy countenance allowed, and the spirit of cor-
diality took on a small freeze, but he pocketed the
incivility in his desire to please the Bank Inspector;
and, aware of the sensitiveness of deaf persons,
sought so to pitch his voice as to be heard, and yet
not remind his visitor of his infirmity.

"I believe it's your first visit to our city, Mr.
Stone."

"Yes. Impressions charming. The first man just
now to meet me, was a cabby, who tried to cheat me,
and got me in a devil of a heat—see !"

"I am sorry, indeed, Mr. Stone. Such things *will*
happen anywhere sometimes. I hope your stay will
be long enough to give me the pleasure of showing
you our bright side. If not the 'Hub' itself, we
claim to be one of the shapely spokes"—saluting his
supposed humor with a captivating smile.

Stone, however, didn't see the humorous point, or,
if he did, failed to recognize it, and all the while
was bending forward and frowning and distorting
his face in painful efforts to hear—co-operating, as
it were, with Dalguspin, who kept on raising his
voice, to get the comfortable gauge of his visitor.

"Yes," he gruffly rejoined. "Hail from the 'Hub'
at large. More immediately from a *hubbub* in our
Bank, which I hope you'll be able to quell."

"I hope so, indeed, Mr. Stone. Anything I can
do for you, will be done, you know, most cheerfully,
Mr. Stone."

"Stay's brief. On business only. Letters intimate your serious involvement in Weston's failure.

We've a balance with you and feel concerned."

"It's a profound mistake, Mr. Stone. Our losses are small, Sir, and the Bank's affairs straight as a shingle. Who gave the information, Mr. Stone?"

"Ah-h! little bird has been singing."

"Then, 'twas a *Mocking* bird, Mr. Stone, whose notes are all counterfeit," said Black Isaac in loud and earnest words, for the moment forgetting the sycophant in his defense of the Bank, which, as touching this particular charge, was entirely just. "*Our* notes are *sound*, Sir, perfectly sound, whether uttered by me, or by the Bank."

"Yes," Stone answered back in a huff, "your notes *are* sound, Sir, *loud* sound, *disagreeable* sound, Sir. You're *bullying*, Sir!"

Dalguspin was thunderstruck and thoroughly nettled, yet restrained himself, and had the prudence to reply in obsequious and lowered tones :

"*Bullying*, Mr. Stone! My dear Sir, what can you mean? You're mistaken, I assure you. I'm *not* bullying, Mr. Stone, but simply defending the Bank against an injurious impression, and naturally spoke with some warmth. That was all, Mr. Stone."

"Wha-a-t?" asked Stone, with hand behind ear and bending towards Dalguspin.

"I was saying," replied the latter in a high key, "you're *mis-tak-en.* That———"

"My ears are not the best, Sir," broke in Mr. Stone with great irritation. "Yet I'm not as deaf as a post, Sir. It's annoying, Sir, to have thrust on me so vigorously a sense of my infirmity."

"Damn the old Red Stone!" rapped out Black Isaac, but *sotto voce.* "Capital specimen of brimstone! And I'd be glad to see him Inspector of the brimstone district!"

"Sorry I can't hear your sentiments," said Stone, who had been keeping hand behind ear, in the effort to hear. "Have no doubt they're o. k.—Did you ask whether I'm Inspector still? Think I caught that word. Yes, I'm still Inspector. Shall inspect your books to-morrow. Am doing my work *thorouhly.* It's a day of wildcat speculation and official dishonesty, Sir. *Officials, Sir, are proving very efficient robbers.* Be ready for me at 10, Sir. Good day, Sir."

As his visitor turned his back for the door, Black Isaac railed upon him, *sotto voce :*

"A derned old seven-sided fool!"

But his chafed feelings, which all along he had been endeavoring to keep under control, when allowed an exit, shot forth with a little over energy, and unhappily the invective reached his visitor's ears. Stone turned—bent on Dalguspin a stormy look—then spoke, measuring his words and giving every syllable its full weight :

"My seventh side, Sir, I presume, is my deaf side. You'll find, Sir, to-morrow, when I inspect your books"—grimly smiling and shaking the finger of menace—"that I have no *blind* side."

"Whe-e-e-e-w! Men and Brethren! Is the fellow crazy!" exclaimed Black Isaac, as the Inspector marched out. "*Never* in all my born days, have I

seen so cross-grained an old wretch, such a compound
double extract of spleen ! He should be strung up by
the thumbs and beaten on his depraved back, until
the blood runs down to his heels.—And I believe,
too, his deafness was all pretense and that the old
Red Head heard every word I uttered ! And what
could he mean by emphasizing "officials are proving
very efficient robbers ?" He pauses and reflects.—
"A devil of a fix ! That Bank deficit I've managed
to keep covered up. But the old Red Head will go
through our books with lynx eyes." Anothe pause.
—"Our scheme comes off Thursday night; and if I
should go to the old Cuss and could placate him and
get him to postpone the examination for a day or
two. But no, it's no use. I've stirred his gall."
Another pause.—"Ah ! well ! I'll confer with Noals.
He's a schemer. And what can be keeping Noals,
I wonder ? He lives hard by and should'ave returned ere this. Could anything have happened ? What,
if the disguises have been lost or stolen ? Then the
scheme must miscarry."

And altogether, with the serious complication from
Stone's sudden advent on the scene, the Pawn-broker
was so anxious to see Noals and grew so fidgety at
his prolonged absence, that finally he rang up Robert
and ordered him to despatch one of the servants to
Noals' residence, to learn whether or not he was at
home. Presently, an answer came that Noals had
left the house at half-past 7, and had not returned.
The Pawn-broker was meditating upon the matter,
and had concluded the "things" were kept down

town at the office, somewhat further off, when the
door-bell rang, much to his relief.

"Ah! there's the fellow at last," he exclaimed.

It was a thorough disappointment, therefore, when
Robert entered, and announced that a stranger had
called.

"Where's his card?"

"Has none, Sir."

"What's his name?"

"Jones."

"What's his business?"

"Wouldn't say—only that it was important."

"Didn't you tell him I had a special engagement,
and every moment in expectation of the visitor?"

"Yes, Sir. But the man said he could not wait,
that his errand was of the most serious nature, and
he would not keep you five minutes."

"Let me see him," said Black Isaac, with a shrug
of the shoulders.

Jones came in, a wretched looking old man, with
shoes and trousers and coat of vagabond type—long,
dirty beard—grey, matted hair—body half bent—in
one hand a supporting stick, in the other a battered
hat—voice thin and squeaking. Evidently, a dilap-
idated specimen—a regulation tramp.

"My name's William Jones, Sir, your servant,
Sir," he said, bowing very low and very humbly.

Black Isaac did not deign an answer, but drew
back from the ragamuffin (he had dealings with such
at the Pawn-Shop, but knew them not at his residence), and rang up Robert, to whom he spoke aside:

"*Why* did you admit the vagabond? I'm astonished at you, Sir!"

"I did refuse him, but he begged so earnestly, and declared most solemnly he bore a communication of great interest to yourself."

As Robert turned to retire, Black Isaac recalled him, and whispered a caution to let the door remain ajar and stand himself just outside, as tramps sometimes meant robbery, deeming it the part of prudence and no reflection upon valor, to match two against one.

"What d'you want?" asked Black Isaac with look and tone of supreme disgust.

"I lodge, Sir, with vagabonds——"

"Not the least doubt at all about that," broke in the Pawn-broker. You look very much like one yourself."

"I may *look* like one, Sir"—very humbly' spoken —"but I ain't one. I was not always as I am now. Once——"

"*What do you want?* I say," the Pawn-broker impatiently and disdainfully interrupted.

"If you please, Sir, I want to tell my story. *You* have an interest in it.—Once, I was going to say, I had money and influence and position. But I took to drink and went down—lower, lower, lower; and at last struck bed rock."

"And your whistle being dry, you've come here for money to wet it," the Pawn-broker contemptuously suggested.

"No, no, no, Sir. I don't do that now. I can't do

that now.—I got to bed-rock, Sir, as I was a sayin'.
My wife and child died in want and wretchedness.
My relations disowned me, and I was left alone in
this miserable world, begging my bread by day, and
lodging——"

"Here! here!" broke in the Pawn-broker sternly.
"I warn you. Enough of this rigmarole. For the
last time—*tell me why you are here?*"

"To pay you a debt, Sir."

"To pay me a debt!" cried Black Isaac, with that
low little laugh of his, amused at the idea in spite
of himself.

"Yes—poor old Billy Jones is come to pay a debt
to the Banker, *by showing up a conspiracy.*"

Black Isaac looked at old Jones in a half doubt-
ing, half believing sort of way, as the latter continued:

"When I was a goin' down, down, Sir, there was
one friend that stuck. He was your Father, Sir.
He gave me money and counsel and tried to raise me
up. 'Twas no use. Yet I remember it all, and am
here to pay his son a debt of gratitude."

The old man paused from weakness, and Black
Isaac began to look interested. He saw, too, no
danger was to be apprehended, and thinking, withal,
there possibly might be disclosures which a third
person should not hear, stepped to the door and
whispered Robert to leave.

"I lodge, Sir, as I was a sayin', with tramps and
thieves. They're mostly foreigners. I've picked up
some of their lingo; and last night, when they thought

me asleep, or mistook me for a pile of rags in the corner, I *over heard 'em planning to rob a Bank"*—the Pawn-broker now all attention. "That there door there behind you, Sir, is little ajar. Please, Sir, shet it, as I want no one else to hear this."

As Dalguspin turned towards the door, with his back to Jones, the latter suddenly straightened his form, drew and leveled a pistol, and thundered out:

"Hands up ! ! !"

Black Isaac turned horror-stricken, to find himself confronted by a robber. In his terror his skin became goose-skin. In other words, the integument bristled; or, to speak with complete regard for scientific accuracy, the microscopic muscular fibres stood on ends. His knees trembled. His voice forsook him. He felt he was unable utterly to shout for help. He could only gasp:

"Spare me ! Here's my purse !"

"Ha ! ha ! ha ! I'll eat my old hat, Dalguspin, if—"

"Heavens and earth !" broke in the Pawn-broker with lifted hands, immensely amazed and immensely relieved. "Can that be you Jimmie ?"

"No-o-o ! It's the *cracksman.*"

"Good Lord, let me get my breath !—'Twas risky," my friend. Suppose I'd been armed ?"

"You wer'n't, though."

"But, devils and damnation ! did you confer in this guise with Robert, and then allowed him to admit you just now ?"

"Don't think me a greeny. I've other outfits, my Boy. Lock the doors, and let me off with this rig."

Noals kicked off outer old shoes, threw off outer garments, and was seen well dressed.

"You shed well, Jimmie."

"Ah! wait till I shed these fixings 'bout my head. You'll see something *red*."

The Pawn-broker looked with wondering eyes at the transformation going on before him, and as the "fixings" (wig, &c.) were removed and Noals was seen with very red hair and beard and in attitude of arrogance, he sang out :

"Goodness gracious! Edward Stone !"

"Yes"—mimicking the Inspector—"it's Stone, Sir —damned old Red Stone, Sir—capital specimen of brimstone."

, "He! he! he! Good! good! good !"

"What did you say, Sir ?"—mimicking, with hand behind ear. "I've a seventh side, Sir, a deaf side."

"He! he! he! capital! capital !"

"Well, Dalguspin," said Noals, who had now removed the last wig, &c., "you wished to note my bearing in disguise. How do you think I fill my part, old Boy ?"

"You make a *perfect* villain, Noals, you're a born Rob Roy. Villiany sits on thee, as though your trade and only joy."

"Ha! ha! Well, in *your* part be half as great, and *we're* all right, or my old hat I'll *masticate*."

CHAPTER XIV.

A stranger to the dissipations and even ordinary recreations of young men, Thomas Ruffin sought his bed, when work and attentions to his Father were over. An enforced fast kept him thin; but he was sound of body, rose regularly before the sun, and heartily enjoyed the early day. If often he felt worn out and discouraged towards night, he would awake with a measure of joy. The fresh, inspiring morning was a daily resurrection.

The morning following the interview with Sister Jessica (it is necessary to carry the reader back somewhat), he rose earlier than usual. He was to receive that morning a notable letter. Would it be from Amy, or from the Sister? Would it be sent to The Home, or to the *Bank?* And what would be its tenor? These thoughts had filled his mind during the night and kept sleep from his eyelids. It was Friday. Could there be anything sinister in that? He believed not. He remembered that Friday, many times, had been to him a white day. He looked out, to see if an omen he could gather from the weather. It was fair. A sharp wind whistled from the north, whirling the dust on the earth beneath, and in the heavens above driving athwart a cold clear blue sky, the skirling scud of yesterday's far away storm-cloud.

After an early breakfast with his Father—it was always earlier on Thomas' account these Friday mornings, and Sabina, as usual had provided for him an extra portion—he hastened to the *Bank*. At half past 8, William, the Watchman, brought the mail. The letter had come. There it was, he felt sure, as he saw the superscription. He turned it over and examined it carefully before opening it. There was no envelope. The sheet was folded on itself simply, making its own exterior, as customary in those days, and addressed in a small fair hand, even as print. It was not Amy's hand, as he remembered it. He broke the wafer and read with a heart beating high :

To Mr. Thomas Ruffin :

Sir :—In supplementing our short interview of yesterday evening with certain explanatory particulars, let me say at the outset, that I have not mentioned the discovery to Amy Sanford, nor shall I. It would do no good, and possibly might do harm.

An ardent object with Amy has been to do what she could to soothe your Father's lot. Her own Father died heart-broken a few months after removal to New Orleans, victim to the ruin which the failure had brought upon himself and others. His kinsman's stroke had affected him even more than his own, and Amy has looked upon it as providential that your Father is within her reach. Though in compassing his affliction Mr. Sanford had been an innocent agent, yet there stood the agony he had caused ever before her. It haunted her like a spectre; and, God helping her, she would make the sufferer what returns she could. If only she could visit him at least, and place her hand softly upon him, and speak gently to him !

But the difficulties seemed insuperable. It was almost certain, she thought, that John Ruffin was enraged against her Father and his house, as the criminal author of his ruin. You, yourself, too, she had grounds for believing, was embittered and estranged.

Under these circumstances I readily consented to gratify her most passionate desire and visited your Father as her representative; and when, happily, as a result of these visits, I was soon able to correct the impressions touching your Father's sentiments and your own towards her, yet she was aware of your Father's antipathy to meeting old friends and of what might be the ill effects of such interviews; and when, further, from my reports, she felt that visits in her own person might not be unwelcome, still there were personal considerations that prevailed with her to maintain the incognito.

For Amy Sanford's circumstances having radically changed, she has felt she must change with them. She has been left penniless. It is necessary, she feels, that the past should all be forgotten, and she should endeavor to fit herself to meet new and exacting conditions; and the course of life she has resolved upon, she could pursue, she thinks, with more singleness of aim and better prospect of success, by living, temporarily at least, in retirement.

Let your mind be wholly at rest touching her welfare. She has made devoted friends, among whom she lives, and who are aiding her, lovingly and effectually, to accomplish the object before her.

The occurrences of yesterday make these statements, I think, obligatory. I have only to add, that you will be trusted to respect the seclusion Amy Sanford has thought it meet to throw around herself, and which by an accident has been revealed. The pledge given me is to be kept inviolate. There are to be no disclosures, no inquiries or attempts at searching out. Matters are to go on just as though there had been no discovery. Otherwise, Amy must know what has happened, with the effect of nullifying her endeavors respecting your Father, and a tendency to nullify them touching herself, and a disposition, I do not doubt, to withdraw further from observation.

The grace of the Lord Jesus Christ abide with you.

SISTER JESSICA.

As Thomas read a brood of confusing apprehensions sprang up. What could the Sister mean by saying Amy's past was all to be forgotten? he asked himself. And what could be the character of this course in life that made it at all necessary or expedient to remain apart from those whom it would be supposed naturally she would live nearest to? And who were these devoted friends she had made, and who were aiding her so lovingly and effectually? All this was

bewildering. He could not understand the letter.
Only he had a sense of being stricken. Again and
again did he read it, before its meaning began to
clear up; and, as it did, a hope perished. He had
had a firm persuasion that Amy and himself would
meet again, and the hope of what might be one day,
had become rooted. He had not stopped to weigh
the difficulties. He had never considered how the
changes that had occurred, should bear upon such a
hope. It was an enchanting vision kept hidden far
down in the secret chambers of his heart, yet shed-
ding, unconsciously, a certain light and an influence
through all his life ; and at hallowed moments he
would lift the veil, as it were, and gaze directly
upon it. The letter was fatal. The vision had fled.
The dream was over. Its impossibility and folly
broke upon him, as he dwelt on the words which
burned into him.

He could see well why, at the first, Amy should
have Sister Jessica minister to his Father in her
stead. But when, through the Sister, she came to
know that his Father understood the circumstances
of the failure, that he was not angered, that his own
affections were unchanged, and that personal visits
might be made, why did she remain still in retirement, if not to avoid the encouragement of hopes
which, under altered conditions, could not be realized ? Amy must know all about him. Was not the
letter sent to 222 N. G. Street, with the sign of the
golden balls ? Sister Jessica knew what that meant,
and Dalguspin's reputation, no doubt; and Amy,
through her, must know just how he was situated.

Was he not reduced to the uttermost, with a stricken
Father looking up to him, a ward of charity, and requiring more than he could possibly do? God for-
give him for permitting one personal thought beyond
his Father's care. It was a folly, this hope he had
allowed to entwine about his life. How could he
think of such things! Amy was right. She herself,
penniless, was struggling to adjust herself to new conditions. It was better she should pursue her course
secluded and undisturbed, and establish herself in
life without hindrance. He was glad she had made
loving friends. She would make them anywhere.
He could rejoice at this, though it strangled a hope
and a light in his heart went out. For in his sentiments towards Amy there was, he felt, no change.
He still loved her and would love her on. She was
his dear Cousin still. The Moss was still his flower.
The locket was and would be as precious as ever.
And Amy's heart was towards them, he was sure.
The past in this sense had not been forgotten—could
not possibly be forgotten. The care she had taken
to send this Sister marked her depth of love. But
the impossible must not be hoped for. It may have
cost Amy herself something to think so. Yet she
felt bound to think it, and the Sister's letter, as reflecting her mind and purposes, was a plain declaration.

All that day and the next and the next, and on and
on, such thought currents went surging and crossing
and running counter in Thomas' mind. That Friday
evening Friend Peale dropped in. He realized immediately that something had happened. But

Thomas could not speak; and when he intimated as much, on the big-hearted Quaker's holding out an opening, the latter in a general way became unusually sympathetic and encouraging. Thomas must bear the burden alone. He was estopped from friendly counsel and comfort. He had bound himself to speak of the discovery to none. Later that evening, when he had called to say good night, he appeared to his Father excited, and was full of talk about Sister Jessica—so much so that the old gentleman was fain to remark upon it. How could it be otherwise? She was the symbol of Amy's affection. The last bouquet he carried to his own room. He would fondle the flowers—take them apart and put them together again—gaze upon them—press them to his lips. They came from Amy herself. Her own hands had touched them. Her slender fingers had arranged them. As for the Mosses, he preserved them all; and the Monday morning following his interview with the Sister, his Father happened to find one of the faded blooms upon his pillow.

Thomas, poor fellow, was all wrought up, and his mind in a confused, vacillating, contradictory state. In one sense, he loved Amy still, just as before, but, he considered, as his Cousin. In another sense, by the stress of circumstances she was removed outside the orbit of his destiny, and he had given up a hope. The effect was a changing one, almost constantly. At times he felt stricken through and through— borne down by the thought, that Amy should be so near, and yet so far away. All within was so lonely and dark and wretched. Then, again, his spirits would revive. He would laud the act. His Father's condition, Amy's, his own, all demanded it. 'Twas dutifully done, if painfully, he would say. And he would draw himself up at the thought of the self-sacrifice and seem an inch taller, and feel he would have been glad for his friends to see how morally fine he appeared. But Thomas was young, and this Power dealing with him was old—a god the ancients named it, the strength of whose embraces is masked by their soft and bewitching character; and if by one bound the young man had really freed himself, he had performed a feat that many a swain has supposed he has done, but whose accomplishment lay wholly in the supposal.

John Ruffin had hoped Sister Jessica would call again the Saturday subsequent to the meeting with Thomas, as he wished to let her know at the earliest hour the impression she had made upon his son. Towards the close of that evening there was a rap on his door. She has come, he said. But when the door opened, it was Miss Kitty who presented herself, with three little children accompanying her. John Ruffin had expressed to the Housekeeper a wish to see some children—a sign probably of a general improvement in his condition; and she had brought Annie and Mamie and Harold, children of one of the members of the Board, all clean and sweet and dressed up nicely, and full of artless free life. She knew they would give the old gentleman no trouble—just the contrary; for Miss Kitty was a manager, and to one who could manage at all, she would say, children gave no trouble, till they become (to use her language) yearlings and young men. They were taken up, to be introduced and to shake hands with John Ruffin, and then allowed, by his express wish, to be at perfect liberty to do just as they pleased. John Ruffin sat and watched them with evident enjoyment. They were all curiosity itself and tested everything in the liveliest way, yet under Miss Kitty's eye. They tried the springs of the window-shades, the door knobs, the shucks and the splits, and the work on the chairs —everything, even to the cocks in the bath-room. On returning thence to the main apartment, little Mamie, with the tooth-brushes she had just seen in her mind, approached John Ruffin in quite a thoughtful way, when the latter, supposing the child had something special to say, stooped and gave his private ear, to which Mamie made the following serious communication :

"Mr. Ruffin," she said, "my Mama had two nail-brushes—but she lost them !"

Whereat the old gentleman laughed heartily. Then Miss Kitty, she began to laugh heartily, too. Then Annie and Harold joined in. Then, Mamie. And here they all were shaking up in laughter, with tears almost in their eyes—and no one knowing the cause but John Ruffin.—When one child spoke about anything, the other two spoke up also, and all talked together in the most rapid and excited manner. Presently Miss Kitty took them out, seeing John Ruffin was satisfied and knowing the supper hour was drawing near.

CHAPTER XV.

And how, Audrey? Am I the man yet?
Doth my simple feature content you?

—*As You Like It.*

The Saturday afternoon succeeding that whose incidents are recorded in the last chapter, John Ruffin thought a visit from Sister Jessica very probable and was eagerly anticipating it. One or two door-knocks has proven disappointing—it was Sabina or some other servant on matter immaterial; and, it being late, the old gentleman had abandoned hope of a visit and was at work on a chair for Sandy Johnson, when another tap came. With a frown at what he supposed was a servant's interruption and in a begrudging tone (for the Shoemaker was to call for the chair that evening) he gave the invitation, and Sister Jessica entered.

"Ho! ho! ho!" he cried, with a changed and happy manner, and brushing aside his work, "it's *you*, my little angel. Glad, glad to see you, Miss Jessie. And so you've brought me flowers again"— the Sister had given him the posy. "And I'm glad there are Moss Roses here again; for Tammie now likes 'em so."

"Does he?"

"Yes. It's strange you should bring the very

flowers he has taken such a fancy to. I can't understand it, but Tammie has lately changed so about flowers."

"Has he, though ?"

"Yes, yes, he was always fond of flowers, and Pinks were his favorite—old fashioned, sweet Pinks —he had his own little Pink bed at Cloud Cap—" and John Ruffin bent his head in tears.

"Don't cry, Mr. Ruffin," said the Sister, in her sympathetic tones. "I must cease bringing flowers, if in any way they cause you grief."

"No, no, Sister Jessie. Don't mind me. I can't speak of dear old Cloud Cap without being a baby. Yes, yes, all along it has been Pinks! Pinks! with Tammie, but here lately it's nothing but Moss Roses. He has a Moss almost every day in his button-hole. And—would you believe it, Miss Jessie ?—last Monday morning I found an old faded Moss on his pillow. I was so sorry I threw it away; for when I told Tammie that night, he seemed really distressed, and said it came from a friend."

"Indeed ! I wonder from whom ?"

"I should like to know myself. I can't understand it, why Tammie has changed so about flowers. I've asked him over and over, but he makes the same answer, that a young friend of his likes Mosses, and so he has come to like Mosses, too."

"And does that seem to you altogether unreasonable, Mr. Ruffin !"

"No-o. But then, you see, I want to know his friend's name, and Tammie won't tell me."

"How undutiful!"

"Not undutiful, Miss Jessie. Tammie can't be undutiful. Just a little self-willed, you know. He has always opened his heart to me so fully about everything, that his holding back the name makes me suspicious and fearful."

"Shame! he should distress you."

"He doesn't mean to, dear child. Last Thursday night I got almost mad with him, and told him, if he wasn't so old, I'd have half a mind to 'give him jessie' for refusing me so."

The unconscious word-play provoked a little laugh from the Sister, whereat John Ruffin remarked :

"Why do you laugh, Miss Jessie? You do just as Tammie did."

"How did *he* do?"

"Why, when I spoke to him about 'giving him jessie,' he broke into a laugh, too. And what d'you think he said?"

"I really can't imagine, Sir."

"Why, he said he was ready for punishment any moment."

Sister Jessica was constrained to repeat her laugh, and John Ruffin again remarked upon it :

"And here you're laughing, too, when it's so serious with me. I can't understand it—I can't understand it." And he started up with cane in hand, and made a shuffling turn, in more real mental worry than the good Sister was aware of.

"It's quite amusing," she remarked.

"Amusing, Sister Jessica!"—the use of "Jessica"

indicating a little stiffness or ripple of indignation.
"How can you say so? It's serious with *me*, serious.
I hope Tammie isn't making bad acquaintances—"
he added with a sigh.

"I hope so, sincerely."

"I hope this friend won't lead him off. He's all
I've got now."

"You needn't be at all uneasy," spoke the Sister
encouragingly; for she now realized that John Ruffin
was in dead earnest touching his fears.

"But there are so many fast young men in the city
—so many temptations."

"I do not think your son, from what you tell me
of him, at all likely to be led astray, Mr. Ruffin."

"I know he's good, almost an angel. But young
men are young men, Miss Jessie, flesh and blood, and
apt to be as those they run with. You see Tammie
has caught already this young man's fancy for Mosses, and if he has bad ways, I fear Tammie may get
there."

"Mr. Ruffin, you need have no fears, I think."

"I wish very much I knew who this young man is.
—Miss Jessie," he continued, after a moment's pause
in reflection, "Tammie tells me he has met you, and
he has been talking a great deal about you, and I
want to let you know, likes you so much. He may've
spoken to *you* about this friend. Have you any
idea, Miss Jessie, who he is?"

Sister Jessica now had occasion for a pause herself, and was framing a reply, when Sabina broke in
and made a diversion in her favor.

"O Mr. Ruffin! Mr. Ruffin!" exclaimed the negro woman with her usual enthusiasm, at the same time exhibiting a torn and uprooted rose bush, "dat nasty stinkin' little good-fur-nuthin' dorg gone and scratched up Mr. Thomas' Moss Rose."

"Well, Sabina, make a hole and put it out again."

"An' dey kin make a hole fur dat dare little dorg, too. Mister Thomas'll *kill* him. He'll be all-fired mad"—closing her period with a vigorous guffaw. Observing now Sister Jessica—the Sister was sitting apart and it was towards evening, and she had escaped Sabina's eye—the negro woman hastily retired, having the audacity, as she passed out, to give Sister Jessica a most irreverent wink.

"Miss Jessie," continued John Ruffin, as Sabina closed the door after her, "I can't get over Tammie's refusing to tell me his friend's name. He has never done such a thing before, and I can't help feeling anxious."

"You need not be, Sir, I repeat, from what you've told me about your son. Don't worry, Mr. Ruffin."

"Yes, yes"—suddenly assuming confidence—"I'm an old goose for feeling so, I know. Tammie's safe. Ain't he, Miss Jessie? *You* don't suppose this young man will lead him off?"

"I hope not, Sir."

"You *hope* not!"—with disappointed air. "Can't you be a little more positive?"

"I think not."

"You *think* not! Is that all-l, Sister Jessica?"

"I am *sure*, then, Mr. Ruffin, your son's friend will not lead him off."

"Thank you, Miss Jessie," he responded, speaking up.

"I am sure this friend will not do him the least harm."

"O thank you, thank you, Miss Jessie," he again responded, greatly pleased.

"I feel certain this friend's influence, as far as it may extend, will be around him only for all that's pure and good—that she———"

"Wha-a-a-t ! wha-a-a-t !" John Ruffin interrupted, with amazement and alarm. "*She-e-e !* Is it a *she-e-e*, Miss Jessie ? My God !"

Sister Jessica saw she had touched with a needle the morbid sensibilities of this old gentleman respecting his son, and paused to consider how she would smooth over her slip of the tongue.

"I say, Miss Jessie, is it a *she-e-e ?*" he vehemently asked again, his alarm gathering force at the Sister's delay to answer.

"Mr. Ruffin, there's no reason in the round world for any alarm. Suppose it might be a she ? I reckon the she's are as good as the he's."

"Oh-h-h ! Miss Jessie," he cried out, and speaking in sentences interrupted by tears and sobs, "but this must be a bad one. It's some bad one has turned my Boy's head. That's the reason—he's so shy about it—and won't tell her name. Here's my poor Boy—been sleeping night after night—with an old faded Moss—from one of these she-devils—and they'll draw him—into their dives—and the first thing you know—he'll be in trouble—and get—into prison ! "

He ceased ; for he had blubbered outright, and could proceed no further. The Sister was amazed. She was fully aware of John Ruffin's morbidly exaggerated sentiments towards Thomas; but had never seen in him before anything approaching this. Going up to him, she spoke to him sweetly, as she placed her hand softly upon his bowed head :

"Mr. Ruffin, you must not do so—you must not do so. I declare my saying 'she' was a slip of the tongue."

"Is it a 'he,' then?" he asked, eagerly catching at the hope.

"It's dark and I must be going. Just one word : You needn't have a particle of fear for your son— not a particle. *I* know this friend of his—indeed, I'm intimately acquainted with this friend."

"O I'm *so* glad, Miss Jessie," he spoke up with a reassurred, happy, smiling manner. "Any one you're intimate with must be all right."

"And I tell you most positively, that this friend, whatever be the reasons your son may have for withholding the name, is *not* a bad one, is *not* a she-devil, nor one capable of harming in any degree your son's body, mind, or soul. Be satisfied with this, Mr. Ruffin."

"I am, Sister Jessie, I am. I'm glad it's not a 'she.' I'm afraid of them, when boys are in it."

"And don't you think the 'he's' need some watching, too?"

"No, no—it's the '*she's*' need it, Sister Jessie, the 'she's.'"

"Very well, Mr. Ruffin; and now I must bid you good-bye. Be satisfied with what I have told you."

"I am, good Sister, I am."

Upon the Sister's departure John Ruffin rang up Sabina and told her he was going to the Park, and requested her to ask Miss Kitty to say to the "Shoemaker," should he call for his chair, that the work was not done, and that he could get it Monday evening. Sabina delivered the message, and presently Miss Kitty thought it worth while to look in and see if John Ruffin's room was in proper order. Probably, if the full truth were know, another reason may have had its weight. Sandy Johnson long had been laying siege to her heart, and while Miss Kitty was not deaf to the eloquence which, in its way, he undoubtedly possessed (for she had a fund of sharp sense herself and could appreciate it in others), and in truth liked the man, yet there lingered a feeling, that the Housekeeper at The Home was a little above the position of a shoemaker. This feeling, however —it really had no sound support—had almost, if not altogether, given way before Sandy's pushing and captivating address and his improving condition. For Sandy now was one who saved his money. He had accumulated a little pile—had a cosy home—never got drunk these days—and, not the least, Friend Peale, whose name was weighty at The Home, was his fast friend. Withal, each had known the joys of wedded life; for she was a widow—and he, a widower. It was not unlikely, therefore, that one of the reasons for looking into John Ruffin's room at this particular time, may have been Sandy's anticipated visit. Be that as it may, it is certain, that, when she came in, she gave evidence of having bestowed more than usual attention upon her personal appearance and was smarter looking than common.

Before long there came a rap at the private entrance door, followed by an admittance.

"Mistress Kitty!" exclaimed Sandy Johnson (for he it was), agreeably surprised at the meeting. "The peace o' the e'enin' to ye, Mistress Kitty. Yer ainsel's the daisy ye hae iver been."

"Be aisy, Sandy Johnson, be aisy with yer blarney. I'm in a quandary a managin' The Home. Don't I look so?"

"In a quandary? Na, God bless us a'. Indeed, ye don't."

"Well, I *am*, and can ye help a troubled soul what to do?"

"In quandaries, some say, cut the Bible for a cue."

"Cut the Boible for a cue?"

"Yes, yes, Mistress Kitty—that's what *she* used to do, me auld wifie Sue—rest her soul" (signing the cross). "In ony trouble she gaed aside wi' her Bible, cut the Buik, and the first words her een lighted on, gied her guidance. That's what I ca' cuttin' for a cue."

"And do you think I'd juggle the loike o' that with God Almighty's Holy Word?"

"Noo, Mistress Kitty, juist let me gie ye a story.

I hed it frae me wifie's crony hersel', wha was a Bible-cutter, too. It's her ain real experience, and a'true to the verra letter."

Miss Kitty was attention, and Sandy proceeded :

"Weel : 'Twas late ae lonely night, when the city was a settlin' into sleep beneath the simmer stars, that her son, a walkin' hame, cam up wi' a lassie, whase manner showed sae great distress, that his tender soul spak kindly to her. At the word she burstit into tears, sayin' she hed juist reachit the city, knew naebody, and hed nae place to gang to. The young mon was touchit, and, acting on the impulse, took her to his hame and asked his widow · mother to lodge her. The auld leddy was dumbfounded—in a *quandary*, Mistress Kitty. Wha was this lassie? A thief? or worse? or what na? But she wadna turn her into the street again. The only bed was by her daughter's side, and that she gied her.

When a' hed retired, the auld leddy, sa troubled in mind, sought her Bible for guidance the morrow. Thrae times she cut the Buik—*thrae* times, Mistress Kitty. First she read :

'Let britherly love continue.'

Thin :

'Use hospitality ane to anither.'

Thin :

'Some hae entertained angels unawares.'

Weel, weel ! she cried within hersel', as she pressed the Holy Buik to her heart, surely the Lord's finger is guiding me. The lassie maunna leave.

Next day employment was found for her. A

correspondence followed, showing her in a gudely light, and confirming her story, that she hed fled frae a step-father's heavy hand.

And what's mair, Mistress Kitty, the young mon fell in love—*fell in love*, Mistress Kitty. They were married, and now are happy in each ithers arms.— *That's* what I ca' cuttin' the Bible for a cue."

"Begone! with sich divilment, Sandy Johnson."

"Aweel! aweel! Hae yer will—hae yer will. But the story's naething, if na true. And what a blithsome eending, Mistress Kitty! If your quandary cud only hae an eending like that!"

Miss Kitty saw matters were getting interesting and maintained an equivocal silence. Sandy thought the circumstance not unfavorable, and continued:

"And as for quandaries, Mistress Kitty, I'm in a quandary, too. Canna *ye* help a troubled soul what to do?"

"Yes—eat yer own dish and cut the Boible for a cue."

"Sae I hae, Mistress Kitty, sae I hae. Twice I opened the leaves; and what d'ye think I read?"

"Most loikely where it's said jugglers and sich loike are burned up thegither."

"Na, na. I read: 'Love ane anither.'"

"And what think ye I read next?"

"Begone! Sandy Johnson, with yer foolishness and rhyme."

"Mistress Kitty, I read:'Now's the accepted time.'"

Miss Kitty again was silent. Sandy saw it was the opportunity of his life and resolved to do his level best. As he went on, enthused by his subject, the various shop terms—pegs, last, awl, wax, &c.—came in handily, indirectly and directly, to illustrate his affection, and reinforce the amatory appeal. And further, he had carefully composed and committed a triplet of rough lines, setting forth both the extent of his assets and the strength of his devotion, to be cast the first chance at Miss Kitty with lover's aim; and he realized the moment had now come to use the lines for all they were worth, as the climax of his effort. So, drawing his chair close to her side, he said softly, as he looked sweet upon her :

"Mistress Kitty, ae wee word frae you and wha, in a' the round world, wad be sae happy as Sandy Johnson ?"—Pause.

"Mistress Kitty, how to bring matters to a pint, that's *my* quandary. I hae tried and tried to win yer consent. A lang, lang time hae I pegged awa' at it. But ye wad pat me off. Canna ye say that wee word noo ?"—Pause.

"Mistress Kitty, ye're the last I shall iver gie hand and heart to." (Sandy—while in the term "last" assuring Miss Kitty she was the only one who would ever capture him—had in mind, too, no doubt, the needful wooden model to which he had stuck so long and so faithfully, as technically and fitly illustrating how faithful he would prove to the Housekeeper). "Ye're my all, I canna wark or live without ye." (Here again, perhaps, Sandy speaks somewhat in a figure, and it is a question whether his utterance should be written down "all," or "awl," the indispensable

tool of his craft. Very probably he means another
alluring pun). "The thread o' my life rins sae close
to yer ain, whyna twist and wax the twa thegither?
Scotch and Irish union beats creation."—Pause, and
then Sandy crowns his appeal:

"Mistress Kitty,

I wark sae and sae, but I wad wark like a nigger—
I hae a wee pile, but the pile wad get bigger—
I hae a snig hame, but me hame wad be snigger,
Gin ye wad only say that ae wee word."

Miss Kitty had been giving a willing ear, and
Sandy had found her hand, and his arm had stolen
round her waist, when, most unfortunately, an interruption was precipitated. John Ruffin had now
returned from a short stroll in the Park. He had
come in by the main door, and Sabina accompanied
him to his room, to do the routine evening service.
The inner door of his apartment was ajar and moved
noiselessly on the hinges that Sabina kept well oiled;
and Miss Kitty and Sandy, with backs towards this
door, were absorbed so entirely in each other, that
they did not hear their partial entrance.

"What's up there?" whispered John Ruffin to
Sabina from the door-way, peering with his dim eyes
through the twilight gloom.

"Sh-h-h! de Shoemaker and Miss Kitty," Sabina
responded *sotto voce*, shaking one hand for silence,
and with the other stuffing into her mouth, as she
ceased speaking, a corner of the apron, to suppress
the guffaw.

"The scamp!" John Ruffin whispered back. "He's
measuring her middle instead of her foot."

It is barely possible that Sabina's power of self-restraint, aided by the apron, could have managed the guffaw, even under the stimulus of John Ruffin's observation. But, unluckily, it was just at this particular moment that Sandy sealed what he considered a surrender with a smack, and the guffaw that had been struggling and gathering force, burst out rousing and irrepressible.

"Mother o' God!" exclaimed Miss Kitty, suddenly rising at the discovery and flirting away Sandy and scowling on him with virtuous indignation, arms akimbo, "what d'ye *mane*, Sandy Johnson! It's little I'd thought ye'd take sich liberty! Beelzebub fly away with ye'! Ye're *drunk*, Sandy Johnson, and if me brither Mike was here, he'd be afther givin' ye a blackthorn! Out with ye, ye haythen crayture; and whin ye be sobered, ye may come for the cheer!"

So saying, Miss Kitty marched out; and Sandy, too, after a word from John Ruffin touching the chair, soon left by the private door, on the whole very well satisfied and enjoying a hearty laugh in his sleeve.

CHAPTER XVI.

"One of the most trying ills of life is this long-continued, clear, dry, beautiful weather," said the gum-shoe man.

Truly, the day was lovely, for the season. A glorious sun shone bright and warm in a sky without a fleck of a cloud; and while "Bob," under Noals' guidance, is awaiting an opportunity to entrap Thomas Ruffin and get an impression of his Bank key, the reader will be told how the latter availed himself of the fine open weather for gratifying an earnest wish on the part of Friend Peale. The warm-hearted Quaker never had laid eyes on John Ruffin, since he had left him at death's door in his wife's hands at Cloud Cap, and often had expressed the wish that he might see, unobserved, his old friend. At first an arrangement was out of the question. The state of John Ruffin's health and wintry weather kept him within doors almost the entire time. Under change of environment and good nursing his condition began to improve—slowly, yet perceptibly. The Winter, too, drawing to its close, grew less rigorous, with many an open balmy day here and there; and John Ruffin would go out, often with Thomas, sometimes with Sabina, and of late not unfrequently by himself.

To-night (Thursday), his night at The Home, with weather prospects so favorable, Thomas thought a meeting could be arranged in the Park. At noon, therefore, having a half hour off, he saw Friend Peale and designated the particular spot where he and his wife (for Friend Peale declared Martha would not miss accompanying him) should be at 8 p. m. In a certain part of the Park or Square, well known to Friend Peale—he often had occasion to pass through the grounds—there was a narrow, encircling walk, and at a certain point in said walk a side seat, and just opposite to this seat were double seats; and the shrubbery and lamps were so arranged, that the former seat was in full light—the latter, in shade. It was arranged that at the above hour Friend Peale and his wife would be occupying one of the double seats.

That afternoon Friend Peale met Sandy Johnson, spoke of the arrangement, and suggested that Sandy go with them. Sandy readily assented, saying he would meet Friend Peale at his residence, and bring, too, the pair of shoes due this day. The jolly Quaker was especially fond of the jolly Shoemaker. They had known each other long and well, and a further bond at present was a common interest in the Ruffins. Each possessed a fund of humor. Rarely did they meet without trying conclusions. It was rare, too, that the Shoemaker came out second best. Sandy was on full time, with shoes in hand, and, while Mrs. Peale was getting ready, one of the usual little encounters occurred.

"Ah! ah! walk in, Alexander, walk in," was the hearty salutation of Friend Peale, who had just had a visit from one of the preachers of his church. "O thou mender of soles, had thee been somewhat sooner, thee would have met a fellow-worker. One of thy craft has just been here."

"And wha might *he* be?"

"A preacher."

"Ha! ha! ha! a preacher! By the bye, I hae a gude ane on a preacher."

"Thee is ever ready with 'good ones.' Well, what new jest is this"

"Laist week a preacher moved frae a hoose near me ain. Yesterday, an auld leddy moved in. And what d'ye think she told me she found in a back closet?"

"Old sermons most likely—full of spiritual consolation."

"Ha! ha! ha! The covers were thar, but the consolation a' gane. She found *twenty-five empty whiskey bottles*, labelled frae almaist as mony different drug stores."

"Come! Alexander, spare the cloth."

"Sae I will—let me feenish; for the label read: 'For medeecinal use only.' Ha! ha! ha! It's a gude ane, or I'm nae son of St. Crispin."

"Thee is a better son of St. Pasquin—as full of jibes as the old Naples cobbler."

"I gied a fac', na a jibe, Sir."

"But a sort of fact"—Friend Peale remarked, smiling genially—"thee seems to hug and dance over. Cobblers are railers by trade, eh? So much cutting and punching at the bench, beget a cutting, punching habit in the mind, eh?"

"It's wrang, Friend Peale," responded Sandy with mock solemnity, "to pint oot a wrang and use nae effort to right it. Ye hae mad an ugly charge upon me character, and ye'll be in the wrang yer ain sel', gin ye canna gie a remedy."

"Well—turn Quaker."

"Humph! I'm a quaker noo. Yer ain sharp tongue maks me a quaker— a quaker for me reputation."

"Ha! ha! ha! Where's a better wit than the cobbler?"

"I may cast a spark and mak wit to be in ithers, if nae mair."

"Thee shall be called the merry cobbler, Alexander."

"A merry cobbler! Weel a day! If ye wad see me a merry cobbler, gie me a sherry cobbler."

"Ha! ha! ha! Thee is Alexander the Great—in thy way.

Well, I see thee has the shoes. Thee is ever punctual. This be the day and the hour to deliver thy handicraft."

"Punctual as the pay, St. Crispin bless yer Reverence."

"A truce to '*your Reverence*,' Alexander. Ill it sits on Scotch lips; for it savors not of Scotch faith.

And thee *will* apply it, when thee knows we Friends set little store on its under thought of priestly form and ceremony."

"Oor faiths are nigher kin than some may think, Friend Peale. The corn grows wi' a husk. The kernel lies sweet in its shell. The church hae a form and a ceremony. But sure, Sir, the church hae anither side, and her ain sel' is where mon gies mon his hand in the Master's spirit. These mony years hae I seen that spirit in Friend Peale deep and pure; and 'yer Reverence' is a way I hae of touchin' me cap to it."

Friend Peale, of course, had nothing else to do but reply with a profound bow; and Sandy, in responding with another of like quality, made a vigorous scrape with his right lower extremity, bringing the calf into violent contact with his chair, plumb against a healing but tender ulcer.

"Umph!" he cried out lustily, with a twinge of that morbid exaltation of sensibility called pain, as a scowl sat upon his face and the palm went rubbing the wounded member.

"Good lack! Alexander! What ails thee, man?"

"Hit the sore on me leg, Sir. A bad, bad ane. A week it laid me up."

"And has pulled thee down, too. When I think of it, thee looks a little worsted. The doctor's salve, I hope, is making thee whole."

"Makin' me whole! Ha! ha! ha! It mad the hole worse, yer Reverence. Ane o' thase pill-an'-powder laddies tried his hand. He gied it a lang name, physicked a lang time, and hes, nae doubt, a lang bill."

"And thee had no benefit ?"

"Na. The ulcer grew worse. Pains ran a' down into me foot and toe and I thocht I hed the goot."

"I can tell thee, Alexander, where thee will never have the gout."

Sandy gave a look of inquiry, and the response came :

"In thy tongue."

"Ha ! ha ! ha !"

"Ah ! well. Thee may doctor thy broken skin thyself. Thee is familiar with skins and patches."

"Sud I gang a doctoring, yer Reverence, I wad hae a doctor's wisdom and na doctor mysel'. Na, na. An auld woman cam in, clapped on her poultice, and here I be up and oot. Nae mair doctors to pat up a job on me."

"Well, well, let's see what sort of a job thee has put up on myself.—Why, look here, my man, these 'soles"—scrutinizing the shoes—"seem somewhat broad."

"And gude reason, yer Reverence—yer *foot* is somewhat broad."

"Come ! come ! Alexander. There was a 'drap' too much, I ween, when thee made the measure."

"I'll lose the wage on a misfit, Sir. *Try* the shune. It's the shune o' thine ain sel', broad-brimmed and broad-soled"—no doubt Sandy meant to include "broad-souled"—"frae tap tae toe."

"A smooth and ready tongue thou · hast.—Thy

wage"—handing the money. "The sum I know by
repetition. With rise and fall of awls and pegs and
hides, through all these years the price hath kept
one point"—(nod and grin of satisfaction from Sandy)
—"placed high and safe in profit's margin."

"Ha! ha! ha! A sharp turn, yer Reverence."

"Thee has taught me such tricks. But I must
leave thee a moment, and wish thee profitable reflections, while I hurry up the Madam," continued
Friend Peale, as he consulted his watch. "It's time
we be going."

"Thar gangs a *mon*," was Sandy's comment, as
Friend Peale left the room—"fu' o' juist preenciples
and seentiments—a chreestian wi' a polish on—a
head light, nae penny dip!"

Friend Peale and wife anon appeared, the latter
in garment of fine texture and true Quaker style—
neat, simple, comfortable, and distinctive—and superior, pure taste should say, to the shifting fash-
ions of the day. They at once left for the Park, and
at 8 p. m. were occupying the seat that had been
chosen.

To revert to Thomas—he reached The Home earlier
than usual, soon after dark. The evening was a
beautiful one, as he had anticipated, clear and starry
and mild; and after supper he proposed to his Father
a walk in the Park. It was a favorite resort to John
Ruffin, as has been said. The cosy seats and shelters,
showy shrubbery, smooth clean walks, and well kept
grounds generally, made it one of the most inviting
Squares in the city; and under its brilliant lights it

was frequented by night, as well as by day, even in
Winter, when the weather allowed.

To John Ruffin there were two special attractions.
The fine trees were one, whereof there were many,
with almost as many varieties—Pin Oak, Ash, Elm,
Silver Maple, Sugar Maple, Tulip Poplar, Button-
wood, &c., &c. He never had seen them in foliage.
But they were noble of size and proportion—many
venerable for age—a number representative of Cloud
Cap flora—all representative of the woods and the
forest to which he had been accustomed, and hence
objects of specific interest.

The other attraction were the ancient churches,
either bordering the Square, or but a stone's throw
away, all memorials of the preceding century, showing thorough workmanship, walls so ample, no mean
saving of material, and architecture all of correct
type. Here stood one of Doric style, with plain
massy pillars, curling capitals, and extended portico.
And near this, a Corinthian edifice, with channelled
pillar and garish frieze. And over against these,
on the other side of the Square, an ancient Quaker
Meeting House, marked by the rigid simplicity
characteristic of that denomination, no tower, no
spire, no clerestory, gable fronting the street, and
encircled by a wall, with coping and gates, all so
high and thick and strong and massive, as to resem-
ble rather the inclosure to a fortress. It delighted
John Ruffin to wander through these historic edifi-
ces, as he had done recently by himself once or twice
—and note the solid handiwork, and fine arches, and

square-boxed pews, and read the mural tablets and the marble set in the aisles, commemorative of personages and heroes and statesmen of old who departed this life in the odor of sanctity.

Thomas found the Peales and Sandy Johnson seated, as had been agreed upon. With his Father leaning upon his arm in a way so clinging and contented-looking, he slowly walked a number of times up and down just in front of, and near to, the settee. Next, they seated themselves on the settee opposite, with the light directly upon them. The Peales had a full view and scarce could believe their eyes. They were prepared to see great change, but not the wreck before them. Could this man—so old, so gray, so bent and broken—be the remains of the hearty, bright-eyed, high-bred John Ruffin of less than two years back? They were astonished and never would have recognized him.

Presently, there was another walk, and then Thomas, with his Father by him, took the vacant settee abutting that occupied by the Peales and Sandy. These settees were on the inner side of the circular walk, and, conforming to the curve, their abutting ends made an outer angle in such wise that Thomas, who sat next to the Peales, cut off their view from his Father. As they turned to be seated, John Ruffin noticed the presence of strangers, but not seeing them after being seated, directly he forgot them, spoke freely to Thomas and was overheard easily.

An incident gave the first direction to the conver-

sation. Scarcely had they become seated, when a
beggar approached and extended his hand. He had
recognized John Ruffin on his entering the Square,
and had followed, watching an opportunity to ask
an alms. The reader has been told that John Ruffin
often asked Thomas for pennies, to give to the "poor
beggars" he would meet on his strolls. The beggars
soon came to know their man, as well as his customary walks and hours, and would be on the lookout
for him. And in the course of this narrative it will
appear there were at times thievish characters among
them, and they would impose on John Ruffin, after
getting a penny going ahead and soliciting again at
the next corner—a matter the Blue Coats had begun
to notice, and more than one of these characters had
been threatened and driven off.

John Ruffin began fumbling in his pocket, but
Thomas, though he did not relish the fellow's looks,
anticipated his Father and gave the penny. As the
beggar walked off, John Ruffin observed, evidently
with a personal bearing in the thought:

"That poor beggar may be happy, Tammie, though
the world doesn't think so."

Thomas had his own notion touching the fellow's
being a poor beggar or a worthy beggar, but replied
to the general idea in the latter clause of his Father's
sentence:

"The world, Father, often thinks one way, when
the truth is just the other way."

"That's so, Tammie."

"The world, for example, thinks it nonsense to say

the rich are wretched, or that happiness stands in tears," continued Thomas, having in mind how often in his own trials and prayers, refreshment would follow a flood of tears.

"That's so. I used to think Tammie never would catch on and kept heaping up a pile to take care of him, and here Tammie's taking care of me."

"And you mean, too, Father, you're not so unhappy, because it's so."

"I do, I do, my Son. Ought I to be unhappy, when I'm like the Lord?" replied John Ruffin, an attendant upon whose affliction was the development of a strong religious vein. "Wasn't the Lord poor, Tammie?"

"Yes, He was poor, Father—born poor, lived poor, and died poor."

"And had no place to lay His head—not as well off as the tramps, Tammie."

"And so is a comfort to the poorest."

"And the angels ministered to Him, too."

"Yes—on one occasion at least, the Bible tells us."

"And *you*, Tammie, are sent to take care of me, and I thank God and am happy, my Son."

"I wish, Tammie," he continued, as another thought came across his mind, "you could go out with me oftener in the day."

"I wish so, too."

"I would show you, then, the churches here."

"I've seen them, Father—often. What would you show me of special interest?"

"The pillars and the carvings. They're fine. Such

fine work. But finer, I've read, in the old world."

"And finest, Father, in the other world, as you'll one day see," remarked Thomas ; for religion is in harmony with the love of the ideal that slumbers in every breast.

"What d'you mean, Tammie?"

"I fear you would not understand me," replied Thomas, who saw now his mistake in having suggested an idea which he should have known would excite his Father's curiosity, yet one it would be difficult, perhaps, to explain to him.

"But I *must* know, Tammie, what you know about the other world."

"I mean, then, that wise and holy men who write about such things, tell us that all these beautiful things that come from man's hand—do you understand me, Father?"

"I think I do."

—"that all these beautiful things, as a painting or a chiseled marble, or the beauty we see in these things—I fear, Father, I shall only worry you by talking so."

"No, no. Go on, Tammie. Anyhow, I love to hear you talk."

—"that the beauty we see in these things, such as paintings or chiseled marble, are just the shadows from patterns or originals of perfect beauty that fill the heavenly world and make a delight for those who go there."

John Ruffin paused in reflection, and presently Thomas added :

"I am reading a holy book that tells of these things."

"I'm glad you're reading and thinking of the other world. All these troubles are good, if they make you think of the other world, Tammie."

"Very true, Father."

"*I* think of the other world every morning, when I get up, and every night before I go to bed—and all through the day. It's the only question. Isn't it, Tammie?"

"Yes, Father, the only real question. Every man in his senses must solemnly ask it some time or other."

"There is a church near here," Thomas continued, "in which I myself have a warm interest."

"Which is it?"

"The old Quaker Meeting House over there."

"O yes, I know—with the high wall."

"It's a very old church—built years and years ago in the far away past."

"I like what's away back," remarked John Ruffin, catching at the idea of the "past," which, as an outcome of his misfortunes, had taken on exceptional magnitude and worth. "Everything in the past looks to be bigger. Things were better then, Tammie—men were stronger then, Tammie."

"Yes, Father," replied Thomas, whose admirations also lay in the past, "I believe pretty much as you do. The men of past ages appear to have been stronger."

"To be sure, Tammie. Sampson was in the past, and wasn't he the strongest man?"

"I don't speak of muscle, Father, though it may be true of muscle. I speak of life in its higher forms. Life seems to have been stronger, more intense then on every line. Religious life was more intense, with the hermit for its representative."

"Those who prayed in caves, Tammie?"

"Yes, Father.—And political and military life was more intense, with the nobleman for its representative."

"You've been reading another book, haven't you, Tammie?" asked John Ruffin, with a general idea of what his son had delivered.

"No, Father. What I've said is from the same book I spoke of just now."

"You and the book are right, Tammie. No use talking—no times like the old times. No such men these days. No noblemen these days."

"But, Father, we mustn't go to extremes. There are many strong and good men now, as there were many weak and bad men in the past. We are speaking of ages, or the tendency or drift of ages—do you understand me, Father?"

"I think I do."

"And our age, as an age, appears to me to be one intense only for loving and for making money; and its representative is an acquaintance of mine in this very city named Black Isaac."

"What! what's that, Tammie. Are you making acquaintances among *black* men?"

Just at this moment there happened to be on the other settee a little commotion, yet audible enough,

Thomas feared, to attract his Father's attention. He cleared his throat once or twice and looked around, pausing necessarily, and his Father, in ignorance of the cause of the pause, repeated the question in tones significant of deepened astonishment:

"I say, Tammie, is it possible you're making acquaintances among *black* men?"

"No, Father, no—I mean he's a black-hearted man."

"Good gracious, my son!" cried out John Ruffin in consternation and turning full upon Thomas, "making acquaintances and friends among BLACK-HEARTED men!"

There was another little shaking up on the adjoining settee, and Thomas had occasion again to clear his throat very distinctly, yet was prompt to answer and reassure his Father:

"No, no, no, Father—you don't understand me. I'm not intimate with any black-hearted man, I assure you. Certainly not. But in the Bank I have business dealings, more or less, with persons of such character. I simply know this man. He's no friend of mine."

"O!" responded John Ruffin in an accent of relief.

"I was speaking, Father, of the old Quaker Church. It has a special interest for me, because a good and true friend of mine worships there."

"What's his name?"

"I had better not say, perhaps."

"Yes, but you *had*, Tammie."

"It might not please you."

"But it *will* please me; for isn't any friend of yours a friend of mine？ And I promise to like him before you name him."

"It's Friend Peale, Father."

John Ruffin was silent.

"Don't you remember Friend Peale, Father？" Thomas asked after a moment's pause.

"Yes."

"Don't you know how fond of him you used to be？"

"Yes."

"You haven't changed towards him, Father, have you？"

"O no—but he may've changed towards poor me."

"I tell you, Father, he has *not* changed. He is still a dear and a close friend to me—and to you, too, in spirit—dearer and closer than ever, and it would delight him to have you let me bring him to you, that he may tell you himself how warm his heart is towards you."

Thomas was conscious of a movement on the other settee, and feared lest the warm-hearted Quaker, under the unexpected circumstances of the situation, might come forward and make a scene. He cautioned with a backward movement of the hand, as his Father replied :

"You know, Tammie, how I've felt towards some other people."

"Yes, Father, I do; but I hope you're getting over that feeling. You don't feel altogether as you did, Father, do you？"

"May be not."

"And if you can't see Friend Peale now, you may let him see you one of these days?"

"May be so. Come, my son, it's getting late. Let-us go."

On the way back to The Home Thomas had good reason for indulging in pleasing reflections. He had just recognized for the first time an evident change for the better in his Father's sentiments touching his friends of other days. Never before had he spoken to him so directly and plainly respecting them, and he rejoiced to find no repulse. It was another sign of a general improvement. He felt he saw the day approaching, when his Father would welcome Friend Peale and other old friends and acquaintances, and an opening up of channels of happiness—for himself (so much needed now), as well as for him—which affliction's hand for the time had held closed.

The Peales and Sandy parted for home at the entrance to the Park, after some earnest words touching what they had just seen and heard. The Peales walked on in silence, each absorbed in renewed reflections upon John Ruffin's pitiable fate. The tragedy never had appeared so vivid—yesterday the magnificence of Cloud Cap, so goodly a heritage, such fullness of substance and of joy—today stripped bare and inmate at The Home!

"The changes of earth!" exclaimed Friend Peale within himself, as he dwelt on all this—"how sudden! how unforeseen! how overwhelming! No change there," glancing up at the stars, whose singular radiance caught his eye at the moment and gave direction to the thought. "Change, change here! None there among the everlasting stars, since the first records of the constellations were made, hundreds and hundreds of years ago—but the same calm, serene, peaceful appearance! There is the identical configuration," he continued within himself, noting the Great Dipper at the zenith, "that my Father pointed out to me, when a boy—that Galileo, and Plato, and Aristotle have described, speeding their giant spheres athwart the heavens, unchanged by the minutest fraction of an inch that science can discover! And there, descending the western sky, are the "Pleiades" and the "Bands of Orion," just as Job beheld them in the land of Uz, unchanged through thousands of years! Change, change here! No change there! Perhaps they are our homes, our final homes, these mighty spheres, and their changeless courses signs of our destiny, tokens of rest and peace without change, without end—their very movements day by day, through the Creator's beneficent hand, suggesting visibly, to those with eyes to see, a support against all change and bitterness below!"

CHAPTER XVII.

BOB'S JOB.

The thread of the plot concocted in the fertile
and malignant brains of the Pawnbroker and Noals,
was dropped at the point where it had been settled
that the globe-trotter, Robert Small, should hocus-
pocus Thomas Ruffin out of an impression of the
key for the *Bank's* rear door. The thread will be
picked up here. This key, it has been stated, had
been given by Black Isaac to Thomas for his personal use. The former, indeed, had fulfilled his
promise to provide Noals with a duplicate key.
This had been done the day following the last interview between them, already detailed. Yet it was
deemed expedient to have Bob do the job, though it
necessitated some delay, as a test of his skill and
good faith.

It was arranged, therefore, between Robert and
Noals (the interview, as all the others, being under
cover of darkness, and Noals, of course, disguised
as a cracksman), that Robert, in disguise furnished
by Noals and representing a Pen and Ink Agent or
Pedlar; should try to get in his fine piece of work
the following Wednesday evening at early candle

light.   Should he succeed, the key would be made
next day, and that night (Thursday) the scheme
finally carried through, with Robert's departure
abroad on the morrow.

Bob, whose appetite for adventure had become
sharpened by long abstinence, entered into the
scheme with spirit; and being withal the smartest
sort of a fellow, whose wit had not been dulled a
whit by his manifold experiences, he had made, as
he conceived, a brilliant preparation, whereof a feature were certain lines puffing the Pens he was to
hawk, and which he repeated to Noals, to the latter's complete satisfaction.

Now, it fell out that John Ruffin, that identical
Wednesday evening, made one of his secret visits to
the *Bank.*   It will be remembered that he had early
expressed an earnest desire to visit the *Bank*, both
to see his son's surroundings, and to make the acquaintance of Dalguspin—towards whom, at that
time, he cherished the most grateful sentiments, but
that Thomas, for the reasons there given, had persuaded him against the step, satisfying his Father
with the prospect of his visiting Dalguspin at his
residence later on.   But John Ruffin had become
most unhappy about his son—his growing thinness,
especially.   Nor could the latter avoid breaks here
and there in his carefully guarded exterior aspect,
disclosing disturbing symptoms to his Father's suspicious and watchful eye.   The assurances Thomas
gave were quieting for the moment only.   His

Father's fears would spring up again and prey upon him secretly. Finally, nothing must do but to visit the *Bank.* Something, he thought, might be learnt. He would see something at least with his own eyes, and know better how Thomas was getting on.

To do this, without his son's knowledge, it was necessary the visits should be made after dark, and the "seeing" confined to looking through the windows. The *Bank's* location he readily found out through Sabina. It was not far off; and he had made one or two of these visits prior to that here recorded. The building fell very far short of expectations, and at the same time Dalguspin's stature shrank anew. Of the three balls John Ruffin took no notice. Upon points of special interest—to wit : the cause of Thomas' thinning so, and the reason for those unusual broodings at unguarded moments, &c.—the visits of course threw no light. Still, it was a joy at the least to see his dear son at the desk, working such long and patient hours, and all for him. He would stand and stand and gaze in through the window, unconscious of anything that might be occurring around him. On this particular Wednesday evening he was making the third visit, and had been at the window perhaps twenty minutes, when he saw Thomas leave the "cage" hat in hand and pass out through a side door. Fearing discovery he turned to slip away, and, as he did so, became conscious of a crowd very near him, and loud excited talking—a circumstance that further hastened his steps.

Let it be observed that, as John Ruffin started down the street Friend Peale entered the *Bank* from up the street, for a special call upon Thomas—to be informed by William, the watchman, that Mr Ruffin just that minute had left—that he had passed out through the Loan Office, to speak to the clerk there, otherwise he probably would have met him at the door—that Mr. Ruffin had told him he would be back in half hour—and that he had a deliberate and a decided opinion he had gone to the barber's for a hair-cutting or a shave. (By the way, William must stand corrected in one particular—Thomas Ruffin's means were altogether too limited to allow the use of any other razor than his own.) Now, the watchman's weighty surmise brought it to Friend Peale's mind, that *he* had omitted the usual shave that morning, and he reflected, as he stroked the rugged chin, that the barber's would not be an unbecoming place for himself. He took a chair at the round table outside the "cage," undecided as to whether he should remain, or call again presently. He had not met Thomas since the scene in the Park, and was especially desirous of speaking to him touching that interesting meeting. While debating the matter of remaining or not, Sandy Johnson, who had been the centre of the commotion on the street, roughly entered, wagging his head and exclaiming:

"Hut! tut! hut! tut! The Deil tak the Blue Coats!"

"Heyday! What now, Alexander?"

"Ah! Gude morrow, yer Reverence," replied

Sandy, who in the partial light (for Thomas had turned the lamp down), had mistaken Friend Peale for the watchman. "I'll be e'en wi' the mon, or niver cut hide again."

"What's the matter? Thee looks sour."

"And I feel as I look, as the lad said, whan he stole of nights into the pantry."

"Ha! ha! ha! But, my merryman, what's the matter, I say? What has aroused thee so?"

"He wad arrist me for speaking to a beggar-mon, the blackguard!"

"Strange! Alexander. Our patrolmen have the best reputation."

"The Blue Coat was his ain sel', like the brute he be."

"How? how?"

"I'll tell yer Reverence: On me way hither to hae a word wi' Mr. Tammas, I spied ahead me auld tounsman, and, curious to ken his ain, followed juist behind. To ev'ry beggar he wad gie a penny and whisper a word. 'Twas always the same (for I questioned the beggars narrowly): 'Pray for Tammie.' He mad for Dalguspin's *Bank* and stoppit at the barred window thar ower against his son's desk. The street was sae bustling wi' chatty clerks and workmen hurrying hame and the auld gentleman sae absorbed, that I got verra' near and cud see the liftit eye and the moving lip, as he gazed in upon his son. Thar he stood fu' half an hoor; thin turned to gae, whan he saw Mr. Tammas leave his desk."

"I think I'll watch for him some evening myself, to have another look at my old friend."

"Ye may look oot, too, for Blue Coats."

"Blue Coats !"

"Ay ! Yer Reverence; for, as I turned to gang awa', a Blue Coat roughly pat his hand upon me."

"What are ye aboot, said he ?"

"An honest mon's business, said I."

"Ye spak juist noo to a thief, said he."

"He's a beggar, said I."

"He's a bully thief, said he."

"Ye're a bully yoursel', said I, enraged."

"I'll arrist ye, said he, and hae ye caged."

"Ah ! Alexander, what says your poet Robbie Burns ?: 'Prudent, cautious self-control is wisdom's root.' The Blue Coat, when I think of it, no doubt did his duty."

"To arrist me for speaking to a beggar-mon ! Why, yer Reverence, to save mesel' frae prison, I hed to tak the mon aside and tell him a' John Ruffin's story. E'en thin he dinna scarce believe me and spak most roughly. *I hae nae love for Blue Coats.*"

"And there thee is unreasonable. No doubt the beggar was a thief hard run; and what with thy following up John Ruffin and his stopping at the *Bank* and gazing through the window, truly, Alexander, thy actions looked suspicious."

"A Blue Coat's a Blue Coat, Sir. Wha shot me dog? A Blue Coat. I love him nae and wad drink to him sae" (taking a glass from the table): "A Blue Coat— a weel paid, a weel fed, a weel clad fellow, hard to

find, when most needed" (glass turned off in pantomime).

"And *I*, Alexander, would drink to him thus"
(taking the glass): "Our Blue Coats—the Majesty of
the Law brought down to a fine executive point"
(glass turned off in pantomime).

"Aweel! I'll waste nae mair words on the fellow.
I cam in juist now wi' me crusty side foremost.
But me ither side and me fuller side and me better
side was truly pitifu' wi' thochts aboot auld John
Ruffin. In a' me spat wi' the fellow and the runnin'
up of passers-by, to hear, thar stood the puir mon a
gazin' in on his son and hearing naething of the
hubbub sae near him."

"These visits must be in secret as far as Thomas
is concerned. I am quite sure he knows nothing of
'em. He tells me he has made every effort to keep
his Father away from the *Bank*, or even learning its
location, lest he should recognize the meaning of the
golden balls."

"And where be Mr. Tammas?" asked Sandy looking round. "I hae na spak wi' him sin' oor Park
meeting."

"At the barber's, William informs me—to be back
presently. And I am thinking I need the barber's
hand, too"—stroking his chin. "Will thee wait till
I return?"

"Na, na. I'll juist speak the while wi' a crony
ower the way."

Scarcely had they left, when Thomas came in, and
while the watchman was speaking to him of his vis-

itors, a stranger, with valise in hand, who had been observing Thomas closely through the window, briskly entered.

"Mr. Dalguspin, Jr., I presume," said the stranger, saluting.

"No, Sir. My name is Ruffin. I'm employed in the Bank."

"The very identical person I should see," remarked the stranger, professionally and by species a Pen and Ink Agent—genus, Book Agent—who proceeded to exhibit his wares and to recommend them with all the volubility, assurance, and persistency of his class. "*My* name is Elba Kramer. Backwards, you observe, it spells *remarkable*, and I live up to my name; for I'm offering some really remarkable wares—exactly apropos of a Bank Clerk. You see, Sir, I'm a merchant on foot, and offer wares so excellent, that, for dear humanity's sake, I carry them to the public, waiting not for the public to come to me."

While rattling this off Kramer busies himself opening his valise and pack.

"I'm a Pen and Ink Merchant, Sir," he continued —"a responsible post, Sir; since the Pen, as known of all men, is mightier than the sword, and the Ink Pot—that 'sable well,' as the poet hath it, is the 'fount of fame or infamy.' "

If the Agent's volubility, so smooth and rapid, drew a smile from Thomas, the latter was further taken with what may be called his easy and gentlemanly impudence.

"Here are samples of my stock, Sir, varied and large," he went on, at the same time spreading upon the table a number of pens. The merits of each variety, manually exhibiting them one by one, he then descanted upon in the following Hudibrastic lines given with all the graces of elocution, to the great amusement of Thomas :

Pens of all shapes, shades, and sizes—
At the Fairs have swept the prizes'
Pens of every sort of metal—
Gold, silver, bismuth, steel, *et. al.*
Pens of high and low degree—
Pens with two points. Pens with three—
Bank Pens—Pens to mark up clothing—
Pens Commercial—Pens Engrossing.
Here are stub Pens, coarse and fine, Sir—
Beat creation in their line, Sir.
Here're Pens Oblique—yet Pens that we
'Gainst crooked writing guarantee.
These Falcon Pens ain't much on biting,
But, you bet, are death on writing.
This, the Pen styled Caligraphic.
This, *par excellans*, Elastic.
This barrel Pen I call a knave—
It carries *staff* instead of *stave.*
Here's the celebrated 'U' Pen.
Here's the lady's *billet doux* Pen.
Here are Pens with nibs of rubies—
Rarely bought but by boobies.
My Pens from morn to eve I cry up—
I cry my Pens, and never dry up—
I cry *good* Pens, best of their kind—
If any stick-frogs you should find—
If not the *Pens of Pens*, why, then, .
You may put me in the *Pen*,
With *Penny* loaf for daily dinner,
A *Penetrated, Penitential* sinner !

A hearty laugh from Thomas greeted the eloquent peroration, and the Agent then went on:

"But, my dear Sir, dropping the strains wherewith, on special occasions, I advertise my merchandise, allow me to bring to your attention one bright particular article. A real factor, Sir, in nineteenth century progress, is the English Steel Pen ; and this"—exhibiting the pen—"is the best of them all, the unapproached, the unapproachable *Compound Elastic.* Rolled in Sheffield, the steel was shaped, cut, hardened, tempered, ground, and slit in Birmingham, by that prince of makers whose initials you see stamped upon the shank, J. G.

"This pen, Sir, is worthy of a study. Its polished platina points hold the ink well and glide easily over the paper. Observe, too, this slight hollow just above the nibs, perceptible to a nice touch, the *tactus eruditus* (I've looked a little into Latin, Sir). It enhances the gradual flow of the sable fluid—a great point, Sir, I can positively assure you."— Thomas still greatly amused.

"Above all, you will please notice the manifold devices to promote elasticity. This puncture or aperture in which the central slit terminates, is located, you perceive, below the shoulder, thereby throwing the centre of elasticity between the shoulder and the nibs—another great point, Sir. In addition to the central slit, you see here two lateral, internal, longitudinal slits, with external cross crescent slits meeting them from the slopes. They all respond harmoniously to the gentlest finger pressure, ensuring an elasticity far superior to any product of the gray goose wing."—Thomas continues to be greatly amused.

"The elasticity of these Pens is a marvel, Sir. A gentlemen recently told me he was testing the spring of the nibs on his thumb nail. Something diverted attention a moment. When he looked for the Pen again, lo! it was gone—whether into the heavens above, or the earth beneath, God only knows. Inadvertently he had exerted a little too much pressure, and the Pen, rebounding, whizzed off, clear out of sight and search. It's a positive fact, Sir." —Thomas all in smiles.

"And I can tell you another interesting fact. The use of these Pens is distinctly beneficial to stiffened joints. There is such a thing, Sir, as sympathetic movement, as well as sympathetic suffering, and in using these Pens the peculiar sense of elastic play under digital pressure, coaxes on, throughout the organism a corresponding movement" (twisting about his body in illustration), "that gradually supples up stiffened joints in a manner *mirabile dictu!* An old rheumatic gentleman tells me he has obtained in this way singular relief, and that twenty-five cents' worth of these Pens will guarantee more solid satisfaction than any doctor's bill a yard long. It's *sympathy*, Sir, sympathy—as the young man said, when he kissed the young lady, on seeing the old folks a kissin' each other."

Here Thomas' smiles broke into a laugh, and Kramer deemed the moment opportune to solicit a purchase.

"Let me sell you this box, Sir? Contains one dozen. Costs twenty-five cents. Every Pen worth the money."

"No," replied Thomas. "I am compelled to decline."

"Allow me, then, the liberty to present you with a Pen. Use it and you'll buy, when I call upon you next week.—A stick, too, goes with it—a stick, Sir, worthy of the Pen. Light"—weighing stick on finger—"though overlong,' measuring from butt to point 7½ inches, and 7½ back again, making in all 15 inches. None of your Florida cedar, the common stick stuff. This cedar, Sir, grew on the heights of Lebanon—a stick, Sir, such as were used by those ancient ones out of Zebulon who 'handled the pen of the writer,' and, permit me to add, becomes the hand of so worthy a looking young man as yourself."

"I thank you," said Thomas, taking the pen and staff with a highly amused countenance.

"Now let me show you, Sir, specimens of my Ink."

Kramer dives into his pocket—feels for something —then stops and looks surprised.

"By the Styx! I'm in a fix! I've lost or mislaid the key to the Ink compartment. Will you please lend me your bunch, Mr. Ruffin? I may find a key to suit."

"Certainly," Thomas replied, handing his bunch of keys.

"By the way, Mr. Ruffin, here are some remarkable blotters," observed Kramer, as he drew from the valise several highly ornamented blotters, and, having felt them over rapidly, put two aside.

"They don't blot my reputation, Sir. Into their substance is incorporated a chemical agent that gives them absorbent qualities altogether unique and remarkable—*so* remarkable, that, in using them, a caution becomes necessary. That is to say : A single slight stroke over the sheet"—making the motion— "suffices. Be on guard, Sir. No more than this, no continued pressure, or so much moisture will be absorbed from the fingers, as to dampen the paper through and run the ink. Upon my word, Sir, a gentleman who had been using these blotters without knowledge, found his finger ends becoming shrunken and shrivelled. He called in a doctor who gave a diagnosis of 'Idiopathic Terminal Atrophy, superinduced by some neurotic lesion of Central or Peripheral origin.' He treated the case and ran up a bill as long as the name. But the poor fellow, like the woman of Holy Writ who sought the M. D.. rather grew worse Fortunately, *I* came along, and put a termination to the Terminal Atrophy, as well as the interminable bill, by showing him how to use the blotters."—Smiles from Thomas are again in order.

"Why, my dear Sir, so soft are they and so thick, that I can give you an exact impression of this key. Let me see."

He selects a key from the bunch and presses it in various ways on one of the blotters he had put aside. Then, holding it up, remarks :

"That's not so good. Let me try it on this."

He now presses the key on the other blotter put aside, and, scrutinizing it, remarks :

"Ah! this is better—a perfect impression, Sir"—showing it to Thomas.

"I find no key to suit"—trying the bunch on the ink compartment, and then returning it to Thomas. "However, I shall be pleased to leave with you to-morrow a bottle of my peerless 'Stygian Writing Fluid.'

"Glad to have met you, Sir"—as he speaks replacing into the valise his things, and with them the blotter on which he had last impressed the key—"hope we may meet again, and thank you very kindly for your polite attention."

It was Thomas Ruffin's first experience with a high class peripatetic vendor, and, as Kramer turned to leave, his eye followed him with a sentiment of wonder, that one of such address and humor should not be above Pen and Ink Peddling.

The "crony ower the way" being out, in a few moments Sandy Johnson was back, to await at the *Bank* Thomas Ruffin's return. Seeing through the window that Thomas had company, he remained outside. Naturally enough he was observant of the stranger; and directly had occasion to become an aroused spectator and watched him closely. The specific thing he was doing, he was unable to discover. But evidently he must be doing something or explaining something of more than ordinary interest, he thought, so energetic was his manner and so attentive and amused did Thomas seem to be; and when he saw he was about to leave, Sandy stepped to the door-way and fixed upon him his keen Scotch eyes as he passed. Kramer noticed the scrutiny and made an evident effort to avoid it. Sandy thought this suspicious and followed the man, who, seeing he was shadowed, mended his pace, and in the darkness soon became lost to Sandy, the condition of whose ulcered right leg was still an impediment to unusual exertion. Near the *Bank*, on his return, he came up with Friend Peale, and they entered together. Salutations over, Friend Peale's attention happened at the moment to be caught by the color of the blotters on ths table—so trivial is the circumstance that ofttimes leads up to the gravest results—and he remarked casually:

"Why, Thomas, thee has fancy blotters!"

"A peddler who has just gone, left 'em for trial, as being of superior quality."

"Hey! hey! And what does this mean?" observed Friend Peale, and in a tone of surprise; for, in running his fingers over the blotters, he noticed that one was damp, and he had taken it up and was examining it. "The blotter is damp! Strange it should be damp, Thomas!—And what do I see on it?" he added, as he scrutinized the blotter more closely. "Bless my eyes! if it isn't the impression of a key!" he exclaimed with voice and look that startled his hearers; for Friend Peale remembered having recently seen a newspaper account of an attempted bank robbery by means of a key made from impressions on a dampened blotter.

"Yes—so it is, Sir. And what of that? The peddler said he had lost or mislaid the key to a compartment in his valise, and asked for my bunch, hoping to find one to fit; and——"

"And thee lent him thy keys?" asked Friend Peale, energetically breaking in.

"Yes, I did—and it was neighborly, not serious, I hope," replied Thomas, wondering at Friend Peale's manner. "And he had these blotters on the table, and made an impression of a key, to show their quality."

"What key is this, Thomas, whose impression I see?"

"The key to the rear door of the *Bank.*—But why, Friend Peale, are you so serious?"

"Did he carry off an impression?" Friend Peale asked under evident excitement, and not heeding Thomas' question.

"I do not know, Sir. He did, if there be not two. He made two.—But what can be the matter?"

"There's but *one* impression here, Thomas," said the Quaker, still unheeding the question addressed to him, and eagerly examining the blotters.

"Then the peddler has the other."

"Then he's a *Burglar*, Thomas Ruffin, with designs on the *Bank!*" exclaimed Friend Peale.

"A Burglar!" cried out the astounded Thomas.

"Yea, I tell thee he's a Burglar! The moistened and prepared blotter—the selection of the key—the carrying off an impression—make a clear case. The papers give an account of a recent attempt of this kind. It's the way of these villians—a trick to get a model. Here's the entire key in all its parts— point, pin, collar, bit, ward, rabbit, shaft, and bow! The entire key!"

"What am I to do?" asked Thomas with profound concern upon his countenance.

"There's but one thing thee *can* do. Inform Dalguspin at once, that he may take measures to thwart the attempt. And I fear, my son, he'll make a point against thee for allowing thyself to be taken in.—If thee could identify the man"—Friend Peale observed, after a momentary pause of reflection—"the affair might make a turn in thy favor.—But that would be difficult"—reflecting again—"seeing he was in disguise, undoubtedly.—Is there aught about this peddler" (he added) "in those parts undisguisable—as eyes, or mouth, or teeth—by which thee would know him?"

Thomas paused upon the reply—:

"I can't say there is."

"But I *can*," spoke up Sandy, who had been a deeply interested listener; and all eyes were turned upon the Scotchman.

"I passed the chap"—he went on—"at the door, and because he seemed to shun me ee, I spied him the closer. Somethin' anent the mon I hed seen afore, and I hae been puzzlin' me noddle to place him. It's a' clear noo. I hae been too aft at Dalguspin's to boot him, na to ken his footman, Robbie Small, through a' his disguises."

"Art sure, Alexander?" eagerly asked Friend Peale.

"Sure's Land's eend is na John O'Groats. His cast and play o' countenance I hae watchit too aft to be deceived. I wad swear to the ideentity."

"And I can bring corroborating evidence," chimed

in the Quaker exultingly; "for all thee says does well agree with what Dalguspin has told me, that his footman proves a Wild West dare-devil, in respect to whom he has entertained most serious fears. And what's another weighty circumstance, that the fellow intends this Friday next to leave for England—an information, that, with most evident satisfaction, as relieved from fears, Dalguspin gave me even yesterday. Yea! yea! I see it all. This is Wednesday eve. To-morrow the key's to be made. To-morrow night the robbery. Next day the robber is to run. That's his scheme."

"But we can put a spoke in his wheel and beat him a' round and clear through," surmised Sandy.

"Yea, we can and will, and all by ourselves. Through Thursday's night we'll watch the *Bank's* rear door, with officer of the law, and nab the fellow in the very act. That's *our* scheme. Then, before Dalguspin we'll honor thee, my son"—with a rallying pat on Thomas' back—"as worthy of most praise in the affair, and thee will play winning cards for his favor."

"Thar's a 'pull' upon a 'puller,' by the soul of St. Crispin," jubilantly observed Sandy.

"Yea, yea—thee's in luck, Thomas, after all. If evil there must be, good it is for evil to yield advantages to honest men. And now for the office of the Magistrate, to swear out a warrant against the footman—this night, this hour, this very minute; for scarce could thee do so to-morrow without risk of revealing too early *our* scheme to Dalguspin."

CHAPTER XVIII.

"What a fine, delightful, rainy day, Sir!"

The reader is informed that this sentiment did not proceed from the gum-shoe man, but from Miss Kitty —a sentiment expressive of a banter to John Ruffin, as well as the actual impression of The Home's hearty Housekeeper.

Yes—let it rain in the interests of husbandry and trade; for isn't the rain-fall lessening—the level of the lakes, lowering—the volume of the rivers, shrinking—and drouths becoming, more and more, a serious national concern?

Yes—let it rain and lay the dust, the city man should say with an emphasis; for is not this dirty dust, made so rapidly, and whirled along the draught-creating streets so readily, and into one's eyes so annoyingly, a most pronounced nuisance? Then look at the scientific side. This horrid dust, with a percentage of output, originally, from diseased lungs and noses and other foul sources, that has become dessicated, then triturated beneath wheels and the heels of men and beasts innumerable, may involve in its breathing — barring the aesthetics of the thing — the deadly bacillus. And even though the bacillus that would kill us might be done up right by the guardian leucocyte, the lifting of this pulverised and irritating filth and settling thereof upon the delicate schneiderian membrane, originates, perhaps, 60 per cent. of the colds, as the ordinary cold lies at the root of, perhaps, 60 per cent. of the one hundred strictly differentiated diseases to which human flesh is heir. Let it rain, therefore, and lay the dust, the dust, the dust.

It is scarcely probable, however, that Miss Kitty took into her calculation the bacteriological consideration. No doubt but that she was one of those persons not uncommonly met with, whose nervous system is so poised as to experience a depression at the approach of a storm, with a rebound when the storm breaks—the rebound not a negative quality merely, but the outcome of certain atmospheric conditions of an exhilarating character accompanying falling weather. At all events, to cut the matter short, the simple fact was, that Miss Kitty felt better on rainy days, though her governmental cares and "quandaries" were increased from the inmates' being kept within doors, and the muddy shoes of those who must go out *would* defile her well scrubbed floors. Hence her sentiment and rally to John Ruffin this early Thursday morning :

"What a fine, delightful rainy day, Sir !"

It was the day following the events related in the

last chapter. Miss Kitty affirmed her weather view, seeing that John Ruffin, the evening before, had expressed the hope the day would be open, as he wished to make a visit, and had asked Miss Kitty's opinion touching the prospects. She allowed her bones and joints to return the answer—one far more reliable than the prophets of the street-corner or goods-box could give, and which, within limits, rivalled in accuracy the weather-bureau forecasts of these more scientific latter days. With a storm brewing, Miss Kitty's answer was unfavorable, and the state of the weather next morning justified her prediction. However, she now expressed the hope that the clouds might break away by the afternoon, in time for the visit.

To John Ruffin it was a notable day, this particular Thursday. It was the natal day of his first born, the son he had lost, and on whom his early hopes had been set. Among his treasure remnants he had two beautiful miniatures of his sons, oval in form and richly mounted in solid gold; and it had been his custom, ever since this elder son had been given up for lost, to take his miniature from its casket, *in memoriam*, once every year, on his birthday. With the rolling on of time the commemoration grew in interest, and finally took the form of a somewhat solemn ceremonial. At the hour when his son first saw the light, John Ruffin would enter his room (which had been duly prepared), bring forth the miniature from its casket and covering, and commune with the departed. Nor did he forget the

commemoration, though it could not be done so formally, in these latter days of affliction. The devoted hour was between 7 and 8 in the evening, and
the thoughts connected therewith belong rather to
the chapter following, which opens at the 7th hour.

Another consideration, for the moment making
this day special, was John Ruffin's resolution to see
Dalguspin touching Thomas. For days and weeks
the thought had been pressing. Already had he set
apart this day for the visit, and when the morning
came he was confirmed in the resolution by Thomas'
failure to bid him good-night the evening before (an
unusual occurrence), or to send an explaining word.
It was all due, he was persuaded, to being so over-
worked, and he would give the *Banker* his mind.

The fact was that Thomas *had* called. But it was
very late. The candle at the window had burned
out, his Father evidently was asleep, and he
would not disturb him. There had been difficulty
in securing the services of a magistrate, to issue the
warrant against Robert. The first one sought was
at the theatre. The second, at a feast. The third,
indeed, at home—but there were preliminaries; and
by the time the paper had been executed, and Friend
Peale and Sandy and Thomas had fully talked over
at the *Bank* the scheme of capture and arranged details, the lateness of the hour prevented John Ruffin's
getting the usual good-night.

Thomas Ruffin's appearance and manner at this
time really were calculated to breed concern in one
less anxious for his welfare than his Father. The

latter was in error touching the main cause. It was
not now, or not so much, overwork. Since the in-
ception of the scheme of robbery, with involvement
of young Ruffin, Dalguspin had turned artfully towards his clerk. It was a feature of his malignant
character to approach the victim with a velvet tread.
The half dollar was added to the weekly wage, as
has been stated. Nor was Thomas kept now quite
so long at the desk, the *Banker* himself sharing what
had been his undivided work. And Black Isaac's
demeanor, too, was less churlish—nay, even kindly.
The raised spirits growing out of the prospect of deliverance through the robbery, naturally affected his
general behavior; and as to Thomas Ruffin, in particular, he realised it was the proper thing to allay,
or try to allay, the suspicion with which his keen
eye saw he was regarded by him. He was not effus-
ive, as at the first. That would have defeated his object very probably, he felt; for he had learned to
recognize a greater power of discernment in his clerk,
than in the beginning he had given him credit for.
But there was a general let up, and Black Isaac had
reason to be satisfied with the effect of the manoeuvre.
Thomas protested to his Father that the situation at
the *Bank* had improved; but the latter would not
listen to it, in view of what was before his very eyes,
that Thomas daily was falling back; and when
Thomas drew attention to his getting to The
Home earlier, John Ruffin felt that his son strained
and rushed through the days, just to make it seem
to him he was less burdened.

That Thomas Ruffin was now unhappy and droop-
ing, was evident, and for the cause we need not go far.
There is a sin (it has been observed), as common as it is
secretive—the first to be seen in our fellows, the last
to discover in ourselves—whose peculiar deformity
lies in its banquetting upon the misfortunes of
others, fattening on their follies and falls—a sin,
that condemns one to be soured in his associates,
unless they are inferior, without gifts or attractions
—and which, many a time and, oft, involves the
blackest little lies, as when, under the pressure of
our social customs, we are constrained to congratu-
late another on some godsend, whose happening
really grates upon us; or commiserate him for some
misfortune, with which secretly we are very well
pleased—the odious sin of Envy ! It has its grada-
tions, in its extremes involving hate, rancor, revenge.

Now, if Thomas Ruffin morally was much above
the average young man, still he was flesh and blood,
he was human; and when, a certain evening, he
might have been seen sitting communing in his garret room, eyes half closed, upper eylids drawn down
over the eyeballs, eyebrows knitted, expression deep
and intense, the physiognomist would have read in
that countenance not only a sentiment of envy, but
that the object of envy was mentally there before him.
Undoubtedly, that object was the florist. We will
not say he really hated the florist. But we run little
risk touching violation of the truth in declaring that
his sentiments towards him were not of the pleasing
variety. Every word Sister Jessica had either spoken

or written respecting the florist, he had weighed most carefully. This florist was "our friend"—*ours*, Amy's, as well as the Sister's, and Amy's especially, he must be, of course, he thought. Then, he fur-. nished gratuitously the lovely flowers, because he was "*interested*" in their purposes. Why interested? He had never seen his Father. If he knew aught concerning him, it could have been only through Amy. And must not any interest he might have in the object these flowers were meant to serve, spring from a personal interest in Amy?—Then he had a decidedly disagreeable sense of the Sister's having spoken of the florist as a *young* man. And further, since the interview with Sister Jessica, he had been diligent in inquiries respecting the general complexion of florists, and disabused of an impression. He had discovered that the florist, in large cities, may be a representative of wealth, character, and position; and if this particular florist was not a man of means at least, how could he afford, he considered, to give away so many rare and costly blooms, even in the line of roses alone?

Out of all this grew a picture, from which Thomas Ruffin was unable, as though dominated by a spell, to withdraw his gaze, yet oppressing him with heavy, wearing thoughts. On this certain evening, when we have attempted a photograph, a Moss Rose was in his button-hole. It caught his eye. He looked down upon it a moment—dallied with it a moment— then drew it forth, and tossed it upon the table. Had it become too faded, to be worn? Or did it now have other associations?

To preserve consistency with that surrender of a hope he had made so magnanimously, he deceived himself in the reflection, that all this heart-ache was what a relative naturally should feel. His anxieties were all on account of his *Cousin.* The florist might not be a man of character, or such a character as was worthy of Amy, and she might be throwing herself away. And Thomas would worry and torment himself almost to death—till, in a moment of clearer reason, the vision would perish, and the florist, the mist about him dissolving, would stand out simply a friend with a kindly heart.

But visions after this kind would be reforming and harassing him constantly. Unhappy days they were. He was sore distressed and could not see the end, and the effect was palpably visible. The rapid fluctuations in his mind, now despairing, now hoping (for it was all a delusion, his giving up Amy)—so perplexed and tossed about continually in contemplating the mystery and the possibilities of her seclusion —the total absence of calm, settled thought—and, not least, being cut off, by the pledge he had given, from counsellor and comforter—all this brought down upon him, indeed, a heavy hand. If naturally frail in appearance, the axe and maul of early days had given him a fairly sturdy frame. But the limit of endurance had been passed. He was failing and he felt it. His appetite was gone. The restored half dollar to the weekly wage, with the liberal pay Sister Jessica had given his Father recently for some small jobs, enabled him to provide for himself somewhat better. Still, he could not eat, so to speak—neither could he sleep. His work·languished—now a miserable drudgery. Of diminished volume, it yet used him up. He bought an Elixir which he saw advertised as covering his case—but without avail. In his garret room he was often in tears. Before his Father it was impossible to assume his usual degree of cheerfulness. Scarce could he refrain, time and again, from breaking down and disclosing all, at the sight of his Father's distress. True, within the past twenty-four hours a change had occurred. The discovery of the scheme to rob the Bank, with the leading part he bore therein, was sufficient of itself to stimulate him to a high degree. Then, as outcomes, he would have a "pull" upon Dalguspin. His good will he would firmly secure. The apprehensions of foul play that had been so disturbing, would all be removed. His pay would be increased very probably. And certainly, his relations with the *Banker* would be smoother at the least to the end of the term. All this made a current of fresh quickening thought, and so Thomas was roused up, and felt a great deal better, and looked a great deal brighter. But his Father had not seen him since this change. As for him, he was in a tumult of fears for his son —felt it was all attributable to over-work—and had settled on this day to see the *Banker*.

From remarks dropped by Thomas, John Ruffin had learnt the street and number of Black Isaac's residence, as well as the time when he would be most likely at home. He had learnt, in addition, there was a 'Bus line (a walk would have been too much for him) but a square off, that ran on this street; and he had put by pennies enough to pay fare for himself and Sabina, whom he would have to accompany him.

Soon after midday the rain ceased. By 4 o'clock the clouds had broken fairly, and John Ruffin, with Sabina, started forth, ostensibly for a walk. He now informed the servant-woman of his purpose, and she, instructed to respect his wishes scrupulously, made no objection—though never had she gone out with him near so far.

The 'Bus soon filled with a typical lot. John Ruffin happened to be seated not at all to his liking; for a frousy old German woman, just from the green-grocer's, had squeezed in beside him, her basket heavily topped with onions, now directly under John Ruffin's nose and towards which ancient and wholesome tuber he cherished a repugnance as marked as that of John Randolph for the wild varieties and their sturdy fecundity—whereof, it is said, he once uttered the absolutely exhaustive malediction, that they should be cut up by the roots, burned, and exposed to hard frost.

There was pressure, also, on Sabina's side, from a very fat man, who, either to compress and ostensibly diminish his avoirdupois, or to support it, was so strapped up in small tights and close-fitting clothes generally, that an unusual amount of blood and tissue, even for *him*, had been pressed up into his neck and face. He seemed, too, to be as uncom-

fortably located as John Ruffin. The cause apparently was in Sabina—whether due to the negro (as
such), or to her squint, or something else about her,
we are unable to inform the reader. More than
once he looked round at Sabina in an annoyed sort
of way; and Sabina, more than once, cut an eye back
at him, as if agog to bestow a guffaw upon his very
stuffy, ill-at-ease aspect.

Having had occasion to notice two of the occupants, we cannot be so impolite as not to glance,
at least, at the others.—Just over against John
Ruffin was a fashionably dressed young lady attended by two lights of swelldom, one on each side,
dudes and dudine—*she* sounding her vowels in the
broad style heard in the drawing-room of the 400,
and *they* looking sweet upon her with eyes giving no
promise of any message to men.—Across from the
fat man was a vulgar city woman, of the Brown
Jones and Robinson set, pointing out to her country
cousin the mansions of distinguished and wealthy
citizens, the public buildings, the monuments, and
other objects of interest, in voice and manner glib
and vain, as if she held a joint ownership in all she
described.—At the upper end of the 'Bus sat side
by side a country-man and a city-man, with phy-
siques characteristic of their respective localities—
the former a strapping, brown-skinned, hearty looking fellow—the latter showing short sight, narrow
chest, weedy legs, and flat feet.—And opposite these
a veritable wooden girl, with small head, long face,
fleshy saddle nose, far apart eyes, and a little mouth

with lips ajar. She sat at the extremity of the seat, in the angle formed by the side and front of the 'Bus, and so still and expressionless, that, but for the wink, she might have been taken for a dummy, belonging to a passenger.

The 'Bus at length reached the street number of destination, the driver was signalled, and John Ruffin and Sabina alighted. The latter was to remain at the street-corner until John Ruffin came out.

A maid-servant answered the bell. Robert, it appears, was absent. Probably he was at the rendezvous—the dim little room on a back street near the *Bank* (the "cracksman" had rented it for the occasion), where the disguises were kept and the conferences conducted. Or, may be, he was off meditating the critical part he was about to play. Already had he received from the "cracksman" the roll of bills which by 8 p. m. he was to endeavor to secrete between the mattresses of John Ruffin's bed, and on the success of which attempt the consummation of the scheme that night wholly depended. It was a much more difficult job than that connected with the key. Here he had made and spread a net beforehand, and Thomas Ruffin walked right into it. There was nothing prearranged. touching the present job. He had been instructed that John Ruffin was deaf, and "off" somewhat. But how far "off?" In the course of his extended experiences he had discovered these "off" characters are sometimes very suspicious, and even sharp. He had settled upon "Grim," as the name to bear—in his disguise representing a workman—and bringing a chair to be bottomed. For the rest he trusted to mother wit and the chapter of accidents. Noals by this time felt confident of his man's trustworthiness; but, to be doubly sure, and to gratify Dalguspin, besides, he had given him this second job, instead of undertaking it himself. The first had been conducted so cleverly and with such complete success, that he entertained no doubt whatever, that Bob would bamboozle John Ruffin and clear the way for their scheme to-night, and hence had an appointment to meet Dalguspin at this very hour for finally talking over the whole matter and completing some minor details.

John Ruffin was received by the maid-servant. Her announcement of "a strange old man," instead of Noals, who was expected eagerly, was a dual annoyance to Black Isaac. But the visitor was in the drawing-room, and all Black Isaac could do (as he resolved to do), was to get rid of him as speedily as possible.

"Who are you, Sir?" he demanded in a tone of irritation and insolence, as he entered the room and saw before him a strange old man, indeed, yet evidently with gentlemanly indications.

"Tammie's Father," quietly replied John Ruffin, apparently not at all disconcerted by Black Isaac's blustering manner.

"And who's Tammie, pray?"

"Don't you know, Tammie?"

"Tell me what you want quick, or get out of here."

"Why, Tammie's your clerk," said John Ruffin, completely at ease.

Black Isaac regarded his visitor a moment. Never before had he laid eyes on John Ruffin. The visitor was something more than he had expected to find. Certain relations existed. Perhaps his manner was a trifle less rude—still, he spoke roughly:

"Well, what's wanting?—hurry up."

"Work's killing Tammie."

"And so you think I'm a brute," observed Black Isaac, resuming all his swagger.

"I'm thinking Tammie may have to leave," was the self-composed rejoinder, though, had Black Isaac looked more narrowly, he might have seen a light beginning to kindle in John Ruffin's eyes.

"The fellow leave me! Teaching him the business, too! Pish! Thankless puppy!"

The last expression having been uttered in a lowered tone of scorn, John Ruffin's dull ears did not catch it, or unquestionably there would have been a scene. He was a type of the Southern gentleman under the old regime—generous, hospitable, courtly, high-strung men, and too proud not to be brave. Withal, John Ruffin personally was no wise lacking in native manliness. If but a wreck of his former self, the old spirit was not dead. Where Thomas was involved, he was ready to dare Beelzebub himself; and in his state of irritation against the *Banker* undoubtedly would have resented then and there his contemptuous remark, had he heard it. Though he failed to catch the insult, it happened that just as Black Isaac finished speaking an insect of some kind, as John Ruflin supposed, pitched on his right cheek and bit. It may have been a neuralgic shoot. At all events, there was a sharp sudden pain, and the old gentleman, with a jerk, raised his right hand, which carried a small light cane, to rub the part affected. As he did so, the cane, borne aloft, shook ominously near Black Isaac's head, who, as cowardly as he was cruel, and supposing his visitor was resenting "puppy," dodged and sprang away.

"Something stung my face, and I raised my hand to rub it," observed John Ruffin. "Don't be afraid" —patronizingly taken, though not so meant.

"Afraid!" went off the *Banker*, chagrined at the demonstration he had made, and advancing as he spoke. "Afraid of *you*, you old simpleton!"

The cane-hand and cane suddenly went up again, and Black Isaac again dodged back from the blows, as John Ruffin remarked :

"There's the sting again"—rubbing the cheek.

"*Afraid*, Sir!" thundered Dalguspin, doubly mortified, and again advancing his step in a menacing manner. "If you dare hint again the possibility, I'll ring up the servants and have you put out, Sir!"

"*You're* not afraid, but *I* am for Tammie," replied John Ruffin, quite at ease, but visibly rousing. "You've promised and promised less time and more pay, and he has been working on, waiting and waiting——"

"And so you come here to call me a liar," broke in Black Isaac in a small fury.

"No. But if you say you can't do better, Tammie leaves right away. He has promised me to leave any time I say so. And he has got a place, he tells me, any time he chooses to take it. He's worried to death, and getting poorer every day; and I say, if you say you can't do better, I'll go right down to the *Bank* this very minute and take him home— *that's* what I'll do."

Black Isaac recognized the absolute necessity to tack about. He thought John Ruffin alluded to his son's supposed hold upon him in the matter of Cameron's note. Be that as it may, there must not be any disturbance for the next few hours at least. Thomas Ruffin must be at the *Bank* to-night as usual. This was enough, even if he had not now marked the fire blazing up in his visitor's eyes. He, therefore, replied, in a manner the most suave at his command :

"I beg you, Mr. Ruffin, to pardon my rudeness. It's my way, Mr. Ruffin. I am free to own my injustice to your son. He's a faithful fellow; and I give you my solemn word, Sir, to make good within a week all I promised, fair time and better pay."

Overjoyed, the old gentleman shambled up— seized Dalguspin's right hand in both of his—shook and shook it most vigorously—and the little cane, again borne aloft, vibrated viciously near Dalguspin's head, which kept dodging about, as John Ruffin cried out his warm acknowledgements :

"O thank you! thank you! thank you! Mr.—

Mr.—" (for the moment unable to recall the name)
"Mr. Gusdalpin"—and then giving it a twist.

With the firm grasp of gratitude John Ruffin kept
up the handshaking and incidental caning in a manner so energetic that Black Isaac was constrained to
expostulate, and that, too—under the stress of the
physical agitation—in a species of quavers, all the
while busy dodging away from the blows :

"I-I've n-no objection to h-hand s-shake, Mr.
R-Ruffin, b-but t-there's n-no n-use s-s-shaking
c-c-cane, Sir."

The sound of the door- bell caused John Ruffin to
release Black Isaac's hand—which he did with a
rousing

"Thank you, Sir !"

"There's a visitor, Mr. Ruffin, whom at this hour
I am engaged to see by special appointment. I must
now ask you to please excuse me."

Bidding the *Banker* good evening, John Ruffin
turned and took a step towards the door. Then
turned towards Black Isaac, face beaming :

"And you're going to promote Tammie ?"

"Certain as the continuance of the *Bank* itself,
Mr. Ruffin. He ! he ! he !"

"God bless——"

The door-bell rang again cutting off the sentence,
and John Ruffin turned and took another step towards the door. Then turned about :

"And within a week, *Mr. Banker ?*"

"Within a week, Mr. Ruffin, if the *Bank* doesn't
break. He ! he ! he !"

"God bless you a ,thou—"

But before he could complete the numerical expression of the blessing, the meddlesome bell rang
again, and John Ruffin, turning, made yet another
step towards the door. Then turned :

"Tammie prays for—"

He was doomed, however, to be beaten by the bell;
for it's ring again broke in, and John Ruffin, turning hastily, took yet another step still towards the
door. Then turned about, and was in the act of
speaking, when the bell, responding to a vicious
pull, rang violently, and the old gentleman, giving
it up, *smacked* his hand to Dalguspin and precipi-
tately shambled out, as the tardy maid ushered in
the impatient Noals.

He found Sabina at the corner, and they went
back as they had come. The visit had been a
complete success. He had glad tidings for his son.
Should he tell him to-night, or to-morrow ? He would
wait and let him know it all just after breakfast, so
that he could go off to his work full of good fresh
morning news. John Ruffin felt and looked brightened up. And nature had brightened up, too, as if
in sympathy; for the day, that had opened with a
down-pour, was closing magnificently. The sun had
just set; but the long narrow stretches of stationary
curl cloud, focussed at the point of going down,
were bathed in his beams, and spread out, over the
entire western heavens, a great fan of brilliant soft

light, ribbed with converging bands of crimson effulgence. A gorgeous American sunset.

They reached The Home in good time. Sister Jessica had called, and, as usual, had left some beautiful flowers.

CHAPTER XIX.

The best laid schemes o' mice and men
Gang aft a-gley.—*Burns*.

It was nigh the same hour, at which John Ruffin returned to The Home, as just related, that Friend Peale and Sandy Johnson called at the *Bank* for a final conference with Thomas touching the watch for the burglar. They all thought it out of question to suppose the robbery would be attempted until at least towards midnight. It was argued that Robert Small must have a confederate, since, in case the Watchman could not be enticed off, it would be necessary to overpower him—that one alone could not do this without great hazard of detection—and that such an expert as Small had shown himself to be, would not run the risk of discovery from a minimum of disturbance, not to speak of observation, until the streets, comparatively at least, should be deserted. This made the matter clear enough, without considering that Small's domestic duties at Dalguspin's did not close until after 11; and that from that hour, with four of them on guard—including the special officer detailed—they could put under close surveillance the front door, as well as the rear.

Thomas informed them that extra work would detain him till at least near 10 o'clock; and then he must go to The Home to speak to his Father—who had not seen or heard from him for two days, and was most anxious, he knew, and would keep supper waiting till midnight—and to let him know, moreover, it was necessary he should remain away at the *Bank* all this night. They parted with the understanding to call again at the half hour to 10.

By that hour Thomas had hastened through his work. Friend Peale and Sandy Johnson returned on time. William, the watchman, Thomas informed them, had been sent for by Dalguspin, but would be back anon. A few moments later Thomas, through the window, espied the special officer who was to meet them on the corner at 10, and went out, with Friend Peale and Sandy, to speak with him. As they were engaged together talking and looking over the warrant under the lamp's light, thirty feet perhaps from the door (to avoid possible suspicion the conference was outside), William—as supposed to be—was seen to enter the *Bank;* and Thomas, calling to him presently from the doorway, that he was going to The Home, to return within an hour, started off with Friend Peale and Sandy, who, having ample time to spare, proposed to accompany him—the officer being instructed, out of abundant caution, to have an eye meanwhile upon the rear door.

In behalf of morality generally, and of the Ruffins individually, it is matter for regret—the degree whereof must tally with the interest this narrative may have raised—that we are compelled to record the absolute failure of the scheme to capture the burglar. It was well laid, and the Peale party were sanguine as of a sure thing, but, like the fore-sight of the famous "mousie" whose nest and nest-lings were disrupted by the cruel coulter, the affair went "a-gley." To write it down otherwise is not possible. True, the story-teller, ordinarily, is a despot over his characters, holding the absolute power of life and death, and his imaginative events, within the limits of probability, he may draw and marshal as he likes. But this narrative has a broad basis of fact, and it must advance on the lines that have been laid.

Nor do such miscarriages involve an arraignment of Providence. Taking the mass of men and con-sidering the course of events, we see that virtue is so often rewarded and vice punished, as to demon-strate that the Deity is the patron of the one, and enemy of the other. And touching the individual, could we follow out his entire career into and through the Beyond, assuredly we would perceive absolute justice to be his portion. But, restricting the eye to his span of life here, it is no less true, that Providence does not always visibly aid the right.

To resume the thread of our story: Friend Peale and Sandy Johnson made a liesurely return, being full of talk touching the capture—among other cir-cumstances, Sandy congratulating himself upon the prospect of saving his "wee pile," he having made

recently some small deposits with Dalguspin; yet, for
no further reason, it may be added, than to show his
animus towards "Mr. Tammas" and have business
occasions to chat him.   Meanwhile, Noals had done
his work effectually.   In William's rig he entered
the *Bank's* front door at a quarter to 10.   With keys
to safe and drawers in hand and the *Bank* already
plucked, five minutes sufficed to leave a burglar's
marks.   Robert Small was on guard for him outside,
and signaling the coast clear, the special officer
being at the *Bank's* rear, Noals passed out as he had
gone in, and, handing Robert his money, pressed on
him to speed to the rendezvous, doff disguise, and
with all diligence make for home, and let the
watchman see him there on duty, if possible.   In
every detail it was a complete success.   Robert was
on time to show William out, to whose inquiry, as
he left the door, he gave the hour as being twenty
minutes past 10.

Some thirty or forty minutes had passed with
Friend Peale and Sandy, when, having reached
the point on the street opposite the *Bank*, they
were thunderstruck by the watchman's rushing forth
(accompanied by a patrolman, whom, happening to
be near the door, William had hurried in to witness
the state of affairs) with resounding cries of

"Thieves! Robbers!"

They rushed over and saw in truth that the
Bank had been robbed.   To the Quaker's inquiry of the watchman, why he had not raised
the hue and cry sooner, William replied that

he had reached the Bank just a moment before.
And when Friend Peale declared that himself, with
Sandy Johnson and Thomas Ruffin, could witness
his having entered the Bank at a quarter to 10, and
that Thomas Ruffin saw him in charge and bespoke
him before he left for his Father's at The Home,
William swore with a great oath it was not so—that
if any one had entered the Bank at that hour, it
must have been the robber—that he was then at the
Banker's house—and that Robert Small, who showed him out and gave him the time, could swear he
left the door at *twenty minutes past ten.*

By this time, though late, a number of persons
had been drawn together by the outcry and report—
among them Noals (known to be a close friend to the
Banker), who said Dalguspin must be informed at
once, and then they would go to The Home, to see
what light the clerk might be able to throw upon
such a piece of devilment—that under all the circumstances, as they had just heard them, *he* ought to
know something about it. Off, therefore, he started,
accompanied by the Watchman, leaving the patrolman to guard the *Bank.*

As for Friend Peale and Sandy, they were in
a maze, not knowing what to think or say. A
darkness suddenly had come down. The former
observed to Sandy, that his swans certainly had
proven geese, touching the supposed identity of
Robert Small and the robber—that the indirect and
unwitting testimony, involved in the Watchman's
statement was conclusive. Sandy made no reply—

only shook his head. As for the hint thrown out by
Noals, that Thomas Ruffin might be implicated, they
tossed it to the winds. True, they had noticed, it
was remarked by each, that Thomas recently had
been in distress, brooding over some trouble and
losing spirit, and had declined, too, friendly over-
tures inviting confidence. But that he should have
had any hand in this matter, was not to be thought
of—unless, under some great pressure (whereof they
were ignorant) and temporary derangement and irre-
sponsibility, he possibly might have been inveigled.
They would await the coming of Dalguspin and party,
and accompany them to The Home. The mere breaking in upon John Ruffin at this late hour would be
serious. And then with such an inquiry, not to mention charge, touching his son! There might be
circumstances of the gravest kind and vitally needing their aid.

The reader must now be transferred to John
Ruffin's room, to learn the course of events there
subsequent to his return from the visit to the
Banker.

Aware of the special character of the day, Miss
Kitty had taken extra pains in providing his supper,
and Sabina had smuggled on the plates an unusually
goodly portion for "Mr. Thomas." The table was
set for two, but John Ruffin refrained from eating.
What was keeping Thomas? He had thought he
surely would be in early this evening. He had not
seen him since Tuesday, and then for a moment,
when he hurried to The Home, to say "good-night."

Should he go to the *Bank?* But then he might miss
his son on the way, and the latter would be alarmed at
finding him out. No, he had better wait. If any thing
had happened, some word would have been sent.
And perhaps it was too early for him. He would
come presently. So the dishes were placed in waiting near the fire. And then all at once John Ruffin
began to bestir himself as it came upon him, that he
was about to forget the day and the hour.

Opening a drawer, he took therefrom a casket. It
contained the miniature of his first-born. A beautiful
specimen of art it was, richly set in solid gold, and
painted when his son was a little boy. He opened
the casket, removed the covering from its contents,
and placed the miniature upon the table. Next, he
knelt reverently in devotion—rose and seated himself at the table—and, taking the miniature of this
lost son, dwelt upon it.—What heart-wrung thoughts
such pictures of childhood have called up in many a
parent under circumstances like those in which we
find this broken, sad-eyed man—picture of some
dear son, who went out never more to return! It
takes us back years and years, when he was a pure
child on our knee, before the world had touched
him. What hopes gathered around him then! In
what dreams did we forecast his career! If he grew
up wild and disappointing, he was our own and
dear to us still. Perhaps it was to break away from
those who had led him off, that he would go forth,
with high resolve to make his mark. How vividly
we recall that parting hour! What heart-ache lay

hidden beneath the smile put forward to encourage him! And how we strained and strained the eye to catch the last glimpse! And now he is lost to view! The great hard world has closed inexorably over him. Oh! what darkness then! What tears of bitterness!

And in process of time came another sinking hour, when the tardy news came, all too late to reach him, that he was about to be no more! Striving in vain against fate, too proud to return with such a record, he had gone down in the struggle far off from us, among strangers!

It was a current of feeling after this kind that found expression in the following soliloquy, as John Ruffin gazed upon the miniature:

"My first-born! The beginning of my strength! Lost! Lost!—'Tis his very image. How innocent and sweet he looks here, as a little child! I remember this little jacket he used to wear—and this ring upon his finger, I remember so well the day I put it on."

He pauses in tears.

"What a fine fellow he was, so bright and handsome! How tenderly I watched over him! What pride I took in him! How thankfully I thought of him as the staff and comfort in my old age!"

He pauses in meditation.

"But he grew wayward and roving and *would* go off. Ah-h! that day he left us, that bitter, bitter day! How well I recall it! I can't recollect what happens now, but I recollect that. 'Twas a sweet day in May, full of sunshine and warmth—so unlike my darkened wretched heart. A smile was on his face, and he spoke so hopefully of what he *meant* to do—poor fellow !"

Again he pauses in tears.

"He stood on deck waving adieu, and we stood straining our eyes till the boat rounded the river's bend; and as he became lost to view, it seemed as if some evil spirit had come down, and closed around him, and gathered him to itself, and parted him from me forever !".

John Ruffin breaks down completely, weeping aloud. Then dwells in silence on the miniature, and becomes more composed after his tears.

"At first he wrote often and in such high spirits. He had troubles, we heard, but *he* never spoke of them. By and bye letters came less and less frequent, and hope seemed to be going out. Then short hurried notes, far apart, saying only he was well. At last no letters, and we could hear nothing from others !"

He again pauses in tears, which end in an outburst of passionate grief :

"Is my boy dead, my first-born ? Or has evil come to him—has he gone down, low, low, low—and ashamed to write ? O God ! O God ! if he be living yet, give him back in my day of trouble, and let me see his face before I die !"

Touching this soliloquy we have to observe: John Ruffin spoke generally in a slow broken way from difficulty both in comprehending and in expressing ideas. If the above (well conceived and smoothly

uttered)—as well as other passages in this narrative
—should seem out of place in a daft man, let it be
remembered, that John Ruffin's intelligence, while
weakened, had not been destroyed. There were,
moreover, mental ebbings and flowings—at times a
combination, a strange combination, of shrewdness
and the baldest simplicity. Again, his general condition really was improving; and his mind always
acted better, too, when turned strongly, as here,
upon some definite point of interest in the far away
past. And in regard to this particular soliloquy, it
was in no small degree mechanical. That is, while
the sentiment was fully there, the course of thought
and expression—the hopes that had centred in this
lost son, the lamentations, the supplication for his
return—had all been repeated substantially, year
after year, on his hallowed birth-day.

John Ruffin was about to replace the miniature,
when Sabina entered, to say a man had come with a
chair. In momentary expectation of Thomas, he
would have turned the man away, in all liklihood,
if his and Sabina's 'Bus fares had not exhausted his
pennies. So he told Sabina to bring the man round
to his door, supposing he would be detained by him
but a second. Presently the man came in, a rough
looking workman. As he entered he was seen to
reel and tremble, and, drawing a flask, drank from it.

"Who are you? Drunk?" John Ruffin sharply
asked, offended at the man's apparent condition.

"Grim—John Grim. No drunk. Got touch o'

the staggers. Have'em sometimes. This stuff'll set
me up.''

"There's a glass and a pitcher of water," said
John Ruffin who was partial to grog, pointing to the
things on the table, and speaking in a kindly voice,
the atonement of conscience for the unmerited im-
putation.

"No water, thank ye. I'm like the fellah who
said, no prohibiton in his'n."

"What do you want?"

"A jam-up bottom to this here cheer here. I hear
ye're cheap and puts up a good job, and them's the
terms as suit me to a T."

"There's my work," pointing to a specimen chair.

"Snug job," remarked Grim, as he examined the
chair.—"Yer price? Mind, I'm poor."

"That's no disgrace."

"No disgrace, but it's onhandy.—Yer price?"

"Half dollar."

"Well, twis' me out a bottom like this here, and
the money's yourn. And it's worth a dollar, too,
and here's the ready money cash down," placing in
John Ruffin's hand a new bright silver dollar.

John Ruffin really was delighted. It was such a
nice looking coin, and so timely. He would give it
to Thomas to-night, instead of putting it into his
own purse.

Grim, who had been eyeing the room, as if for a
purpose, looked up at the print on the left wall,
with the remark:

"I'll take a look at yer picturs. *Mighty* fond o' picturs."

John Ruffin's good-will having been secured by the dollar, he made no objection. Grim, therefore, moved round the room apparently giving thought to the prints, but furtively watching John Ruffin, whose back was towards him. As he reached the bed, over which hung a print, with a quick glance at his man and sudden movement he drew out a roll of bills and was about to thrust it between the mattresses, when the old gentleman turned towards him and unconsciously frustrated the attempt.

"Been in the city long?" asked Grim, seating himself on the bed.

John Ruffin replied with a negative movement of the head.

"Been twistin' shucks long?"

John Ruffin remained silent.

"Reckon not, old friend. Yer fingers don't look horny like. Reckon you've seed better days."

John Ruffin continued silent, showing symptoms of annoyance.

"Where did ye come from?"

"That's *my* business."

"So it is—darn my buttons, if it isn't," said Grim, who, if his speech was scrubby, really had a kindly winning tone and manner, as good policy required. "'Scuse me. Didn't mean to worrit ye. Ev'ry feller has round him his own little circle like, and a stranger's foot dasn't go in."

"Whe-e-w!" he presently remarked, all the while

on a lookout to discover, or make a way for, an opening to get in his work, "this here room of yourn's hot as old Harry's, and I've ketched a *git-tarrh*"—giving, as do the illiterate, a strong accent to the first syllable. "'Spose you open the door."

Hard of hearing, John Ruffin looked at Grim in a puzzled way. Then rose and turned towards the door. Grim, seizing the chance, made a quick move-ment, and was on the point of thrusting the money-roll between the mattresses, when John Ruffin again unwittingly frustrated him by turning and asking :

"Did you say you fetched a *guitar* to the door?"

"Ha! ha! ha! No-o-o, my old friend. I said I'd ketched a *git*tarrh, a *git*tarrh in my head—a bad cold, don't you know?—and wants fresh air. What *d'you* call the tarnation thing?"

"Oh-h-h! replied John Ruffin, who by this time had lost the full dollar's worth of patience, "if you want fresh air, you can leave."

"Now, ye'll let a feller rest a bit, as what's brought a job, and paid double price cash down —won't ye? He mought have another."

John Ruffin thought upon the new bright coin in his pocket and of the pleasure he would have in pre-senting it to his son, and Grim's argument had weight enough at least to arrest his hintings. In resuming his seat in silence he directly faced the bed, and Grim, whose work was to be effected within narrow time limits, saw something must be done to change his position. He had noticed a miniature upon the table. Rising now from his seat on the bed, he took the miniature in hand, and began a haphazard sort of conversation, in the hope it might lead in some way to his getting a chance.

"It's fine!" he said, holding the portrait admiringly before him. Then, having rubbed the setting and smelt the finger, he broke out:

"Blast my buttons! if this here rim and back here ain't real gold!—Whose pictur?"

"Mine."

"O do tell me somethin' I doesn't know. Whose *likeness* mought it be?"

"My son's."

"Reckon yer look at it ev'ry day."

"I look at it once a year."

"Once a year! Ge-e-e whillikens!"

"I take it out on his birthday."

"This his birthday?"

"Yes."

"How old?"

"Twenty-six."

"Where is he?"

"Don't know."

"Living?"

"Can't say."

"Spiled in the raisin', p'r'aps."

John Ruffin was silent.

"Did he leave you?"

"Yes"—after a pause.

For a moment Grim stroked the full grisly beard of disguise. Then, as though struck by an animating thought, he advanced, extending the hand:

"Yer hand, my old friend, I'll be dog gone ef we ain't paddlin' in the same cunnoe."

"What do you mean?"

"Why, *my* boy, too, lef' me four year back ; and I hain't heerd a word frum him a hul year las' peach time. But I'm 'spectin' him to turn up, I is."

This struck a warm deep current of sentiment in John Ruffin, who immediately became interested in his visitor. With sparkling eyes Grim saw the hit and worked the idea for all it was worth.

"I is, in truth," he went on. "He's my oldest boy, and times *is* hard. It's a purty bad bread-and-butter scuffle, and takes a mighty hard pull to git along, with my old woman and little ones to tote. But, says I to myself, says I, one day, when I'm in the straits and all down-hearted, and feel I'm all forsakin, and the world's all agin me, I'll hear a tap at the door."

"Hear what?" John Ruffin asked, not catching the word.

"A tap at the door.—Come in, says I, and in comes my boy, with a smile on his face, and gold in his wallet. Ha! ha! ha!"

"I hope so," said John Ruffin, looking full at Grim with eyes of sympathy."

"Yes-sir-re! I'm 'spectin' my boy to turn up *yet;* and, mebbe, yourn'll turn up, too. Yes, I guess he'll come back alive some day, like Jonidab frum the whale's belly. Patience, patience. Don't yer know mulberry leaves in time gits to be satin?"

"I'm praying for his coming every day."

To secure John Ruffin's interest was a primary condition, since it involved acquiescence in his remaining, and Grim felt he had made a critical hit. Still, the minutes were flying and no chance in sight, till John Ruffin spoke of his praying every day for his son's return. Grim now thought he perceived how he could change presently his posture without creating suspicion, and have the game in hand. So he began a run on "praying," conjugating it in all its moods, tenses, and inflexions:

"You're a prayin' man?"

"I am."

"Ever git anything?"

"Get anything! My prayers are heard so often I'm almost afraid to ask God for anything."

"Why so?"

"I might ask for something I ought not to."

"Ge-e-e whillikens!—Reckon you love to go to meetin'."

"Love to go to meet him? Do you mean Tammie? I love to to meet *him.*"

"Ha! ha! ha! Way off the track. I mean, do yer love to go *to church?*"

"Oh-h!—Sometimes. Can't go in bad weather."

"Why so?"

"I haven't any money to buy a seat, and they put me in a back corner behind the pillars, where it's cold and I can't see or hear. But it's a good place to pray."

"Behin' the pillars! Darn my buttons! ef some

of these old fellers a prayin' behin' the pillars, ain't the pillars theirselves."

"The pillars!" exclaimed John Ruffin, not fully catching Grim's words, and puzzled as to his meaning.

"Yes, the biggest sort of pillars; but the preacher, he can't see 'em. He sees them as set in the front pews and shells out, and calls *them* the church's props. But more an likely the blessin' as what holds up the hull consarn, is some poor old neglectit shinin' soul in a back corner, a prayin' behin' the pillars. Them's *my* sentiments."

"You must pray too, remarked John Ruffin, with an interest in his visitor enhanced by his apparent religious character and the special quality of his views—a quality seemingly all the finer, as proceeding from so rough looking a fellow.

"Be dog! ef I don't," responded Grim promptly; "and I feel like prayin' this very blessed minit. Let's git right down here and pray fur our poor boys."

John Ruffin made a movement as if to get on his knees facing Grim and the bed, when the latter interposed :

"Stop, my friend, stop! Look a here! Ain't yer goin' to pray to'ards the *East ?*"

"I don't know what you mean."

"I mean it's better to pray to'ards the East. I allers do."

"Why?"

"Why!—Don't yer know, when the Lord wus born, His star 'peared in the *East ?* And don't yer

know, when He comes to jedge, with a great light all
about Him, and all the shiny angels a follerin', He's
to come frum the *East?* And don't yer know, when
the grave-diggers dig their graves, they dig their
heads to'ards the West, so that, when they rise up,
they won't have to turn all round to see Old Master
a comin' frum the *East?* And don't yer know all
the churches have their halters at the *East* end;
and so, when the people are all a prayin', and have
their necks bent to the halters, they're a facin' of
the *East?*"

"I didn't know."

"It's so, fur certain and sure. And now lets git
right down here on our marrow-bones, both on us,
and pray fur our boys. *You* pray to'ards that there
door there. That's to'ards the East."

"Will you really pray with me?"

"Will I pray with yer! In course I will. I'm a
prayin' man frum the word 'go.' I can make a
prayer as quick as ye can shuffle a deck; and I can
pray, too, as long as any man. *Try* me. Try me
and see."

"Let us pray, then."

If ever it be true—as no doubt it often is—that the
sincerity and depth of a prayer may be measured by
the exteriors of the suppliant, the air of unaffected
humility, the subdued and mindful reverence, transparent in this afflicted man as he knelt, was the
counterpart to the swell of pure tender sentiment,
which, inspired by the hallowed hour, he presented
before God. Grim, too, knelt—at the bedside; and

immediately he made use of the chance to hide away
between the mattresses the money-roll. The job
had been a difficult one, and his wits much longer
on the stretch than he had anticipated. He consulted his watch. Time was up. He was to meet the
cracksman, to stand guard outside the *Bank*, or the
scheme would fail. To make the meeting now was
barely possible. Unfortunately, he reflected, he
had flung down the glove to a prayer contest; and
while John Ruffin was sincere every whit, with no
thought of a profane physical endurance, Grim, seeing his spiritual turn, did not know how long he
might not remain kneeling, and to pronounce, therefore, a loud "amen" and rise, was an absolute necessity. John Ruffin, whose memorial prayer had been
offered already, rose, too, and reverently.

"Hope yer prayer will bring yer boy," remarked
Grim, preparing to leave.

"I hope so."

"I'll call fur the cheer next week. God bless yer."

"God bless you, too."

Grim's gumption and kindly way had held secure-
ly John Ruffin's attention, to the exclusion of other
thoughts. As he passed out, the latter looked up
at the clock, and suddenly becoming conscious of
Thomas' prolonged absence, exclaimed, with dismay
written upon his countenance :

"Good gracious! It's long past Tammie's time.
Why, why don't he come!"

At once he is agitated profoundly, the mental
condition finding expression in divers movements,

now hasting up and down the room, now wringing the hands, now stroking the head, stirring the fire, touching up the table, &c., &c., in the vain effort to lessen the pressure of thought in one direction by dividing it. Finally, he kneels a moment in prayer. Rising, he bewails the hour:

"He's here these late Thursdays a little after 7. It's now after 9. Oh! I wish he would come!"

Now he hurries to the window and looks up and down the street, muttering, as he lowers the sash :

"How those stars glitter! so cold! so pitiless!"

Again he bestirs himself about the room in a whirl of distress, pitiable to behold. No human being knew the depth of the suffering his morbid anxieties inflicted. Reflecting a moment, he breaks out in a degree of agony :

"Gracious me! he may've been *robbed!* My God!"

He kneels and prays a moment. Then, all beside himself, in a state of excitement seemingly approaching a paroxysm, he flies to the window and scans the street again :

"My-y! my-y! nearly every light is out! Oh! I do wish he would come!"

Scarcely had he lowered the sash, when, catching a foot-fall, he raises his head and listens intently.

"I believe that's his step," he whispers between hope and fear.

He looks from the window. The anguish has passed. The pressure is gone. A light and happy heart rings out :

"Yes, yes! It is, it is! O you winking, laughing little stars, you've got another face now."

Thrice happy, indeed, was John Ruffin to meet his son—looking, too, so animated and improved; for the work in hand to night had inspirited Thomas. Again and again he embraced him. Again and again, by word and by action, did he manifest his joy. Observing on the table the flowers Sister Jessica had brought that afternoon, Thomas presently disengaged a Moss Rose and transferred it to his button-hole.

"I'm glad," remarked his Father, "it's not a *she* who sends the roses."

There was a twinkle in Thomas Ruffin's eye, unobserved by his Father, as he recalled how cleverly Sister Jessica had extricated herself from a certain difficulty; for John Ruffin had been careful to detail to his son the conversation with the Sister respecting the sender of these flowers. But the prevailing thought was in another quarter. Thomas, now brightened up and in a sanguine hopeful frame touching everything, had taken the rose full of tender sentiment towards Amy Sanford, and what his Father *did* observe, was, that, as he spoke of the roses, the blood mantled his son's cheek.

"What on earth's the matter?" he anxiously asked, peering into Thomas's face.

"Nothing, Father—nothing at all."

"Yes, I'm glad it wasn't a *she*," John Ruffin went on, touching the same sensitive string. "One of these days, when you get older, will be time enough to be thinking about *she's* and *sweethearts* and—there it is again," breaking in upon himself on observing again the mantling blood. "Your face has all at once colored. Something *is* the matter. Why *do* you look so, my son?"

"The cool night air may have brought the color."

"I never thought of that. I'm so glad to know the reason."

"And I'm glad, Father, to see you so bright to night."

"Bright! Oh! I'd almost forgotten. I've got something bright for *you*. Here's the money for a chair"—showing the dollar. "See! What a nice new coin! And now it's *all yours*"—pressing the coin in his son's hand, "and I'm so glad I can do a little to help along."

"I am glad you can help along, Father, but far more glad to see your thoughts so clear. It's many a long day since I've heard you talk so well."

"This is your brother's birth-day, Tammie, and I've been thinking and thinking about *him*—and then about the time when he left us—and then about the time when he was a little boy at Cloud Cap. I think better, when I think of things way back. And my thoughts to-night about these way back things, have been so clear, that I seem to think better about everything. And I feel strange, too, my son, as if waking from a dream. And a dread is on me, too, as if something might happen. You know they say clouded minds sometimes brighten up, when the light's about to go out for good."

"I'm delighted to hear you speak so much like yourself," said Thomas, struck by his Father's unusual fullness and clearness of speech, and embracing him. "My dear Father, your are so much better. And let us thank God for it."

"I *do*, my son—I do."

"And put away the dread you seem to have of some evil about to happen.—There *is* something going to happen——"

"What is it? what is it?" quickly interrupted John Ruffin with look of alarm, drawing his chair close to that of his son and seizing his hand, as if to shield himself from some impending danger. "I feared so, Tammie."

"Nothing bad, Father, I assure you. It's going to happen to-night, and——"

"To-night!"—his fears again interrupting.

"Yes, Father, but don't be alarmed. I must leave for the *Bank* directly after supper. I've some special work on hand there, and may be kept away all night."

"All night, my son!"—alarm increasing.

"Yes, Father. But you *must not* be uneasy. It's not bad, I say."

"Is what's to happen anything to do with the *Bank?*"

"Yes."

"And can't you tell me what it is?"

"Not now, not well now"—his Father would have been frantic, had he known Thomas was to be engaged in watching for a burglar. "I'll explain it all to-morrow. Believe me when I tell you it's not bad, but something for my good, as well as for the good of the *Bank*."

John Ruffin reflected a moment, and then joyfully exclaimed :

"O Tammie! I know what it is. The *Banker* is going to promote you."

"I can say this much, that what's going to happen is very likely to result in my being promoted."

"I thought so. O I'm so glad. You deserve it, my son. You've worked so hard and for so little pay. And *I've* got some good news for you, too. But 1 shall keep it till to-morrow, just as you do yours. And there's money in it for you, too."

"Yes, Father, I think I can count now on having more money, and being able to provide for you better."

"My son, you provide for me now very well, indeed. You've just given me these nice flannels I've got on; and when I go out and the wind blows cold and I feel so snug, it seems to me as if these flannels were your own arms round me, making me warm and comfortable."

"But I shall provide for you better still."

"My dear, dear son !"

"And I shall be able, too, to put by something every month. We will save and save, and put by more and more."

"That we will, that we will."

"And after a time," went on Thomas, flushed by his environments and with the future rosy before him, "I shall be able to go into business on my own account; and we shall have a home of our own—"

"My dear, dear son !"

"with every comfort round you—"

"Dear, dear son !"

"and servants to wait on you."

"My dear, dear son !"

"And my business will grow and grow; and after a time, when the money's in hand, I shall go down South and buy back for you"—Thomas pauses an instant, and his Father tightens the grasp on his hand and looks up at him with beaming expectancy —"what d'you think, Father? Why, I shall *buy back dear old Cloud Cap !*"

At this John Ruffin burst into tears. Then rising, he put his arms about his son's neck, and, as Thomas went on, murmured out his joy upon his breast.

"And we shall put a man in charge, Father, and have it cultivated, just as you used to cultivate it. And we shall spend a part of each year at dear old Cloud Cap. And you'll ride over the fields that knew you before. And I shall see again every old familiar spot I loved when a boy, the places where I set my partridge traps and hare snares, and the old branch crossing where I used to build my mud dams and run my corn-stalk flutter wheels; and, Father, we shall be so—"

Thomas suddenly paused at the sound of hurried feet and voices on the steps, as of men making for the door. In alarm father and son part from their embrace.

"What's that Tammie?"

"I don't know."

There was a rap. Thomas rushed to answer it, and, as he opened the door, faced Dalguspin.

"For God's sake, what's the matter?" he cried, as his glance revealed others in the rear of Dalguspin.

"I'll tell you in a moment. Let this officer in."

Thomas' first thought was for his Father. Dreading the effect of such a demonstration—and at midnight, too—he hastened back to his side, amazed and bewildered. The officer was followed in by the Watchman and Noals—Noals being followed by Robert Small, who remained apart in the rear. A moment later Friend Peale and Sandy Johnson entered and stood back near the door, resolved to see the end of this most strange affair. Meanwhile the investigation had begun.

"The *Bank* has been robbed, young man! What do you know about it?" asked Dalguspin, addressing Thomas who stood breathless, with his Father trembling behind him.

Thomas made no reply. That he, a party to capture the robber, should be charged or suspected of being in any sense a party to the robbery, absolutely confounded him. He stood speechless and pale as death, looking Black Isaac full in the face, but unable to utter a word.

"What do you know about it, I say?"

"Nothing," Thomas stammered out.

"Nothing! Why then leave before the Watchman's return?"

"I did not."

"You did! you did!" asserted William, speaking up and advancing.

"*I did not!*"

"*You did! you did!*" repeated William.

"*I will swear* I did not leave before your return. I left a few moments after you came in, and everything was straight then."

Had Thomas Ruffin seen Friend Peale and Sandy Johnson, no doubt he would have called upon them to witness his words. But they were standing far back and somewhat to his side, with a single candle to give light to the room. And even had they been within the line of vision, their presence would have escaped him; for, under the tremendous excitement, he saw not a soul save the person he was addressing. Friend Peale, on his part, did not think the moment opportune to speak, seeing he had made already a statement to the Watchman and others at the *Bank*.

"It's a lie as God's my witness!" avowed William. "At what hour did you leave?"

"A quarter to 10."

"By the *Bank's* clock?"

"Yes."

"Now, see how you are caught: When I entered the *Bank* I found the safe had been robbed and at once gave the alarm. This officer"—pointing to policeman—"was at the door when I came up. He saw me go in and rush out. The interval was not one minute. I took him in, to see how things were, and called his attention to the time, and the *Bank's*

clock showed *forty minutes past* 10! Isn't it so,
Mr. Officer ?"

The officer nodded assent.

Thomas made no reply. He could make none
against the statement of William, supported by the
officer. He was dazed. The only thing clear to him
was his innocence. He was unable to see how an
error might have occurred—how the person whom
he had taken to be the Watchman could have been
any other than William. Was there a conspiracy
against him—it flashed into his mind—on the part
of William and the officer? Or was he the prey of
some evil spirit, doomed to be entangled and led on
to ruin? He stood silent and confused, with the
blood mounting into his pallid countenance.

By this time the Institution, which had been all
abed, was aroused. Miss Kitty and Sabina hurried
down. The officer was on the lookout at the inner
door for the authorities, to explain. Miss Kitty was
fighting mad to learn The Home had been invaded
in this style, to make such a bastard lying charge
against "Mr. Thomas," and that a million Dalgus-
pins—she knew something of Black Isaac—might
swear themselves black and blue before she'd believe
a word of it. When she entered, a glance at the
situation, the perplexity and distress of the father
and son, wrung her heart, and, intensely roused, it
was all the officer could do, to restrain her from
"pitching in" with a red hot Irish hand, he warning
her that the proceedings were a kind of court, &c.

John Ruffin had been standing aghast behind

Thomas. Recovered now from the immediately paralyzing effect of the shock, he leaped into a flame, and came forward approaching Dalguspin :

"Do you charge my son with robbing the *Bank ?*"

There were a score of persons in the room, with officer of the law. But the awful wrath of this stricken old man who seemed to swell and get bigger under its influence, advancing on him with lips quivering, eyes blazing, and cane (which he always carried) uplifted, was more than Black Isaac's nervous organism was framed to bear. He sprang back, and tremors seized him extending from the cerebellum to the lowest vertebrae of the spinal column.

"Down with that there stick," commanded the officer, interposing.

"Do you charge my son with robbing the *Bank ?*"

"I've made no charge. I'm here to find out what your son may know about this robbery. He has been taken already in a lie——"

"He can't tell a lie !" fiercely broke in John Ruffin, again advancing with uplifted cane.

"Down with that there stick there, I say," repeated the officer, stepping in front of John Ruffin.

"Didn't you hear how your son was caught?" went on Black Isaac, at a discreet distance from the enraged father. "Didn't he say he left the *Bank*, by the Bank's clock at fifteen minutes to ten, when the Watchman entered ? And isn't it proved by this officer, that, when the Watchman entered, the Bank's clock showed *forty minutes past* 10? What d'you say to that ?"

"That my son cannot tell a lie."

"I'll waste no more words on an old fool. We'll have this room searched. Here's the officer to do it."

"Searched for what?"

"Money."

"Money!—Tammie has worked and worked day and night, but you haven't given him enough to lay by any."

Dalguspin saw it would be better to smooth matters over, if possible, and, in a conciliatory strain leading up to the end in view, adroitly said:

"Mr. Ruffin, you do right to stand up for your son. It appears he has gotten into a hole. There's one way out. It may have been the robber, disguised as the Watchman, who entered the *Bank* at a quarter to 10 and deceived your son."

"That's how it was! that's how it was!" ardently exclaimed John Ruffin.

"We shall have this room searched; and if nothing be found to fix guilt on your son, I shall suppose he must have been tricked in this way, and will fully repay both you and him for having hinted such a charge."

This turn—considered a most reasonable view of the case—sent a great thrill of joy through the hearts of Thomas and his friends.

"Will you, *Mr. Banker?*" entreatingly asked John Ruffin, now completely pacified, seeing light ahead.

"Yes.—But, should money in suspicious amounts be found——"

"*Good Mr. Banker! Good Mr. Banker!*" cried
out John Ruffin, eagerly breaking in and taking
Black Isaac's hand in both of his, "you say you'll
do something good for Tammie, if you find nothing ?"

"Yes."

"*Good Mr. Banker!* — Tammie," he continued,
turning to his son, "they'll find nothing, and it'll
turn out for your good. You said this evening something might happen to-night for your good, and it's
going to be so."

"Did you hear that?" asked Dalguspin of the
officer, aside.   Then aloud to John Ruffin:

"What was it you said?"

"I said Tammie told me this evening something
was going to happen to-night for his good."

Dalguspin, aside, nods to the officer.

"Was it anything in connection with the *Bank?*"

"Yes. He said 'twas about the *Bank*, but wouldn't
tell me what.   He said 'twould make him better off,
and he'd be able to provide for me better."

Dalguspin, aside, again nods to the officer.

Here was another turn, and one unfortunate for
Thomas.   He could not deny a word his Father just
had spoken, yet saw how pointedly they compro-
mised him.   Neither had he the presence of mind to
attempt an explanation.   He had noticed the bye-
play between Dalguspin and the officer—as had, too,
all the rest save John Ruffin, dull of eyes and ears.
A deathly sense of being forsaken and devoted came
over him—forsaken by the good influences.   It has
been mentioned in a back chapter, that the superin-

tendence of angels was impressed early and vividly upon his consciousness. He felt now—in his confused, bewildered state of mind—that the evil spirits had him. An awful sense arose of some plot they had formed against him, and to further which they had beguiled his own dear Father to incriminate him in the very effort to defend. As for his friends, a horrible fear began to take shape. They hung their heads. Could such a thing be possible!

"That's all he would say," went on John Ruffin; "but I see how it is now. Will you promote.him, *Mr. Banker ?*"

"Yes. I think now your son will soon have a change of position"—aside to the officer, "*under your guidance.*"

"*Good Mr. Banker ! good Mr. Banker !*"—You may search, but you won't find anything. If you haven't paid Tammie to-day, there's only one silver dollar in this room, and that's in Tammie's pocket, and that I gave him myself. If you find any more, you may take Tammie. Yes, you may *take my Tammie*," turning to his son and taking his hand, "if you find any more than that.—But, Tammie, they'll find nothing, and it'll all turn out for your good."

"Make the search," said Black Isaac, addressing the officer.

With the dispatch and skill of an expert the officer went through John Ruffin and Thomas, finding on the latter a silver dollar and one or two pieces of small change. Then, turning attention to the bureau, a few moments sufficed to finish his work there.

"Nothin' but the silver dollar just as Pap declared," he said to Dalguspin upon the completion of the search. "Looks, Gov'nor, like a water haul."

"Why don't you search the bed?" suggested Noals. "Plunder would be more apt to be hidden there than anywhere else."

"That's so," replied the officer; and going to the bed and turning over the upper mattress, he finds something which he seizes and examines with great interest. The attention of all suddenly is roused to a high pitch.

"Have you found anything?" asks Dalguspin advancing.

The officer turns, holding something in his hand, and, for a moment, looks fixedly at Thomas. Then addresses him in low, incriminating tones:

"Where did this come from?" extending his hand, as he speaks.

In his distraught state of mind Thomas had followed the search fascinated, not knowing what bedevilment might not turn up. He was in a species of trance and absolutely unable to answer the officer's question.

"Where did this come from, I say, young man—this roll of ten fifty dollar bills?"

Screams burst from Miss Kitty and Sabina—a cry of horror from Friend Peale and Sandy Johnson. John Ruffin's deafness had not caught the officer's words, yet he realizes something appalling has happened and asks excitedly :

"What is it, Tammie?"

"I'll tell you," said Dalguspin. "Five hundred dollars have been found hidden between the mattresses, and your Tammie is a thief and a bank-robber!"

John Ruffin, his body thrown back and hands clasped upon his breast, stands staring at Dalguspin and trembling, in an attitude of terror.

"Yes—*that's* what was going to happen to-night, I suppose, and *that's* how he's to be able to provide for you better?"

At this John Ruffin releases his son's hand—turns facing him—fixes on him awful, unspeakable, pitiful eyes—and with a great and exceeding bitter cry: "Oh! Tammie!" sinks into a chair, as if life were going out of him.

Thomas throws himself upon his Father's knees: "Father! I am innocent! I am innocent!"

"Arrest him!" said Dalguspin to the officer.

The officer seizes Thomas, who, with tears and imploring hands, repeats the agonizing cry:

"Father! I am innocent! I am innocent!"

His Father could not speak. He could only raise his eyes to Heaven.

Robert Small's hour had come.

"Stay, officer!" he cries, rushing forward. "He *is* innocent! I hid that money there!"

Huzzas irrepressible burst from Friend Peale and party. Dalguspin and Noals turn to escape by the outer door, near which Friend Peale and Sandy are standing.

"Seize 'm!" cries Small to the latter. "*They* are the robbers ! Can you hold them, while I explain?"

"Aye ! aye ! Sir," replies Sandy, who had Noals as secure, as Friend Peale had Black Isaac. "I'm lively and happy. In fact I feel like a jay-bird."

Miss Kitty and Sabina were now exceedingly nigh the borders of a fit; and had not Sabina possessed a handy method of letting off excess of sentiment, the fit would have been inevitable. Her explosions were truly remarkable. As for Miss Kitty, fearing Noals in his struggles would get away, she rushes to the aid of Sandy, who, getting his arm well around her waist, charges her:

"Haud me tight and gude and he canna rin awa' wi' us."

Meanwhile, some hurried whispered words pass from Small to the officer, and the latter releases Thomas, and puts Black Isaac and Noals under arrest. Thomas rushes to his Father, whom the sudden turn of affairs and whirl of emotion have brought to his feet. He folds his son in his arms— then turns to give thanks to the stranger.

"Whoever you be," he said, approaching Small, "God bless you for ever and for ever for saying my son is innocent."

"Do you not know me, Sir?"

"I can't say I do. My sight is dim and the light is dim"—peering at him. "But I think I've heard the voice before."

"This is Robert, your lost Boy !"

CHAPTER XX. ·

With a rage for adventure Robert Ruffin left the most enviable of homes. He was shrewd naturally, yet, starting out devoid of experience, in profitless schemes soon lost his means. He made his way up North into the back country, and when last heard of had enlisted for the Black Hawk war of 1832. The fortunes of that war he followed to its close, and for conspicuous gallantry at the decisive battle of Bad Axe River on the left bank of the Mississippi, was noticed personally by General Whiteside. Drifting· down the Mississippi, he landed at New Orleans battered and out of pocket, yet bent on adventure still. He had friends and kindred in the city, in the House of Thomas Sanford & Co., but was too proud to make himself known. Because he could not write favorably, and would not write falsely, he had ceased writing home. From New Orleans he worked a ship passage to Brazil, attracted thither by the gold reports. A year and more spent in this southern half of the western continent, had for net results nothing beyond an addition to his stock of knowledge of human nature, and a mining experience—an experience which he turned subsequently to good account.

Working a passage back, with the roving spirit on the wane, he again landed at New Orleans. Mexico and Texas were then at war. The war spirit in New Orleans was rampant to avenge the Alamo, and young Ruffin soon found himself in General Houston's army. At San Jacinto he was wounded, but fought through, and towards the close of the battle saved the life of a disabled Mexican officer, who, having surrendered, was about to be bayonetted by a ruffian soldier. A warm friendship sprang up between them, and the officer, about to return to his country upon the declaration of peace, invited Robert to accompany him, out of gratitude offering his benefactor an interest in the mines on his estate.

Young Ruffin was looking homeward wistfully. But seeing an opportunity to return with something in hand, he accepted the officer's munificence. His Brazil experience now stood him in good stead, and he worked his mine so successfully, striking a lode of unusual richness, that within an almost incredibly brief period he had accumulated as much gold as he could carry conveniently belted round him, and, sighing for home, bade his friend adieu.

His purpose was to ship at Vera Cruz for New Orleans. But the first vessel thither traded likewise with the city, where his father and brother were now living, and the character of the cargo was such as to require the skipper to sail for the northern city first. While at the port occurred the incident which led to his entering Dalguspin's service. Respecting the fine imposed by the court, it did not require a second thought to have him act on Black Isaac's suggestion, and not touch the gold. He had just so many pounds of the royal metal. At $16 to the once (its normal value those days) it made a certain round sum which he was especially desirous to take home intact. Again, this gold was packed away and secured about his person in the most artistic and careful manner, and it was advisable to leave it undisturbed, if possible, on the journey. And, withal, he considered that to offer nuggets for sale would involve risk of discovery that he carried treasure, and attendant danger. •

How through Mrs. Peale he discovered the presence of his Father and Brother, and how near the shock came to making a discovery of himself, have been related. Just prior to this, before hinting his scheme to Dalguspin, Noals, having heard of Robert's character through the Pawnbroker and his moonshine about going abroad, had approached him as the Cracksman, intimating that one of the *Bank's* employees might be tricked to bear the burden. Robert's fears immediately were aroused. Wary, too, and needle-witted, he became suspicious and determined to remain Robert Small, the incognito he had assumed upon his arrest, and keep broad awake. By keyholing and otherwise he discovered the real robbers, and finding his Brother was to be ensnared, entered into the plot with the full force of his capacity for adventure, playing parts peculiarly trying—yet necessarily played, to entrap the villians.

The discovery of Robert, following immediately upon the vindication of Thomas, was too much for John Ruffin. He fell into a swoon—from which, however, he soon recovered through the good offices of Miss Kitty, skilled, as the exigencies of her position required, in the administration of simple remedies; and then ensued another transporting scene, the meeting between Father and Son, between Brother and Brother, and between John Ruffin and his old friends; for the sudden great swell of supreme joy broke through the barrier of his antipathies, and John Ruffin wept again upon Friend Peale's neck and Sandy's. Miss Kitty and Sabina, too, were full participants in the jubilation. Miss Kitty said she never rejoiced so in all her life long, declaring solemnly she was so happy she did not intend to say "no" to any human being for a whole week—a remark let fall, as it happened, within Sandy's hearing, and which the wide-awake Scot did not fail, within the time limit, to bring home to the Housekeeper. Even the officer—glad to be on the same side with a citizen of so much consequence as Friend Peale—caught the spirit of the occasion, and delayed with his prisoners to offer congratulations.

Next morning early Mrs. Peale called, with her good man, and the scene of the previous night in a measure was repeated. Before they left it was arranged—the Peales pressing the invitation upon

their old friend and refusing to be denied—that the
Ruffins should come over that afternoon and remain
with them until something might be settled touching the business future of Robert and Thomas.
Friend Peale had a plan of his own, to make the
evening memorable, and was aided, too, by Robert.
For having heard how the latter was belted, he got
his promise to keep it a secret and defer the·exhi-
bition, till after tea.

It was a notable "Tea," that evening. If not as
thronged as "Teas" are nowadays, nor the styles so
fashionable, its joyousness· was unsurpassed. · The
company was all of one mind and one heart, with no
lack of topics of conversation of a highly exhilarating character. Sandy Johnson was there, you may
be sure, an honored guest. In John Ruffin a minor
physical revolution had taken place. He was lifted
up, made anew, running over with happiness. As
his special servant, Sabina, for this particular occasion, had been sent over, to serve; and her face was
illuminated and mouth kept stretched in one un-
broken smile, and her whole body in a quiver of
excitation, as she bustled about the table.

Tea over, they repaired to the drawing-room. Presently Robert was called upon to·repeat the story of
his adventures. He gave a racy narrative, remark-
ing, as he closed with his mining experience, that
he had on his person some Mexican mementoes to
exhibit. Removing coat and vest he showed on
arm and neck the remains of wounds from Mexican
lance and musket.

"This," he said, unbuckling a belt, "is another Mexican souvenir, and happily of another character."

The belt, a most ample one, was of buckskin doubled on itself, with the edges stitched together, except where left open for the mouths of pouches formed by stitching the belt across. It was well worn, indeed, with many bulgings standing out, and sagged greatly, though sustained by broad stout buckskin straps passing over the shoulders.

"This is a trophy from the mines of Mexico," said Robert, exhibiting from one of the pouches a lump of pure gold as large as the thumb, and which shone again from the continued friction of the buckskin. "These pouches," he went on, as he turned towards his Father and laid the belt across his knees, "hold twenty-five pounds in gold dust and nuggets, and the value is five thousand dollars. After all, Sir, my wanderings seem to have been guided by a merciful Providence." ·

The ejaculations and congratulations over, John Ruffin exclaimed :

"Yes, yes, indeed, Providence is filling my cup. He has given me back a son with gold in his hand. And all along He has been giving me and mine friends in this city—all these here—that I didn't know of. And there's another friend, too, He has given me, that I *did* know of. O if she were here to see our joy !"

"What friend is that, John ?" asked Friend Peale.

"Sister Jessica."

"Thee may see her this very evening."

"O do you know Sister Jessica ?"

"Certainly I do. Very well, indeed. She was invited to meet thee, but comes late. I think she has just arrived, and will bring her in"—rising, to leave the room.

As Friend Peale, a few moments after, entered with the Sister, John Ruffin rose from his chair to meet her, when Friend Peale remarked :

"On this special occasion Sister Jessica consents to be uncovered," lifting the veil, as he spoke. John Ruffin drew back—gave an intense look—then opened wide his arms, and Amy Sanford rushed into them.

What followed—John Ruffin's finding a daughter, as it were, and under such circumstances, the cumulative effect upon him of these renewals of great joy; the tumult in Thomas Ruffin's breast as he beheld Amy's chastened and maturer charms, and recalled his confessions to Sister Jessica; the beaming countenance of Friend Peale at bringing about so happy a turn; the swell of deep-felt joy from every heart present, acting and reacting upon each other—we leave to the reader's imagination to fill out. The whirl of emotion received another stir presently from the entrance of Aunt Sanford, she being the last to illustrate this independent and contemporaneous converging of closely related personalities, through a concatenation of circumstances whereby exact truth is often stranger than fiction.

Nestled close to John Ruffin's side Amy now had

to tell *her* story: How failing health compelling her
to leave New Orleans, she had secured through
Friend Peale's good offices, a position in the school
where she had studied—that in a long and critical
illness from enteric fever she had been tenderly
nursed at a Friend's Church Home by a dear Sister
Jessica, member of a sisterhood connected with the
Home—that Sister Jessica took the fever, presuma-
bly from herself, and died,—that she then entered the
sisterhood, taking the name of Jessica, and purpos-
ing, as far as she could, to fill the place of her departed friend—that, as Sister Jessica, she had tried
to minister to him—and that in all things, both in
continuing the incognito and in first assuming it,
she had acted under the advice of Friend Peale and
the physician to The Home—with further particulars and reasons for the disguise, as set forth or
implied in Sister Jessica's letter in another chapter.

Robert Ruffin's gold wrought a change in Friend
Peale's views touching Thomas' business future.
The clerkship he had in view for him, was dismissed.
The young men could now become established on
their own account. Under the ordinary condition of
affairs, the valuation of this sum of gold would have
been five thousand dollars—ten thousand in present
current funds; but at that juncture it was worth a
great deal more. The times then were out of joint.
It was but a month or two prior to the disastrous
panic of 1837. The finances of the country were in
a deplorable state; and gold being at a high premium, Friend Peale found no difficulty in negotiat-

ing for Robert and Thomas a joint interest in an establised and reputable firm of grocers. This enabled the sons to take at once a house and comfortably domicile their Father.

To bring the rest of our acquaintances up to date : Dalguspin and Noals were tried, convicted, and sentenced to fine and imprisonment. Dalguspin died in prison. Noals served through his term, and left the city.—Our friend Sandy, in due time, led Miss Kitty to the altar; nor was it long before his intelligence, backed by the Peale influence, won for him the vacant post of Superintendent.—And Sabina— poor, simple-minded, merry-hearted, good-natured Sabina—she remained a fixture at The Home. Sabina was alone in the world, with no kindred that she knew of, her father, who had brought her from Virginia, having died. She had sense enough to discharge the homely duties of her station. Ignorant and unknown beyond her local habitation, she was faithful to her broom and brush, said her prayers, had a ready hand and a smile for everybody, and closed her earthly account with better prospects ahead, than many a monarch or millionaire.

A few years have gone by. Thomas Ruffin has prospered. It is a winter evening at his happy home. A lovely child is sitting on his Father's knee. It's name is Thomas, and it has full bright brown eyes and chestnut hair just like its mother's. A flower stand holds a posy of Mosses. Thomas Ruffin and the florist are good friends. Amy and himself often visit his conservatory and have many a lightsome laugh over memories of other days.

Ten years more have flown. Thomas Ruffin looks a personable man, of fine presence and robust health. Amy has been all a wife could be. His son, a bright generous boy, is now thirteen —an only child, but in his Father's estimation worth a million. In the order of nature John Ruffin, of course, has declined physically. Mentally, under the influence of the most favorable surroundings, he has risen to the level of his possibilities and is a glad-hearted old man. In the domain of affairs, Thomas Ruffin, keeping his eye steadily on life's aim and using legitimate means, has prospered abundantly. The business of the Firm has passed into the hands of the brothers. "Ruffin & Bro." is a leading House among the city's great merchants. They own ships and import from Brazil and the West Indies. Wealth has flowed in and enabled Mr. Ruffin to realize the dream of his life, the repurchase of Cloud Cap.

Mr. Kyle—who, it will be remembered, bought the property under the decree of the court—being resident at New Orleans and making but flying visits to Cloud Cap, the estate, controlled by a manager, had fallen back. Mr. Ruffin restored it to its old place in the front rank among the splendid establishments of this famous district. We use the word "famous" advisedly. We are writing absolute facts. The reader could be taken to this district to-day and have the localities we describe pointed out. The scenes outlined are historically true. Some of its citizens, illustrating the type, could be called by name—one, at the date of our narrative, being a distinguished United States Senator. It was a district then of magnificent plantations, and represented great wealth, culture, and enterprise—enterprise restricted, by the economic conditions of the day, to agriculture. In a general way it was typical of the South. It is profoundly misleading, as has been truly said, the phrase "New South," if it is meant to be inferred that the old South stands for indolence and ignorance. There was immensely more wealth, more liberal education, more statesmenship, more enterprise in the South then, than now; and "New South" should be rather a shortened phrase for "Renewing South," the South struggling to recover her former self. The owners of these estates, reared under the influence of lofty ideals, were cultivated, intelligent, broad-minded citizens, of high sense of honor, firm adherants to priciple, purity and directness of aim, and—barring perhaps here and there a degree of stateliness—bore themselves with an engaging grace and dignity befitting elevation of character—*gentlemen*, the ornaments and guard of the land. They were the creators and representatives of public opinion, and reflected upon the period in which they lived the hue of their own qualities. With the plantations under the immediate direction of the managers, they had time for the thorough study of affairs, and furnished material for a grade of public men of commanding ability,

integrity, and courage, who, challenging leadership,
wielded vast influence in shaping national legisla-
tion, and with whom the run of those to-day is in
painful contrast.

The social side, in its way, was no less notable for
brilliant entertainments, presided over by the charming ladies of the mansion, and tended by the trained
family servants, the courtly slaves of courtly mas-
ters, with a port and a high breeding and a pride of
character which the Congo negro never realized before, and has not realized since, bookish though he
be.

With a free and loving hand and under the stimulus of a generous rivalry, Mr. Ruffin entered upon
the restoration of Cloud Cap. His heart was in the
South, and he purposed, when his fortune reached
a certain point, to wind up affairs North and pass
here the evening of life. He increased the acreage
—rejuvenated and refurnished the mansion, adding
many improvements and conveniences suggested by
his city experience—restored and retouched out-
house and cabin—put the fields in the best possible
condition—and made Cloud Cap, more than ever before, the pride of the district. The work required
time and repeated visits South. He had kept it all
from his Father. The restoration having been completed, towards the close of that decennary we have
taken from his life, he made known to his Father
what he had done, and announced an approaching
visit with his family to Cloud Cap. As infirm as
John Ruffin now was, the journey, by sail and steam-

boat, was easily borne. And the moring of return! What! what! a morning to John Ruffin! It was the 21st of April, and the weather, as seemly, put on a glorious face for the occasion. Yesterday—so dry, so windy, so dusty and disagreable. A cloud arose in the night. The air thundered, Thine arrows went abroad, and the rain fell. This morning of return all is lovely. The birds are out and gay. The young leaves so soft and velvety. And gentle breezes blow fresh and inspiring, sweet with the flowers of an early spring. Of course it's a holliday for the slaves, very many of whom are there that John Ruffin remembers. Of course they are all in Sunday rig and line the avenue of approach to the mansion. And when the outrider, with spaniels bounding at the horse-heels, herald the approach, what cheers go up! And how the cheers deepen and by turn are answered back from the files, when the open carriage, with grey-haired Cupid on the box, rolls through, and the old master, remembered for his considerate kindly heart, after years of affliction and trial, has come again into his own.

Leaving affairs in his brother's hands, Mr. Ruffin, with his family, passed a portion of the winter and spring of each year at Cloud Cap, dispensing a splendid hospitality and giving entertainments. which were the events of the season. It was during the last visit in this decennary that his aged Father, perfectly satisfied with the portion Providence had allotted him, was called to a higher home, resting in the arms of his beloved son, and for his gift thanking

Him with his latest breath, to whom in his affliction he had drawn nigh.

Those who insist upon having a story to end pleasantly, should put by the book here. The reader who would follow Cloud Cap to its actual historical close, may do so in the few lines that ensue.

Ten years again pass. A horror of great darkness has settled over the land. Red-handed war has severed states and parted father and son!—Mr. Ruffin, having transferred to the South the greater portion of his wealth, was winding up his affairs preparatory to final removal to Cloud Cap, where his son, enamoured of life there and now a young man of majority, had been more than a year in charge, when the war-cloud burst. With the profundest concern he had followed the preceding angry discussions and deepening threats of rupture. War nowadays may be topic of senatorial flippancy. To one of Mr. Ruffin's mould it was the unspeakable horror it really is. By sentiment and by interest Thomas Ruffin was a Southern man through and through. His heart was in the South, his property concentrated there, his home now practically there. But he was one of those Southern men who could not bring himself to think, and was vigorous in impressing the opinion upon his son and others, that the circumstances of the presidential election of 1860, as much to be deplored as they were, alone and in themselves could justify a disruption of the states, whatever might be the view held touching the nature

of their political union. But his son, high-spirited as
he was dutiful, was in intimate contact with the fiery
Southern leaders. With the first cannon a torrent
of passion swept the South. Especially in this district of great plantations and multitude of slaves,
the effect was indescribable. San Domingo of 1791
was before the eyes of the citizens—its awful scenes
of uproar, butchery, and beastly outrage. The furor
was overwhelming. The young men flew to arms,
and this son was among them. Mr. Ruffin made
every effort to get to him, or at least get news.
The embargo cut him off by sea. Repeated attempts
to penetrate the lines proved fruitless. Weeks and
weeks of fears and sore distress passed without
tidings. At last they came—that Cloud Cap had
been confiscated, as the property of an enemy; and
his son slain in battle.

An individual dies. A race abides. Mr. Ruffin
lived on a retired noble life, quietly dispensing in
manifold charities—the Old Men's Home first among
them—the means he accumulated, an unassuming
considerate man, humane and courteous. His remaining years are of less concern, than the section
and the people, of whom he was one.—What is
Cloud Cap to-day? The reader could be taken hither
and his own eyes witness the desolation. It is in a
portion of the South that has not felt the renewing
hand of these latter times. The district—once so
famous for its cultured, refined, beautiful homes—
has been given over almost wholly to negroes; and
its chair in Congress, then adorned by one who stood

for the best type of all that is full-minded and high-minded and thoroughbred in bearing, is now filled by a coarse demagogue—an illustration of a present pervading and portentous malady, the decadence of functionaries, that mediocres and vulgarians obtrude, that so many more in private life are more learned, honorable, and qualified, than in the halls of council —which, if true of the nation's legislature, is truer of the state's—truest, of the municipal, where so often our splendid cities, in place of being in the hands of representative citizens, the great merchants and business men, the flower of the land, are controlled by low, inferior, trading sets, propagating a blight from these pregnant centres!—Thus much in passing. The great plantations of our district have been divided and subdivided into small farms, and cultivated so unskillfully and so long without return to the generous soil, as barely to support the wretched blacks upon them. The superb residences are falling into ruins, and upon the site of the Cloud Cap mansion stand negro huts with chimneys built of sticks and mud!

But the Renaissance will come hither yet and this region blossom forth again. The South, as a whole, is advancing, and under conditions that bid fair to send her forward beyond her former self. Her climate, her soil, her mineral wealth, are the one factor. The characteristics of her people, the other. Did she not bear a glorious part in the Revolution and in the war with Mexico? And if in the last dreadful conflict every succeeding battle field was but another tribute to the manhood of her rank and file, the eminent strength of character they displayed subsequent to the close of hostilities, when, stripped bare, they were compelled to educate their former slaves and stand disfranchised in the presence of the voting negroes, is more admirable still, and the gage of a people whence will arise citizens and patriots of renown. Confessedly, it is the most American section of our country. Since colonial days its blood has run mainly in one channel—the purest representative of the men who fought the Revolution and framed the Constitution—of that organizing, indomitable, historic race, which, had not its sea-girt limits forbidden expansion at its centre, long since would have dominated Europe, and whose powerful settlements on every continent self-interest and the advancing spirit of solidarity must yet combine into a confederation dominating the world—and dominating it beneficently, as the best exponent of the two paramount civilizing forces, commerce and religion.